The envelope was plain, white, the kind you buy in boxes at the office-supply place, three blue lines in the upper left-hand corner for the return address, left blank. It carried an ordinary stamp and was postmarked somewhere unreadable in New Mexico. I slit it carefully with my letter opener, taking out the single sheet inside. Block letters, printed, not a clue as to age, sex, anything.

To whom it may concern:
Twenty-one years ago death came to innocents.
Death in life pays for death of life.
The accounts will be closed.
Let it be. . . .

By A. J. Orde
Published by Fawcett Books:

A LITTLE NEIGHBORHOOD MURDER
DEATH AND THE DOGWALKER
DEATH FOR OLD TIMES' SAKE
DEAD ON SUNDAY
A LONG TIME DEAD
A DEATH OF INNOCENTS

Books published by The Ballantine Publishing Group
are available at quantity discounts on bulk purchases
for premium, educational, fund-raising, and special
sales use. For details, please call 1-800-733-3000.

A DEATH
OF
INNOCENTS

A. J. Orde

FAWCETT CREST • NEW YORK

A Fawcett Crest Book
Published by Ballantine Books
Copyright © 1997 by A. J. Orde

http://www.randomhouse.com

Library of Congress Catalog Card Number: 96-90772

ISBN 0-449-22519-4

Manufactured in the United States of America

First Edition: July 1997

10 9 8 7 6 5 4 3 2 1

one

WHILE GRACE AND I were on our honeymoon in the Bahamas, she told me in the nicest possible way she didn't want to live, as she put it, "over the shop." I was not particularly surprised at this. Grace had alluded to this preference once or twice during our recurrent discussions about getting married, and I'd already decided not to make a big thing about it. Even though "over the shop" was the upper floor of a very pleasant old Denver house, large enough for a couple by anyone's standards, it wasn't a space Grace and I had furnished together, and it was also totally deficient in outdoor space, which Grace considered essential for any long-term residence.

"It's not that I'm such a fanatic gardener or anything," she explained. "But I have been reading about it a little, and when I decide to put in a tulip bulb or a lilac bush, I don't want to have to take something else out to make room for it. All you've got at Jason Lynx Interiors is that tiny little area out in front, and Mark has that full of stuff." Mark McMillan has the title of associate, but he actually runs Jason Lynx Interiors as much as or more than I do.

I gave Grace a sympathetic hug. "Mark has mentioned he'd be interested in moving into 1465 Hyde Street if

I want to move out. Since I want to live with you, and you want to live elsewhere, I guess Mark has a deal."

"Ooh, Jason," she cooed, snuggling. "I'm so glad you don't mind."

"I don't mind," I said loftily, ignoring the coo for the persiflage it was. Grace is not the cooing type. "Not *mind*. But you do realize finding a place that suits us both is going to be a pain in the ass. You with your incredibly high standards. And me with my penchant for perfection."

At that juncture I thought I was making a mild joke with no intention of being prophetic. Neither perfection nor high standards had been a factor when I'd moved into the apartment at 1465 Hyde. It had been Jacob's place, my foster father's, and he'd had a stroke, so I came to help him out, with my wife Agatha and our baby son. We'd gone on occupying the place while Jacob was hospitalized, because it was there and it was furnished and we didn't have the money to do anything else.

Jacob had outlived both my wife and son, though not by many years. They'd all been gone long enough that I'd worn out the anger and the guilt that the idea of either moving or marrying again had aroused only a few years before. Grace had been a major factor in exorcising the ghosts, and by now the two of us have been together almost five years, long enough that we had no lingering doubts when we finally made it official—lengthy honeymoon and all. Finding a place to live happily together was just the next step, and I was sure we could handle it without any great difficulty. Best laid plans, and all that.

Country, she said. Or small town. Anything but suburbia. Town house, I said. Or, a remodeled old house with a big yard.

"Let's really take time to look," she said, there on the Bahama beach, with the sun turning her hair to silver. "Maybe we'll both fall in love with something."

I told her I already had, and one thing led to another, and we didn't talk about houses for a while. Grace is a cop. She's tiny and very blond. She eats like several starving stevedores. She's smart and intense and incredibly loving. Even while I was holding out for a city house, I figured if she wanted country, we'd find something that would do. She'd grown up, at least partly, in the country, and I know it can become an addiction. My country friends claim they would curl up and die if forced into urban life.

"Do you want to keep your apartments?" I asked. Grace had remodeled her grandmother's old Queen Anne Victorian into four units plus the one she'd occupied, and they brought her in a nice additional income.

"Sure," she said. "I'll get someone to live in my place and manage it for me. That's my security blanket."

I approve of security blankets. Too many things could happen to people who thought they had it made. Grace agreed. The work ethic, she said. If you're raised on it, you can't get by without it. By the time the honeymoon was over, we'd thrashed out most of the details of our own work ethic. Mark would be offered the apartment at 1465 Hyde when we found another place, and Grace would keep her apartments. Together we would find a house for us, and together we settled on how much we could afford and what terms we could manage.

The Bahamas were eternal summer. When we returned to Denver, it was fall, edging into winter. We got back on Friday morning, and Grace didn't go back to work until Monday, so as soon as we got home we told Mark and Eugenia Lowe, the showroom manager, that we were house hunting, then Grace and I sat down at the kitchen table to go through the real-estate ads in the newspapers. Grace had decided we would do this before we unpacked, so we could make appointments for the weekend. After an hour of this, I was already tired of looking for a house. One simply knew that all this hype could not be true.

"Maybe we should just get a real-estate agent," I suggested. I'd done work for several, one or two of whom I had liked.

"Let's narrow it down to some possibles before we do that," Grace insisted. "A real-estate agent can't do us any good until we know what we want."

I gave in. We each chose four ads that seemed to offer possibilities. We called the real-estate agent involved. We made dates to go look over the weekend. In addition, we circled a few open houses, where we could drop in without making an appointment.

When we'd done that, I caught up on business while Grace unpacked her stuff in the front bedroom and bath, the former guest suite, which was now hers. Grace wanted us to have separate sanctums. She said when she was busy at the cop shop and had to work overtime, she wanted a place she could come in late, read for a while, maybe do her exercises, eat a sandwich, crawl into bed when she felt like it without having to tiptoe or feel self-conscious because it was two in the morning. Which was fine by me. We both thought of lovemaking as an event, not a habit, and we both had a need for intermittent solitude, either by habit or inclination. In our new house, we told one another, we wanted an area we could turn into a suite, two bedrooms with a little shared sitting room (for lazy mornings), two half baths, and a big shared tub and shower. We hadn't talked about other space much. We'd just make sure we had plenty of room and see what developed.

While Grace was busy marking her territory, I drank coffee with Mark and Eugenia and heard about what had happened while we'd been gone. Wilson Credable wanted to rent some antiques for the set of an Ibsen play his theater group was putting on, though why he would need to rent antiques, God only knew. He had a house full of them. However, Mark had worked out the insurance, so I said fine, let them rent. Our Yellow Pages ad was up for renewal, did we want to have one at all? We talked about that for a while. Yellow Pages ads bring you all sorts of weird inquiries that take time to answer, and they're less likely to bring in any profitable business than some other kinds of advertising. Eugenia thought she could reword the ad to cut down on the nut calls ("I have this china dog that my father won for my mother at a state fair in 1923, and it looks like an antique," etc. etc.), so we told her to go to it.

"Valerie French has located an item she wants you to look at," said Mark. Valerie was a former customer who seemed to have an antique sensor built in. She homed in on good pieces of furniture like a guided missile.

"What? Did she say?"

"Some kind of chest. She doesn't know what it is, she just knows it's nice."

"Well, set a date. Where is it?"

"In her garage. She says she's got it on loan from the owner just so you can look at it."

There were a couple of other trifling things: some materials we'd ordered that hadn't arrived as specified (nile green is *not* apple green, no matter what the tile supplier says) and a chair that a customer found uncomfortable. The chair wasn't custom, so we'd take it back and find her one that fit better. When Mark and Eugenia went off about their business, I sat at my desk to look over the bills and itemize some invoices. When we sell furniture, we describe it in great detail on the invoice, just so there will be no misunderstandings later. If it's a reproduction, we say so. If it's not all original, we say so. If we have our doubts, we say so. I had learned that it prevented a lot of trouble later on.

Evening came; the staff went home; Grace and I settled into our habitual routines. Bela, the big white Kuvasz dog, and Schnitz, the Maine coon cat, had their walks and were brushed. Grace's cat Critter, Schnitz's daddy, had his walk and grooming. We were hoping Critter and Schnitz would learn to get along. Schnitz was neutered, so there shouldn't have been any competition, but thus far their relationship consisted of hisses and lightning-like flashes of paws, claws fully extended. Critter felt insecure, Grace said. It wasn't his place. Now that he had his bed in Grace's room, with her things around, that room would be his territory, it would smell like home, and we hoped he'd settle.

To make him feel more secure, I visited Grace in her room rather than the other way around. Critter was used to me in Grace's bed, though he did tend to settle all thirty pounds of himself into any crevice left between us. I was more tired than I realized, and I dozed off while she was still reading, sleeping so deeply that when I woke, Grace was already up, coffee smells were drifting down the hall, and Critter had worn a semipermanent hollow into the front of my legs.

Our first real-estate agent appointment was at ten. A big old Georgian house on a corner lot, in the Park Hill area. I thought it had possibilities; Grace hated it. Too formal, she said. Our second appointment was an old farmhouse on an acreage out toward Littleton. Grace liked it. I pointed out that the place was an architectural monstrosity, badly built, needing everything from a new foundation to a new roof, and we decided against it.

Thereafter we saw a faked Tudor, a re-muddled Victorian, another farmhouse built by a do-it-yourselfer who had done it himself, without instruction in the use of either a plumb line or a level. Then we saw an "executive's estate," which meant a pretentious, many-leveled house in Cherry Hills Farms set so close to its neighbors you could hear them expressing themselves in the bathroom. We actually stopped in at four separate "open houses," two of them sort of countrified, two in town.

By Sunday evening we were tired and decidedly snappish. "Wrong," I said, pulling Grace tight against me. "We're going about this all wrong. Instead of looking at houses we don't like, why don't we concentrate on ones we do. What house do you like best, of all the ones you've ever been in?"

She thought about this for a while. We started talking about things we liked and things we didn't. I made some notes. Grace didn't want to see neighbors. She didn't mind hearing them, provided they didn't play rock or rap at top volume, but she didn't want to see them. She wanted the illusion of privacy. She didn't want a house she had to live up to. I agreed to that. Comfortable surfaces, renewable when soiled. No white carpet or fragile wallpaper. She wanted a big kitchen, not large in work area necessarily, but in space, so she could have a sizable table and really comfortable chairs to loll about in.

Since we both work, it needed to be a house that could be kept fairly simply, including the outdoor space. Plenty of room, but natural landscaping, not formal lawns to mow. Neither one of us mentioned children, though we were both thinking about them. Grace didn't mention it because of my son who had died. I didn't mention it because Grace had said several times she wanted children but was getting nervous about her biological clock. We sort of agreed that the house should be "large," and left the reason for later discussion. Even people who know each other as well as Grace and I do seem to have these little tender areas that need to be stepped around.

By Tuesday night we had our list, and on Wednesday morning I called Edna Maxwell, a real-estate agent I'd done some work for a couple of times. Edna's about fifty, indomitably energetic, very successful, with the rare quality of being able to listen when people talk. We made a date for dinner that night, at Addy Brewster's, which was convenient for both of us, since her office was in Cherry Creek. For a wonder, Grace got home on time, and we made it to the restaurant with several minutes to spare.

I got a kick out of Edna trying to keep her face straight as she watched Grace eat, but aside from that, she was all attention, and we shared our list right down to the preferred exposure of the kitchen windows. When we turned the conversation to ourselves, it turned out she had a nephew who was a detective on the Lakewood police force. Grace had met him, and this gave them something to talk about.

"Are you frantic?" she asked, over the coffee she and I drank while Grace enjoyed two servings of mocha torte with almond ice cream. "Do you have to move right now?"

I said no, and Grace, handicapped by a mouthful of cake, shook her head.

"I'd rather not overexpose you," Edna said. "People get frantic and look at everything, and then they get tired and cross and end up buying something they don't really like. I'd rather take my time, come up with properties as close as possible to your needs, and show you only those. All right?"

We agreed, all right, and that's the way we left it. Grace, now that she knew we were definitely doing something, wasn't in the mad rush she had been the week before, letting us settle into something approaching patience.

Valerie French invited us to her place for a drink on Thursday evening so we could look at the chest she had in her garage. At one time Valerie would have dragged it into her living room and thrown a recently purchased rug over it, then stacked it with several smaller acquisitions. Since Mark and I had decorated the place for her, she kept it very neat, and it looked to me as if she enjoyed living in it. Valerie still looked like a rose in full bloom; every time I saw her, I hoped she'd find someone really good to share her life with. Grace and Mark and I had saved Valerie from a disastrous marriage not long ago— though Valerie didn't know we had—and it was time she met someone who'd appreciate her.

We carried our drinks out into the garage, and Valerie turned on the overhead light, a bare, hanging bulb that glared in our eyes. The light wasn't flattering to the squat, dusty chest, throwing harsh shadows along the sides, but I caught my breath, nonetheless. I'd have to look it up to be sure, but oh, it looked like the genuine article.

"I liked the looks of it," Valerie commented, head cocked to one side and a pleased smile on her face.

Grace was running her hands down the front of it, incised with an overall design of tulips and leaves. The chest stood about forty inches high and was about four feet long, a foot and half deep. Above short, stubby legs, two long drawers, one over the other, were surmounted by a three-paneled chest with a top that was flanged at the rear sides and hinged on hardwood pegs. The lid made a slight overhang at front and sides. The knobs on the drawers were turned. The wood of the paneling, drawer fronts, and stiles seemed to be oak, once stained or painted black, though when I raised the lid, I could see that the top was pine.

"What?" asked Grace, bringing me out of my stupor. I'd been bent over, focusing on the inside of the lid. The date carved there, 1709, was the same as on the center panel, where it was enclosed in a heart along with two sets of curly initials.

"What?" Grace demanded again.

"Dower chest," I said, coughing a little. "Probably made in western Massachusetts, almost three hundred years ago."

"Oh, lovely," gushed Valerie. "How wonderful. It was a hope chest, then?"

I nodded. Grace evidently thought I needed help, for she asked, "How much is it worth, Jason?"

"Oh," I said, trying to be casual, "something over thirty thousand, if one can find the right buyer."

Both their mouths dropped open. Well, so had mine,

figuratively speaking. "I've seen only three authentic Hadley-type chests in my life, and I've never seen one with the original top before. It's always the top that breaks or cracks. I wonder if there's provenance. . . ."

Valerie overflowed again. "Oh, how wonderful for Mrs. Mills! She has the family Bible, Jason, and it goes clear back eleven generations, to the people whose initials are on the front. It's a great-great-great-grandma, way back, married on that same date, 1709. She said it was the only thing she had, and she didn't think it was worth much. I said I thought it might be."

"Providential provenance," I said. "You mean it's actually a family piece?"

"That's what I said. See, one of my friends is a therapist. She does home visits, for people who are crippled up with arthritis or muscle problems, you know? Anyhow, she and I were going to a movie last week, right after her session with this really nice old lady who never has any company—Mrs. Mills. So I went along, and we got to talking, and it turns out the old lady needs repairs on her house and she hasn't any money, and she doesn't want to leave home because it's *home*, you know."

I did know. Grace and I shared sympathetic glances.

"So, I saw she had old furniture, and I said maybe she had something worth something, and she said probably not, only there was this really old chest in the guest room, which is like *stuffed* with old boxes, so we had to dig the chest out, almost with a pick and shovel, you know. So, anyhow, I looked at it, and I told her I'd take it and see if you said it was worth anything. That's when she showed me the Bible."

"So you're selling it on commission?" asked Grace.

"Oh, heavens, no," she replied. "I wouldn't take anything. I know Jason has to, because he'll have to show it and advertise it, won't he? But I couldn't take any of it. I just want to help out."

"Twenty percent," I said firmly. She was right. I would have to show it, and clean it up, and be sure it was what it seemed to be. And Valerie would get half of that, whether she would or no. I wanted to encourage her! "And, Valerie, I'll be glad to up front the money for Mrs. Mills's repairs, providing it's a reasonable sum. I'll have to see the Bible first, so we can make copies of the names and dates and have a notarized document prepared. What is it, the usual marriages, births, deaths?"

She smiled happily. "All the way back to the 1600s. I think that's wonderful."

She agreed to make a date for us with Mrs. Mills.

I thought the whole event was little short of miraculous, and Grace and I chortled over it all the way to the restaurant. Grace thought Valerie was marvelous, and I thought Valerie was almost as marvelous as the Hadley-Hatfield chest she'd found, so called because such chests were customarily made in the vicinity of those two Massachusetts towns.

"Actually," Grace confessed, a little shamefaced, "I didn't think the chest was that . . . pretty. Not that graceful. It looks sort of chunky and clumsy."

"It is," I admitted. "I don't think of a piece like that as being decorative, particularly, though one could set it to advantage. It's basically a collector's item. Similar pieces made elsewhere were more elegant looking. It's like the sponge-painted armoire your grandma left you. It looks like a giraffe with a bad case of mange. Ugly as sin, but rare. People pay for rarity."

"And you're going to meet Mrs. Mills?"

"Very definitely. It's always good for a dealer to know the people involved, to be able to say that he knows they actually exist. We know Valerie, but if we didn't, we'd be foolish to take her word that Mrs. Mills is a real person."

"Can I go along?"

I laughed at her. "Unlike your profession, love, mine does not exclude friends and relatives. By all means, come visit the scene of the crime."

And there I was, being prophetic again.

Valerie couldn't wait to give Mrs. Mills the news, and she made a date for us to see her friend on Saturday morning. Grace was free, so we picked up Valerie and the three of us drove out to north Denver, out beyond Federal Blvd. into an old part of town, originally Italian, now partly Hispanic, where we found the Mills house hunkered down in the shade of a tall neighboring wall. The wall had a gaping hole in it where a section had seemingly fallen in, and as we drove into the driveway we could peer through the hole into a wilderness of late autumn trees, some bare, some with leaves still blazing red or yellow. Distantly, through gaps in the foliage, we could see a house.

"That looks weird in there, doesn't it?" said Valerie. "Mrs. Mills says nobody's lived there for over fifteen years. The people who owned it just up and left it."

We got out of the car and stood a moment in contemplation, watched balefully by a large, elderly bulldog who lay on the porch, then we went in to meet Mrs. Mills, a charming old lady in a wheelchair who greeted us like old friends and told us we'd come on a good day because she didn't hurt too badly and was, therefore, more cheerful than usual.

"It makes me cross," she said, with the manner of one admitting to premeditated murder. "When I can't do things, it just makes me cross. Let Chester come in with you. It's time he had his breakfast."

At Mrs. Mills's suggestion, Valerie fed Chester. At Mrs. Mills's suggestion, we called her Kate. At Mrs. Mills's suggestion, Grace made coffee, and we chatted a bit. It had been a while since I'd adopted an old lady, and I made a mental note that this one seemed eminently in need of adoption. Then I made another mental note to explain to Grace about the first mental note. My favorite old lady, Nellie Arpels, lives across the alley from 1465 Hyde, and if and when Grace and I move away, we'll need to be sure that Nellie continues to be a favorite old lady. Maybe Nellie would enjoy Kate. I hadn't had a luncheon with my old ladies for some time, either.

After a sufficient time had been spent in chitchat, Valerie fetched an inlaid wooden box with little round feet and a simple brass keyhole, the Bible was lifted out, laid on the table, and reverently unwrapped from the large square of black silk it was kept in. Someone's mourning shawl, I thought. The edges were perforated with little holes, as though hand-tied fringe had been removed. The Bible was leather bound, the gold leaf ornamentation flaked away almost entirely, the leather itself split in several places along the spine. Kate turned the fragile pages, and I wrote down the entries, one of the earliest matching the initials and date on the chest, the last one made in 1987 and recording the birth of a great-grandchild to Mrs. Mills.

"That's Margaret's boy," she said, pointing. "They live in Australia now. They're the last family left. . . ."

We told Kate what the old chest was worth, maybe, and she turned ashen pale and seemed about to faint. Valerie restored her with coffee, and we settled details.

We were getting up to leave when Grace mentioned the house next door. Did Mrs. Mills think anyone would mind if we went through the hole and looked at it?

"Why, child, nobody'll even know. Chester guards that hole to keep the neighborhood boys from going in there. They do it anyhow, over the top where the big tree hangs over, but Chester keeps them from getting in from my place. Now, I'll just keep Chester here beside me until you've gone through."

We went through, leaving Chester to scowl at us from inside the screen door. We weren't worth barking at, but he knew we were up to no good as we climbed through the hole into the woods. It felt like a real forest. The tall wall was of brown brick, and the trees were so thick along it that it disappeared behind the growth. The ground was carpeted with leaves, last season's and all the seasons' before that. We passed an oak, flaming red in the slanting light, and an even redder maple. Most of the trees had turned gold or pale apricot. We came from among them to the foot of a weed-grown lawn where the remains of several gardens struggled with the grasses.

"Peonies," said Grace, bending to touch bronze leaves and stems. "And iris, and day lilies."

I supposed she was right. I wouldn't know a peony if it bit me. I did know houses rather well, however. This one was shaped like an angular bow, a center block facing south, with a wing at each side slanting off at a forty-five-degree angle, so the house seemed to embrace the lawn and gardens in its arms. It had been built in the early 1900s when Denver had gone through a period of fascination with Spanish-style architecture—tile roofs, stuccoed walls, pillared terraces, and the like. This one was a graceful example of the type.

"Ah," said Valerie.

"Oh," murmured Grace.

I gave her a look, but she wasn't thinking of me at all. We made a slow circumambulation of the house, without encountering any false notes except the presence of a badly designed little enclosed porch that had been added on at the back. It was outside what I guessed to be the kitchen door and might have been intended as a mudroom.

Before I could say yea, nay, or watch it, the two women were clambering about, peering through the windows. I already knew what they'd see: probably Saltillo-tile floors downstairs, walls of old plaster (some of which would no doubt be cracked), perhaps with shell moldings over the doors, and unless someone had done some extensive remodeling within the last twenty-five years, there would be an absolutely impossible kitchen.

However, there would probably also be a lovely staircase with a wrought-iron rail to go with the graciously proportioned windows. In addition, the exposed brickwork was remarkably good, as was the ornamental work at the tops of the windows and around the front door. I caught myself smiling. Taken together with the extensive grounds, it really was a very nice house.

"I want it," said Grace. "Tell Edna."

"Grace," I said cautiously. "It's not for sale."

"I don't care," said she.

"You haven't seen the inside!"

"I want it. I'll sell the apartments if necessary. But I want it!"

Talk about love at first sight! Talk about demon possession! Or the triumph of the irrational! I bit my tongue and said nothing at all except, "I'll call Edna." Let Edna take the slings and arrows of total madness. She got paid for it.

On the way back, we drove around three sides of the place, which enclosed almost half a city block. From inside, it had looked even larger because of all the trees. It had a set of wrought-iron gates for pedestrians on one street, closed and locked, and another set for vehicular traffic around the corner. Also closed and locked. The brick driveway went up to a three-car garage and the gate bore a little sign, IN CASE OF TROUBLE NOTIFY KAMPE AND TENTER, PROPERTY MANAGEMENT, and a phone number.

It didn't look to me as though Kampe and Tenter were managing much. Though their instructions were, perhaps, only to inspect the place once every six months. The padlock on the gates wasn't rusted, so maybe they gave it a semiannual look over.

Nothing would do but we go back to Kate's place, where Grace asked if we could take her to lunch, to pick her brain about the people next door. Kate thanked us kindly, but said she wasn't really comfortable leaving home in her chair, "for personal reasons." So, we picked her brain anyhow.

The house had been built in the twenties. The Monmouth family, she said, had owned it since at least 1961. They had come there as a youngish couple with three children, pregnant with the fourth. The Monmouths had gotten a divorce sometime in the late seventies. Mrs.

Monmouth had kept the house for her and one daughter, and also she'd taken in a family, though whether they were guests, or relatives, or refugees, or emigrants, Kate didn't know. They were foreign, for she'd often heard children playing and talking in some language other than English. Then, in the early eighties, those people had left as well when Mrs. Monmouth had died, such a young woman still, in her early fifties. That had been fifteen years ago. The Monmouth children would be around forty by now, she said. Two boys, two girls. Matthew, Nash, Lucia, and Joanna. Except for Nash, so biblical! But easy to remember.

"Why didn't they sell the house?" Grace demanded. "It's just been sitting there for fifteen years?"

Kate sighed. "My dear, I don't know. I was only a neighbor, never a friend. She was always Mrs. Monmouth. She never referred to me as anything but Mrs. Mills. She never asked after my family, so I could hardly ask after hers, though she always greeted me very nicely when she saw me out in the yard, and when Christmas came, I got a little box of something expensive, chocolates or perfume, just as the other neighbors did. I always thought it was a rather lady-of-the-manor gesture, don't you know, since we weren't her tenantry, but I'm sure she meant well. . . ."

The tone betrayed her. She had resented it at the time and did still.

"You read Jane Austen," I hazarded.

"Trollope more recently," she said, with a faint smile. "How did you know?"

"Tenantry. It's not a word I hear every day."

"What a nice young man you are," she said, with a twinkle. Grace gave me a very funny look.

We talked about picking up the chest, and she promised to keep the Bible safe, and, at my suggestion, also the box she kept it in. When we got into the car, Grace asked, "Do you always come on to old ladies like that, Jason?"

"Only some old ladies," I said. "The ones who were reared on genteel flirtations."

"Genteel flirtations," she repeated, thoughtfully. "I must remember that."

"What did you mean about the box the Bible was in?" asked Valerie.

"William-and-Mary inlay," I said. "Walnut box, the inlay is probably fruitwood. Did you notice the little ball-shaped feet?"

"I missed that!" she said, sounding angry with herself. "I wasn't looking. Is it valuable?"

"In this case, probably, if it dates back to the same period as the Bible itself or maybe a little later. Let's say it will buy Mrs. Mills a new roof if she needs one."

I called Edna as soon as I got back to the shop, gave her the address of the Monmouth house, told her as far as I knew, the place wasn't for sale, but investigate and let me know because Grace thought it was perfect.

"Has she been in it, Jason?"

"That question is totally irrelevant," I answered. "She is being spiritually guided and she knows it's perfect without seeing it."

"I've been down that route before," she said in a grumpy tone. "It's usually a total disappointment, but I'll see what I can do."

Mark exclaimed over Valerie's discovery and sent our truck to her place to pick up the Hadley chest. I made out a check to Mrs. Mills, enough to cover her immediate needs, and then called our sometime buyer in New York,

Myron Burstein, leaving a message for him to call me on Monday. It was late by then, so we closed the shop and Grace and I spent the weekend amusing ourselves and the animals.

When Myron heard about the chest on Monday he waxed ecstatic. He thought he knew just the buyers, a Boston couple who were collectors of early Americana, particularly Massachusetts Americana, so we talked about people for a while, then about some oak and bevel glass cabinets he'd bought from an old brownstone that was being wrecked, and then about a couple of marvelous rugs he'd found that he wanted me to buy though I had absolutely no use for them.

When I hung up, the phone rang immediately again, and it was Edna Maxwell. "Jason, you must have been reading someone's mind!"

"Whose?" I asked, still focused on Myron's conversation.

"The Monmouth house? Remember? Well, the reason it's never been up for sale is that the oldest boy didn't want to sell, and the other two heirs didn't push it. But now, Joanna needs some money, so she got a court order forcing the sale. I've talked to all three of them. They've authorized me to let you look at the place and make an offer. It was appraised when their mother died, for estate purposes, at two hundred thousand."

"Is that all?" I gaped into the mouthpiece. "The land alone is worth that."

"All the gentrification out that way has taken place in the last seven or eight years, Jason. Before that, it wasn't considered to be a good part of town, and it's too big a place for that neighborhood. You know that affects prices. You won't get it for two hundred thou, but it won't cost a mint, either."

She was right, of course. That part of north Denver had been an ethnic enclave for generations, and the place was too big for the other houses around it. "When can we see it?"

"This afternoon?" she asked. "When does Grace get off work?"

"She doesn't go back until tomorrow. She's getting her hair cut this morning. How about this afternoon, around two?"

So, when Grace returned from the salon, looking like a fluffy chrysanthemum, off we went to north Denver again. This time we drove in by the wrought-iron gates and walked along the wide terrace to the front door.

The double door was carved, an overall pattern of oak leaves and acorns, strawberry leaves and blossoms. The front hall was oval, Saltillo tiled in that Mexican natural clay that varies from pale gold to almost red, through every intermediate shade of apricot, rose, peach, melon, and ocher. The stairs swept up in a graceful arc to the concentric arc of the matching wrought-iron railing on the balcony-hallway above. Beneath the stairs an arched corridor led to the back of the house through a pair of wrought-iron doors. To the left were living room, library-cum-den, and a bedroom with bath. The bed-bath suite opened from the arched corridor under the stairs, so it could double as a powder room.

The right-hand wing held a large dining room, with breakfast room, pantry, and kitchen behind it, and behind that, a large, ugly laundry and the basement stairs. It was really very well planned.

On the upper floor, each end of the curved hallway opened on two bedrooms and a bath, and each of the four bedrooms continued out through french doors onto wide, covered porches at each end of the house, giving every bedroom a wall of light to either southwest or southeast.

I noticed, without comment, that the surfaces of the decks were badly weathered. I'd assumed so, since there were leakage stains downstairs in the ceilings of the living room and dining room. Flat roofs or decks are hell in a climate like Denver's, where it can drop forty degrees in an hour and a spring storm may drop three feet of snow that freezes every night and partially thaws every day, building ice dams that prevent drainage and tear the flat surfaces apart.

When we went back downstairs, Grace saw me looking at the brown streaks down the walls and her face was a study in dismay.

"Hey," I told her, "no big deal. The way the house was built, the way the roof line was designed, it's perfectly possible to enclose the upper porches, which will take care of the leaking problem as well as adding space that's usable year round."

"But I like the porches!"

"They can still be porches. But they already have solid walls up two feet around the edges. We'll put sliding glass windows from the short wall up to the roof, and they can stay open in nice weather."

Her face cleared immediately. She really was in love with the place! She didn't want any warts on her prince charming.

So, we looked some more. We went outside and looked. We came back inside and looked. We went upstairs over the garage and looked at the small apartment there. We poked around in the basement. We opened every cupboard and drawer in the very unpleasant kitchen. We were happily surprised by the bathrooms, which, though they weren't as nicely arranged as I would like, did seem to have been done over within the last twenty years.

When at last Edna wandered off to leave the two of us alone, Grace said, "You're right about enclosing those decks upstairs, Jason. It's silly to have flat, unenclosed decks like that!"

One nice thing about having a wife who's managed property is that she knows what makes sense.

"But wouldn't it be terribly expensive?" she asked.

I shook my head. "I don't know. I shouldn't think so. If you wanted to carry the same flooring out there, we'd have a problem matching the floors. Personally, I think I'd do them in tile and keep the drains through the wall so they could be washed down. The decks are sloped and the gutter is already there."

"So we could have a lot of potted plants!" She hummed happily for a moment, then frowned. "We'd have to do the kitchen over. I can't stand that kitchen."

"Any place we buy would probably have to have the kitchen done over. In my experience, no two people ever like the same kitchen. And you're right, it's awful."

"It's so dark and dingy and smelly."

I agreed with her. Only a mole would have picked dark wood cabinets, plus a dark countertop, plus a dark floor for a north room with one small window. Only a mole would have built a dark little shed right outside that one window. Also, the kitchen had an island with a built-in stovetop in it, no hood, no fan, and at least thirty years' worth of greasy smoke hazing every surface.

I came to myself to confront my bride, poised, eyes sparkling, looking at me like a puppy, wanting to play catch. I cleared my throat and made myself sound enthusiastic. "Let's drive around the neighborhood. Let's ask some questions. Then, if we're still interested, we can make an offer, contingent on a full inspection."

"Can we afford it?"

I shrugged, then laughed, telling her I didn't know because we had no idea what kind of offer the family would accept. If they were reasonable, and if we kept the down payment fairly low, we had enough cash, probably, to put in a new kitchen—starting by tearing down that awful back porch—and enclose the porches upstairs. Anything else would have to come later.

Edna came back, and we chatted, and to make a long story short, the following Monday we made an offer which was low, lower than I thought they'd take, and surprise, surprise, it was accepted! I sent an inspection firm to go over the place with a fine-tooth comb, and except for the normal stuff you'd expect in a seventy-year-old house, it was in good shape. A few settling cracks in the plaster, wiring systems that might need some help, and so forth. Married less than two months, and we were homeowners. Grace immediately went off the deep end, ricocheting off the walls, delirious with happiness.

I have personally had three clients who either divorced or separated after living in a house while it was being remodeled. There is no worse strain on a relationship, and I didn't care to risk it. Even when I insisted that we redo that kitchen before we moved in one stick, however, Grace was still ecstatic. Everything up to that point had gone so expeditiously that it should have made me suspicious. Nothing ever slides so smoothly, my foster father used to say, as when it's headed downhill! We got title insurance without a moment's hesitation. The closing two weeks later was absolutely without incident. We didn't even meet the Monmouth siblings; their end of things was handled by their attorney.

As soon as the place was definitely ours, I hired a man we use occasionally for cleanup and demolition jobs, Joe Wagoner, to bring his two sons and clean up the place, rake the leaves, get rid of the trash, mow the long, dried grass, tear out the kitchen cabinets and take down the ad hoc mudroom outside the kitchen. It was early November by then, and I wanted to get the outside stuff done before snowfall. I called an architect friend to come look at the job of enclosing the decks upstairs, and we also got the water and gas turned on, had a telephone put in, and did a scale floor plan so we could discuss placement of furniture sensibly.

A couple of days into the project, Mark and Eugenia drove out with Grace and me to give the place their stamp of approval. When we arrived, I saw the grass had responded to mowing and a late rain by greening up a bit, enough to tell me it was alive. The gardens were trimmed around the edges. All the dead leaves had been swept away from the house, and some of the tangle of shrubbery had been trimmed. In the kitchen, the dark old cabinets and the old kitchen appliances were gone, except for the refrigerator. Joe stuck his head in from the back porch that he and his sons were busy dismantling, and told me he'd like to keep the refrigerator while they were working there, just for keeping lunches and sodas in. And by the way, he said, they'd found some photos behind a kitchen drawer. They were in the living room.

Grace went to get the photos, while Mark and I applied my measuring tape to the stripped room. The emptiness gave me a much better perception of the available space.

"I like it," said Mark, wandering over to look at the

dining room. "You'll need good window treatments in the living room, Jason. And in the dining room. With that south exposure, the rooms will be hot in summer unless you cut the sun."

Grace came back into the kitchen, shuffling through a stack of snapshots. "There are trees out there, all across the front. In the summer, they'll shade the windows."

"What are you going to do here in the kitchen?" Mark asked.

"Light wood," Grace said, tucking the photos into her purse. "Light tile. Light countertops. I like Talavera tile, and it goes with this style house, so we'll probably go for that on the backsplash and around the stove. . . ."

She was interrupted by a yell, out back, one that was more than merely surprise. A shriek, almost. I thought someone had dropped a hammer on a foot, but the sudden eruption of voices out there was more hysterical than warranted by a dropped tool. I headed for the kitchen door, with Mark and Eugenia right behind me.

The roof and walls of the porch were gone, the wood and plasterboard piled on the cabinet parts from the kitchen in a long stack down the driveway, ready to be loaded and taken away. When we arrived, the Wagoners had been working on the floor, taking up the planks so they could get at the floor joists. At the moment, however, they were not working but rather were hovering over the floor, bent over, staring at one another. Joe had a pinch bar under a strip of tongue and groove flooring, but he wasn't moving.

"What?" I demanded.

"There's something under there," he said in a strange, rather strangled voice.

"Well?"

"I . . ." He looked around at his sons. "I don't want to."

"What, for heaven's sake?" I demanded. "Skunk?"

"It's not alive," he said, abruptly dropping the bar and running off the flooring, out onto the grass, where he bent over, retching.

"Let me," said Mark, stepping past me. He thrust the end of the curved bar under the loose strip of flooring and heaved back. It came loose with a shriek of nails and a ripping of wood as the tongue tore away from the neighboring strip.

He looked down into the hole he'd made, and with Grace right behind me, I moved over next to him, where I stopped, regretting my haste, regretting I'd been there at all. We were looking down into a terrible face that stared up at us from dried and vacant eyeballs.

I swallowed deeply and said to Mark, "Get me the flash from the car, will you, Mark?"

While he fetched it, I stood back, breathing deeply. Grace knelt by the hole, peering down. Eugenia had drawn away, and the three Wagoners were standing out in the drive, motionless as a monument. Nobody moved until Mark returned with the flash. I used it to illuminate the hole, which wasn't deep, angling the beam to look between the floor joists. It wasn't just a head. The whole body was there, most of it still hidden by the floor, a dried, mummified body stretched out between two joists as though enclosed by the sides of a coffin. My first thought was how small it was. Very small. Still, that idea didn't connect to anything until I heard Grace cry out from beside me.

"It's a child! Oh, Jason, how awful. It's a child."

Grace and I agreed ruefully, angrily, that the last thing we'd ever planned on was having our first home together start out as a crime scene, with crime scene tape stretched around it and no admittance to anybody, including Grace and me. The body was toted away to the pathologist while the four of us and the three Wagoners underwent a lengthy interrogation. Which was silly since the body had obviously been dead for years. Many years. We couldn't tell anyone anything. Still, the sergeant in charge (whom Grace didn't know, had never before met, and didn't much like) was determined to do everything by the book, including tearing out the balance of the floor and looking through the wreckage of the porch. When he heard that Joe and his boys had already hauled away some of the stuff out of the kitchen, he had a fit, as though someone had conspired to remove evidence.

"He's had his stripes all of five minutes," Grace muttered to me. "And he hasn't the remotest idea what to do with them."

Eventually a Lieutenant Martinelli arrived, whom Grace did know, along with some forensics people, and when the Wagoners were given leave to depart, Martinelli joined the other four of us at a neighborhood restaurant. Hunger was the motive, but we also wanted to give Martinelli any help we could. We didn't know who owned the place before the Monmouth family; we knew only what Mrs. Mills had told us about the Monmouths, and we repeated every scrap we could remember. Then Mark and Eugenia departed while Grace and I took the lieutenant over and introduced him to Mrs. Mills, and he got the same story from her.

"I was just thinking how lovely it was to have such a nice boy as a neighbor," she said, patting me on the knee, "and such a pretty wife, and then such an awful thing!

Who could it be? One of the foreign children do you think?"

Lieutenant Martinelli asked, "Who owned it before the Monmouths, Mrs. Mills?"

"An elderly couple. I can't even remember their names. They're the ones who built it, back just before the depression. Of course they weren't elderly then, around fifty, maybe. They wanted a place for the family to come visit, she told me, so they built it sort of divided up. She said she could shut off all the bedrooms upstairs and just live in the lower floor. . . . What was her name? Awful, not to be able to remember things. Georgia was her first name, but I can't remember. . . . Harris! No. Not Harris. Hartford. That's it, Hartford. Georgia and Will Hartford. Anyhow, she died of a stroke in '59, and he moved away, and I suppose he's long dead by now, and that's when the Monmouths bought it."

"Mr. Lynx and Ms. Willis say Mrs. Monmouth wasn't very neighborly."

"Not very cozy, no. Perfectly polite, you understand. But not cozy. Had this man drive her everywhere. I never saw her just walking around in the neighborhood."

"Would you have any idea where the children are now?"

"Lucia ran away when she was in high school. I heard about that from their maid. They had a maid and a yardman and a cook. The yardman lived in the apartment over the garage, but the others lived out. Rosabel, the maid's name was. Rosabel Jones. She came six days a week, well, five and a half, and she used to walk past here to the bus, and sometimes she'd stop to say hello, if I was out on the porch. I don't know if Lucia ever reunited with the family. Nash, he was the younger boy, he left when the mister did, even before the divorce, and Joanna went away to college about that same time. I never saw the boys much after Lucia left. Matthew went to law school here in Denver, and up until his mother died I'd sometimes see him driving by, always alone. His name was in the paper when he passed the bar. I never saw any of them after Mrs. Monmouth died and the house was closed up."

"Do you remember any disappearances?" the lieutenant asked. "Any case where a child went missing?"

"Well, you read about those things all the time. I don't remember any specific one. . . ."

"I meant, in this neighborhood."

She shook her head regretfully. "I don't think so."

Martinelli told us to hold fast for a couple of days, while the forensics people satisfied themselves about the age of the corpse—both prior to and since it died—after which we could reoccupy the place.

I was worried about Grace. Ever since the corpse appeared, she'd been very pale and strange seeming. It could have been just the shock, not a pleasant thing to see as a reality, as opposed to something on TV, made to titillate. Or it could have been the fact that it seemed to overshadow our house, a kind of omen. If the latter, it was going to be a major difficulty. Any change in plans at this point would mean a lot of trouble and time. The place was well and truly ours. We'd have a hard time making a case to set aside the sale on the grounds that the real-estate agent hadn't disclosed the truth about the property. Edna hadn't sold us on the place; we'd asked her to buy it. Besides, who knew what the truth was?

If Grace didn't want the place, we'd have to redo the kitchen before we could offer it for sale. We had a mortgage, not a huge one, but still an indebtedness we hadn't had a few weeks before. Not for the first time in my life, I cursed my propensity for being hit by the fallout from other people's problems.

It turned out I'd been wrong about what was bothering Grace. She told me, that night, when we were softly between the sheets, just at the edge of sleep.

"It's a little girl, Jason. A little girl. Maybe ten years old."

"Now, Grace, you haven't seen the report yet. . . ."

"I know. But that's what it is, anyhow. The clothes are little girl's clothes. Those pictures the Wagoners found, Jason. There are children in those pictures. Maybe Janey Doe is one of those children. All alone like that. Hidden. So nobody knew where she was, or what had happened to her. . . ."

"Except the person who put her there," I said. "I took a good look at the planks the police pulled up to get the body out. They were nailed down with eight-penny nails, and I couldn't spot any superfluous nail holes. Also, the boards are tongue and groove. She, if it is a she, was put under there before the floor was nailed down."

"Before it was *all* nailed down," she corrected me, her lips at my ear. "Part of it could have been finished, and then the body could have been slipped under that part. Particularly . . ."

I knew what she meant. Particularly if the body had been in rigor at the time. It would have been like slipping a plank under there. The child had probably weighed less than a sack of cement.

"So, we need to know when that little addition was done, don't we?" I asked. "Are the pictures of the Monmouth children?"

She murmured. "They may be the Monmouths. I'll give them to you in the morning, and you see what you think. I thought the boys looked happy, but the girls didn't."

That gave me pause for a moment. "I assume you're not going to let Martinelli do all the work on this?"

She said sleepily, "It's *our* house, Jason. I want to know what's going on. I can live very happily in that house, provided we learn the truth. I don't think I could live there if I hadn't really tried to find out what happened."

I gave a slight sigh of relief. She still thought of it as our house, so that eliminated one set of immediate concerns. It did pose another, more long-term one, however. When Grace says she can't do something, she means she can't do it. She doesn't say the words until she's thought it out. If she and I were to occupy that house, it would be absolutely necessary to find out who killed the little girl. Grace is not always rational any more than any of the rest of us, but she is always decisive.

At the moment I was inclined to think this was unfair. Many houses have had people die in them. In England and Europe, anyplace that's been occupied for hundreds of years, people have died everywhere, and not all of them peaceably in bed, either. If I said this to Grace, she would say simply that she didn't know about those people and she did know about this little girl. It wasn't the kind of distinction I could argue with.

Since we couldn't do anything with the house for a few days, and since Grace was busy getting herself back into the habit of her daily round, I decided to concentrate on mine.

An antique dealer in Colorado Springs was going out of business. He'd called me a few days before Grace and

I left on our honeymoon, and I'd told him I'd be in touch when we got back. Monday morning after the corpse was discovered, I drove down to the Springs to go through the shop with Mr. Benjamin "Buster" Brownell. He was not a typical dealer. In my experience we tend toward the effete, or perhaps fastidious, but Buster would have been right at home on a used-car lot.

He touted me this and he touted me that, and I made notes. He wanted someone to take the whole inventory, and I didn't mind doing that providing I could lay off all the stuff I wouldn't handle on someone else. There are people who do glass, and people who do coins, and those who do art, or fabrics, or furniture, and so on. There are also people who do junk, and a lot of what he had was junk. A lot of art deco stuff, some of it pretty bad. In among the junk, however, there were a good many pieces, mostly small, that I could use. Small tables are always in demand, and ones made of lovely wood with excellent craftsmanship do not go out of style. He had two nicely made corner cupboards, things I can always sell. The reason he hadn't sold them was probably that no one ever saw them. They were hidden behind mountains of stuff. The whole shop stank of smoke, and there were butt-filled ashtrays everywhere.

I asked him if he had a complete inventory, which he didn't. I asked him if he was willing to make one, or have one made. He sighed, very put upon, said his lease was up in sixty days, he'd waited until I got back from my honeymoon already, make him an offer.

I made him an offer. Buoyed by my success at buying the house, I made the offer lower than I thought he'd take, and he took it. "Who wants the grief." Buster grinned. "Dolly and me, we'd like some time on the beach before we're too old to enjoy it."

Later I found out he had lung cancer. He and Dolly never did have time for the beach. At the time I merely felt that sixty days didn't give us long. I asked Eugenia to take charge of sorting the contents. Since the Wagoners were, so to speak, on the payroll for the next couple of weeks, I asked them to take their truck down to the Springs and start loading whatever Eugenia said should come up to Denver. When all the good stuff was weeded out, we'd see about disposing of the rest.

"Maybe a nice bonfire," sniffed Eugenia, who hadn't been thrilled by my description of the place. When I spoke to her on the phone the following day, however, she admitted there were some nice things there. "Thank God for the Wagoners," she said. "I need every muscle they have among them! Everything decent is buried six feet deep."

That was Tuesday. Wednesday, having nothing better to do, I went down to the Springs myself and helped out. We sent two loads back to Denver that day, one to be unloaded into our storage facility and one to be taken to 1465 Hyde. Eugenia was in overalls, something I'd never thought I'd see, but the wisdom of her garb was soon made manifest when I snagged my perfectly good tweed jacket on a cow-horn chandelier that someone had left sticking out of an open cabinet.

By Thursday, we thought we had all the good pieces pulled out. We would get enough from what we'd selected to cover the cost of the inventory plus expenses and a reasonable profit. Anything more was gravy. I called Toddy Fairchild and offered to drive him down the following day, if he'd like to look over the mess.

Toddy is an expert on glass and pottery and anything else nonmetallic that has ever been fired or melted. I asked him to suggest someone for the other stuff, and he said the Sullivan sisters. I should have thought of them myself, except that my mind goes into a skid when I think of them at all. I sighed a petulant sigh and told Toddy to call them.

They were named Betty Anne and Biddy Jean; they call themselves Betts and Bitts, fiftyish, twins, not identical, but close enough to make you think of redundancy run amok. They're lizard-thin, pig-eager, and magpie-voluble. They have hair that changes color with the seasons, usually quite different one from the other. One will be silver-blond while the other is auburn, one slightly purple while the other is slightly blue. In addition to having a rather smart little antique shop called Olde What? the two of them together write the gossip column of one of our daily papers under the title "News Who?" It's a very good column, not malicious but always quite accurate. They have spies everywhere. Their chattering squawks, very birdlike, often sound almost like language but make no effort at continuity.

"Dear Jasey," cried Bitts/Betts.

"Such a lovely," cried Betts/Bitts.

I hoped they meant the day, and left it to Toddy to make what passed for conversation during the hour's drive. They got along famously, for Toddy was full of information about this family splitting the property over a divorce, and that one about to remarry, and so on. Among the three of them, they probably knew everyone in Denver or environs who had money or status or notoriety. Once we arrived, everything became busy and businesslike, including Betts/Bitts, who cleared a kind of depot in one corner and moved everything into it that they thought they could sell, voices still going like little radios someone had left on. Toddy did the same in the opposite corner, though more quietly.

Buster dropped by to see how we were doing, and he joined us for a brief lunch hiatus at a nearby fast-food place. We asked for nonsmoking, and the poor guy had to get up and leave the table twice for his cigarette. He was with us when I mentioned the house Grace and I were buying, however, and he pricked up his ears.

"Big Spanish-style place, right? With a wall around it, a lot of wrought iron? I bought a bunch of stuff at the auction of furnishings from that house. Must have been at least fifteen, twenty years ago."

"That must have been after Mrs. Monmouth died," I said.

"Right. The son was there, I remember him. Snotty guy. Kept bitching about the low bids they were getting. Didn't seem low to me, and dealers cleaned out the place. The furniture was nice, but too expensive for my clientele."

How the place had been furnished interested me, so we talked about that for a while. He remembered the furnishings as dark, heavy period stuff. A lot of walnut and mahogany and shiny varnish. The thing he remembered best was a pair of bronze lamps that had stood in the front hall. He'd bought them and made a good profit.

By three-thirty we were finished. I'd called a local flea marketeer to come over at four, which he did, and we rapidly settled on a price for "everything remaining," which included the cow-horn chandelier, a Victorian wrought-iron umbrella holder, and a large something made out of tin which I had been trying for some time to identify, sort of puzzling away at it while doing other things.

I received three checks: a medium one from Toddy, a little one from the flea man, and a medium one from the Sullivan sisters, alias "News Who?" Bitts and Betts opted to go back to town with Eugenia, and that was the week.

"We can go back to our house this weekend," said my bride, over supper.

"The pathologist's report is in?" I asked.

"She's been dead for twenty years or so. We'll know more exactly when we locate one of the Monmouths who can tell us when that little porch was added on."

"You were right, then. It was a she."

"Little girl, ten or eleven years old. If we can't identify her any other way, they'll probably have the face rebuilt on the skull. And there's some genetic stuff they can do to detect racial types. Not foolproof, but maybe helpful. There was hair left, so we know the coloration. She was dark, maybe African American, or in part."

"Cause of death?"

"The belt was still around her neck. She was strangled. The hyoid bone was broken."

"Sexually molested? Or too long ago to tell?"

"Actually, the dryness preserved everything pretty well," she said in a depressed voice. "Her panties were there, but they were under the body, not on it. We can assume a sexual attack."

I shook my head, not knowing what to say. Then I was moved by a sudden impulse. "We can arrange for burial, Grace. She doesn't have to go into Potter's Field."

"I don't think that matters, Jason. Not to me, at least. What's bothering me is that no one knows who she is.

You'd think the disappearance of an eleven-year-old girl would have been newsworthy in the seventies."

"If anyone knew she'd disappeared. Maybe they didn't know?"

"Someone knew. Someone put her there. I talked to Martinelli, asked him if he minded if I nosed around on my own time. He said go ahead, he's so overworked right now it could be days before he gets to any interviews at all. A twenty-year-old homicide doesn't have a really high priority."

"Where do you want to start?"

"You'll help?"

I got up from the table and walked around it to give her a hug. "If you want me to."

"I do. Want you to. It's really important to me, Jason. I can't settle into that house until we've done all we can. Like it was meant that you and I would be the ones to buy that house. Anybody else might not try, you know? They might throw up their hands and have a good shiver over all the ghastliness, but being who we are, we just have to figure it out."

Grace gave me all the information Martinelli had given her, a description of the clothes the little girl was wearing (a pink print dress, a pink sweater, white slip and panties, white socks and brown shoes), her height, probable weight, a description of her teeth (two cavities filled). All this told us she'd been provided for, cared for, seen to. She wasn't a street child. She became Jane Doe, at that point, or little Janey, which is what Grace called her. She had died sometime between twenty and thirty years ago, give or take five. We needed to narrow it down.

There was one thing I could do on Saturday, and that

was go to the library and look through the daily papers for the spring of 1975. I started at the end of February, just to be sure, and got as far as mid-March before I had to give up. Eye strain. I finished up the issue of March 15 and resolved to start with March 16 at the earliest opportunity.

Grace's schedule gave her Sunday off, so we spent it being lazy, trying new recipes, taking the creatures for walks, going to bed early. Monday morning early I called for an appointment with Matthew Monmouth, of M.M.A. Corporation, with an office not far from my shop. Grace would have liked to go with me, but she was busy with six other things, filling in for people who were on vacation, so she laid down some ground rules to keep her out of trouble with the department. I was not to talk about or ask about Janey Doe. That was police business, which Martinelli would get to. I could inquire about the house because she and I now owned the house and we had a legitimate interest in it. I was not to get Mrs. Mills into trouble by mentioning her.

I thought I could keep my inquiry rather narrow. Thus far, the only thing that had appeared in the papers was a paragraph on page eight saying a body had been found in a residential area. Martinelli had refused to specify the address, except to say it was in north Denver.

The office buildings on Cherry Creek North were grouped around a planted plaza arrangement in such a way that the little wintry breeze on the avenue was funneled into a blizzardy gale that threw a few flakes of snow into my eyes as I approached the tall glass doors. They opened soundlessly, letting me and the wind into the lobby. I was five minutes early. Mr. Monmouth's formidable secretary had allotted me only fifteen minutes of

Mr. Monmouth's valuable time, and when I arrived she deprived me of even that brief appointment.

She was apologetic but remained dignified. "There was some kind of emergency out at the yard, Mr. Lynx. If you'd like to drive out to the yard, I'm sure he'd be glad to see you there. I spoke to him a few minutes ago, and he's just sitting there, waiting for some people to show up."

I called her ma'am and was very respectful. I had a chief petty officer like her once. She responded by giving me a map that located the yard in an industrial area beyond the southmost suburbs. It would take me some time to get there, and I asked if she would be kind enough to call and tell Mr. Monmouth I was on my way.

The drive out South Santa Fe Drive past Littleton and along the South Platte River to Titan Road took forty-five minutes, a good part of it along a narrow, winding, two-laned road that had at one time been the main and only road from Denver to Colorado Springs. Back then it had been called "The Ribbon of Death," in honor of the number of impatient motorists who had met their end trying to pass against oncoming and high-speed traffic they couldn't see. Now that the road handled only local traffic, it had a more benign reputation, but I still drove carefully. Even local traffic was copious and erratic, seeming to depend more on the horn than on the brakes.

I turned west on Titan Road (so named for the Titan missiles that had once been manufactured at the Martin Marietta plant out that way) and went past a container yard and a line of warehouses. There was a gravel pit on my left, topped by the long diagonal of a dragline and surrounded by hills of rosy gravel. The tributaries of the Platte had been bringing gravel down from the mountains for millennia. The valley floor was probably half a mile deep in it. The gates to the gravel pit were sagging, one of them lying flat. Evidently nobody much wanted to steal gravel.

Past the gravel pit was a stretch of well-maintained taut fence and the open gate to the M.M.A. yard, marked by a discreet sign. Parked in the fenced area were a number of large earthmovers of various types, plus half a dozen trucks and trailers, one of which was fitted up as a mobile shop. Its rear door was open, and someone was working inside. I heard the scream of a power saw as I drove in. There were two vehicles parked next to the prefab building that served as an office—a battered pickup and a Lexus. As I drove up, the door opened and a man looked out, beckoning me to come in.

Monmouth was about what I expected, a couple of years younger than I, fortyish, very well suited and tied, taller than I by a bit, heavier by quite a bit, very blond, with a neat little mustache the color of pale straw. He looked a little out of place behind the cheap metal desk in this spartan office.

"Good of you to drive all this way," he said, with well-practiced geniality. "The yard foreman called to tell me we've had some vandalism, and I'm waiting on the two security firms who're coming out to take a look at the place. Sorry for the inconvenience. What's this about the old homestead in north Denver?"

Echoing his genial tone, I made my pitch.

"My wife and I bought the property a few weeks ago, and we were wondering if you'd be kind enough to give us some information about it. We know your family lived there up until fifteen years ago, and that it was built by people named Hartford, back in the twenties or thirties. We were wondering when the wall around the property was built, and when the little mudroom was added on the back?"

He sat, nodding, untroubled, completely at ease. "The Hartfords owned the whole block, originally. They sold off lots every now and then, and when Dad bought the property, he built the wall around what was left. That was in '61. He planted most of the trees at the same time. He wanted a kind of private park around the place."

"He certainly achieved the feeling. The trees are wonderful."

"Mother picked them out, the kinds, I mean. When we were little, she used to take us for walks, showing us the shapes of the leaves. In fall, we'd collect them. She even made a screen for Lucy's bedroom out of pressed autumn leaves."

"Lucy?" I asked, eyebrows raised.

"My little sister, Lucia. Three years younger than I."

"Does she still live in Denver?"

For just a moment he lost his aplomb, only a second of discomfort, quickly covered by his moving to look out the window of the office, making a gap in the metal blind and peering out at the road.

"Actually, we don't know where Lucia is. She ran away from home when she was fifteen. I believe Mother heard from her a time or two after she left, but she never returned. Nash and Joanna and I, we thought she'd come to mother's funeral at least, but she didn't."

"That's sad," I said in a sympathetic tone. "Teenagers can be very irrational. I know I was."

He smiled, and returned to his chair, seemingly comfortable again. "What was the other thing? . . . Oh. You wanted to know about the mudroom. Let me think. . . . We had a cook. Mrs. Jensen, Helga Jensen. She was always feuding with Steve for tracking dirt into her kitchen. Steve drove Mother around sometimes, but mostly he worked in the yard. So Dad had that little porch built on, so Steve could take off his boots outside. Let's see, I'd started college that year, so it would have been about 1974 or 1975. Probably '75, because I remember being home while they were building it, and it was springtime."

"Your dad built it himself?"

"No. I think Dad just pulled a couple of framers off some other job for a few days and had them build it. No. I know he did, because his father, my grandfather, was pissed about it." He grinned, reminiscently. "Granddad wasn't ever one to put family ahead of the business."

"Helga must have been gratified. That's quite a reaction to a little mud on the floor."

"Well, she was a good cook, and Dad relished his food. Besides, the feud was upsetting my mother. Mom had hysterics about all kinds of things, and if the help was unhappy, Mom was unhappy, and when Mom was unhappy, we were all unhappy. It got worse, later. Dad was fed up with the constant uproar so he left. A year or two later they got a divorce."

"So your mom lived there alone."

"She got the house in the settlement, but I kept my room there, too. For five or six years, anyhow. After Nash graduated college, he lived up and down California for a while. He was into surfing at the time, and he trained to fight forest fires. What do they call it? Smoke jumping? He was determined to break his neck, or drown. Joanna went away to school, so the family sort of spread out. Helga was still there, though, right up until Mom died."

"Was she still warring with Steve?"

"Oh, Steve. Steve left when Dad did. He was Dad's man, gardener, chauffeur, errand boy. Mom never had liked him. I didn't blame her, really. Steve was a good worker, but he could be hard to handle. I think I could have managed him all right, but Mom still thought of me as a kid."

I gave him a genial nod, playing at casual interest only. "The real-estate agent told us the place had been vacant for about fifteen years. I'm surprised at your letting it go. It's really a lovely house."

"Wrong part of town for me," he said. "Wrong part for any of us . . ."

"Your brother and sister came back here, did they?"

He nodded. "Joanna came back when she finished school. She teaches art at the CU Denver Center. Nash came back when Mom died. He traded surfing for snow boarding. He's in banking. We all hated to sell, the place had sentimental value, but Joanna wants to open a gallery—which in my estimation is a damn fool idea—and the house is part of the inheritance. None of us was interested in buying the others out. Just one of those things, you know?"

I said I did, asked him if he'd mind my calling if I had other questions, thanked him for saying he wouldn't mind, then walked with him to the door and out into the yard where he patted me on the shoulder, expressed joy at having met me, and told me to let him know how things went out at the house, all under the scrutiny of the man in the shop who was still busy with the screaming saw. As I was leaving, a van came in, the logo on the side identifying it as a security firm.

I went down the road to the gravel pit, parked, and made notes before I forgot the details. Helga Jensen; Steve, the yardman; mudroom built a couple of years before the divorce, probably 1975; Joanna leaving for school; Nash graduating, Nash living in California. Matthew Monmouth was fortyish. Mrs. Mills said the older three children were born prior to the Monmouths taking the place in '61. So Matthew had been born about '57; his brother in '58 or '9; the older girl between '59 and '60, give or take a year or two either way. Matt would have left for college at age eighteen or there-abouts, say '74. And the mudroom had been built the fol-lowing spring: 1975, twenty-one years ago. Nothing inconsistent with what we knew to be true.

I pulled back into the road and started home, still carefully. It was late enough now that some people were headed home from work, driving faster than they should, seduced by their familiarity with the road. I was passed by two or three accidents arranging to happen before I got back to the multilaned highway at County Line road. Once back at the shop, I drew up a time line, starting in 1961 and ending at the present, then put what happenings I knew of opposite the proper year. Lucia's leaving home, each of the kids starting and graduating college (assuming they'd done it in four years each), the divorce, Mrs. Monmouth's death. The foreign family. Damn! I'd forgotten to ask about the foreign family. Not that it seemed to have anything to do with anything. They hadn't come until later, according to Mrs. Mills, after the divorce and before Mrs. Monmouth died.

The history was far from complete, but it would give Grace something to look over when she got home. Just for the hell of it, I looked up Helga Jensen in the phone book. There were several H. Jensens, no Helga. I thought Grace might prefer to do the calling, woman to woman, so I didn't follow up on that.

two

WHEN I GOT back to the shop, I called Grace. She wasn't there, so I left the message that the mudroom had been built in 1975. I was just hanging up when Eugenia put her head into my office and asked me rather tartly if I intended to do anything with the inventory of items brought from Colorado Springs. We went down to the basement together and looked them over while I made notes. She had already cleaned up the things that didn't need repair. It's a wonder what soap and water and lemon oil will do.

One side table had a cracked leg that had been badly mended. We chipped some glue out of the crack and put it in water, to see if it would dissolve. If it would, we'd work our way into the crack by packing damp cotton into it until it came apart, then dry it carefully and completely and reglue it with proper clamps. If it wouldn't dissolve in water, we'd try other solvents, and if it wouldn't dissolve, period, we could saw through the cracked section and replace it with a narrow strip of matching wood. None of which would have been worth doing except that the table itself was a very good one.

The corner cupboards were both good, but dirty. The bottoms had panel doors, the tops, glass. The muntins—

the thin wood strips that separate panes of glass—looked
original in both: one cupboard had all the original glass
and the other was missing two pieces. The lighter colored
of the two had slots at the front of the shelves, for
hanging wineglasses, and I doubted very much that they
were original. The wear was in the right places on both
pieces, however. Fake antiques often have "wear" in
places no one could possibly "wear" the furniture in
question. "Wear" shows up where people put their hands,
on drawer and door edges and around pulls, or where
pieces of wood move, one against another, at the sides
and bottoms of doors and drawers and at the base where
the furniture is moved repeatedly on the floor. It does not
appear in the middle of doors or under the edges of
molding, where fakey antiques are often "worn" or "distressed." These pieces had been well cared for in the
main, and I judged them both to date to the early 1800s.
Buster had no provenance on any of his pieces. On the
few occasions when I'd been around him, I'd gathered
that he wasn't interested in what he sold so much as he
was in the business of buying and selling. He bought
stuff and sold stuff, and it didn't matter to him much
what the stuff was.

I went back upstairs to my office just in time to take a
call from Bitts and Betts, both on the line simultaneously,
to say they'd found something interesting in a tin box,
could they bring it over? I wasn't quick enough to think
of an excuse why not.

"Who was that?" Mark asked.

"The Sullivan sisters," I said.

"Oh, Lord," he muttered. "I've got to go get some tile
samples."

"You could stick around to help."

"Sorry, Jason. Last time they were here they stayed four hours in full unintelligible cry. You're on your own."

Which was rank insubordination but understandable, for all that. The sisters showed up suspiciously promptly, making me think they'd called from around the corner.

"Jasey!" Betts entered loudly.

"Such a flapdoodle," chittered Bitts.

"Found us a thing, we did, a veritable thing, not our style, not our kind of thing, your kind of thing," said Betts.

I gritted my teeth and smiled. "What was it?"

They put the tin box on my desk. I remembered it from Buster's place, a very nice oblong box with a humped lid, like a little trunk lid, with a ring on top. It had the brownish look of the old baked varnishes—baked varnish was the best Europeans could do in copying Japanese lacquerware—and both base and lid were brightly decorated in a flower pattern in several colors.

"Very nice," I said.

"Our kind of thing, don't you think, we did, think so, and what's inside should be our thing, too, shouldn't it, but it's not." Betts pried open the lid and revealed what lay within. A sheaf of letters, quite unfaded.

"Lid stuck," offered Bitts. "Stuck tight, took us quite a time, WD-40 you know, squirt squish, until it comes loose. And it's got the name on it, so we thought, well, Jason's kind of thing, his, right, not ours."

I frantically grabbed for clues as to what they might be talking about. "Name?" I said. "What name?"

"Buster told you he bought stuff from there. Monmouth. That's the name. This is some of what he bought. You know, Jasey, at lunch?"

I took the proffered sheaf of letters and turned them over. The envelope on top, directed in a spidery and quite foreign-looking hand, bore the name of Virginia Monmouth at the address of our new house. Virginia Monmouth. That had to be Matthew's mom. The disjointed phrases fell into place, as they sometimes but not always did with the Sullivan sisters. Yes, I had discussed the place with Buster over lunch, using the name Monmouth.

The contents of the letters were impenetrable, being written in both a different script and a foreign language. German? Possibly German. Though I doubted I could tell German from Dutch. I shrugged mentally, deciding these were from the foreign people that Mrs. Mills had mentioned.

"Thank you," I said. "Thank you for bringing them. Do you think Buster bought the box along with other stuff and never opened it?"

"Barely opened it ourselves," said Betts. "Can opener, we thought, about to resort to that, except it's a nice piece of tin, very good, get something for that."

"Nice all round," said Bitts. "Good job, Jasey. Let us know next time the same."

They patted me, one on each side, and then fooled me by departing without further ado, chittering to one another as they went. I couldn't decide if they were more squirrel-like or birdlike.

"Are they gone?" asked Eugenia, from around the corner of the door.

I waved the letters at her and she came to have a look. "That's a real coincidence," she said, noting the address on the envelopes.

"Not really. The contents of the house were auctioned off when Mrs. Monmouth died. Buster is a dealer. He bought some stuff. I'm a dealer, it's natural we'd come into contact some time or other."

"But in fifteen years, wouldn't you think someone would have discovered them?"

"You saw Buster's place. I doubt if he's cleaned house in twenty years or more. The tin box was probably at the bottom of a pile. And the sisters said they had a devil of a time getting it open. My problem at the moment is, what do I do with them?"

"When are they dated?" Eugenia asked, taking them over to the window, where she could get a better light on the postmarks. "Here's two or three in '73. As many in '74. One each December, probably Christmas letters. Then here's one in March '75 and another a few weeks later. Are you going to have them translated?"

"Only if necessary. Mrs. Wills told us there was a foreign family living with Mrs. Monmouth for a couple of years. My guess would be that she, Virginia, was of German descent, and that the foreign family were relatives who wrote to her infrequently but regularly, and then came to stay for a while."

"Logical," she murmured, handing me back the letters. "Not necessarily true, but logical."

I scorched her with a look, which she ignored. When I dropped the letters onto my desk, they landed right on top of the packet of photos, the ones the Wagoners had found, still in their dirty envelope. Grace had evidently left them there for me to look over. I shuffled through them without really looking at them. Pictures of children. Slightly different-sized prints, so probably taken at various times. Nothing jumped out at me. I dropped photos and letters in a drawer, making a mental note to talk to Grace about both.

The Wagoners were working again at the north Denver house, so Grace and I agreed to meet there when she got off, to see how things were progressing and try one of the local restaurants, which were mostly Italian. We found nothing changed at the house except that the pile of trash had been removed. Some of the mudroom floor, the joists and some flooring at the edges, was still there, as though the Wagoners had put off getting to it. I didn't blame them much.

Grace was very quiet during dinner, and not as ravenous as usual. She ate only single portions and didn't ask for my dessert, though I gave it to her anyhow. While she nibbled at it, I filled her in on Matthew Monmouth and gave her the time line chart I'd written out.

"So sister Lucy disappeared when she was fifteen?" she murmured. "She can't be Janey Doe. Too old. Though the timing's right."

"Timing?"

"Both in 1975. The mudroom was built then, so the little girl was killed then, and Lucy disappeared then."

"You think there's a connection?" I asked. The idea had not occurred to me.

"I don't think anything at this point. If one person dies and a connected person disappears, my usual inclination would be to ask questions. Like, did Lucy have something to do with killing her?"

"Lucy was fifteen!"

"Fifteen-year-olds kill people. At this point, we just don't know what reason she might have had to kill an eleven-year-old girl."

"At this point," I said, "we just don't know much of anything. Let's talk about something else."

So we talked about paint colors for the interior of the

house and about the kitchen arrangement Grace had sketched in her notebook. Just as we were leaving, Grace suddenly said, "You know, Jason, we don't know that Mr. Monmouth is gone. Mrs. Monmouth died, and she owned the house, but what about him? He could still be alive."

"We still have to talk to Joanna and Nash," I countered. "We can ask them."

She was almost silent on the way home. When we stopped for a traffic light, the street lamp lit her eyes, swimming with tears. I went through the intersection and pulled over.

"What is it, love?"

"Children," she said. "All day I've been thinking of children. Like Janey Doe, and then today there was an abuse case. Little innocents, just used up and thrown away. Some days, oh, you know, Jason. It just got to me, that's all."

I pulled her close and kept my arm around her the rest of the way home. Grace is tough. She has to be tough to do her job, but as she has remarked to me on more than one occasion, one can't get so tough that nothing penetrates, because if one does, one stops being a good cop (or good anything else) and just starts going through the motions. Grace had cried over cases before, and often the cases had involved children.

"Martinelli called today," she murmured in my ear. "I told him what we had so far. He told me he'd check the missing persons files around 1975: '74, '5, and '6. We figured three years would cover it, just in case somebody doesn't remember too accurately. Then I was just hanging up when Brad Fenwick came over and told me what I was working on reminded him of a case he had

four years ago, child strangled, about the same age. He'd
already pulled the file. Except that she wasn't raped, it
was a carbon copy, Jason. The belt around the neck, the
panties under the body, the whole thing. That body was
hidden in the crawl space of a condo development, just
like Janey Doe's body. The floor was half done one afternoon when they quit work. Next day, when the carpenters came back, one of them brought his dog, and the dog
found her body."

So that was what had been bothering her all evening. I
tried not to sound horrified as I said, "Four years ago?
That's eighteen years after the one we found, Grace.
You're not thinking it's the same killer?"

She shivered. I turned up the heat in the car. The days
were still warm, but the nights were definitely turning
toward winter. "Are you?" I persisted.

"I don't know."

"Was the victim identified?"

"Yes. A ten-year-old parochial-school student, grabbed
while out on her bike. They found the bike before they
found her. The body turned up the following day."

"Meaning?"

"Meaning he'd put her there almost immediately.
She'd been dead for less than a day when the dog found
the body."

"And no arrests?"

"No, nothing." She shivered again. "I keep . . ."

"You keep what, love?" We turned into the alley and
stopped outside the garage.

"I keep thinking, maybe there are more. We've found
two. But if he started twenty-one years ago, or before,
and if he was still doing it four years ago . . ."

I pushed the button on the garage-door opener. In the backyard, Bela uttered an "Is that you?" bark. We drove in. The door fell shut behind us and we just sat there for a long moment, arms around one another. Outside, Bela impatiently questioned the delay. He hadn't been fed or brushed or walked, and he wanted at least two out of three.

"Two similar occurrences don't make a pattern," I said, trying to sound authoritative. "Particularly not when there's almost twenty years between the two! You know that, Grace. If it weren't that the victims were children, you wouldn't think so yourself."

She nodded, wiping at her eyes. "I don't know what's the matter with me, Jason. The last few days, ever since we found Janey Doe, I've felt so weepy."

I bit the bullet. "Would you like to sell the house and make another choice? We can do that. It will take a little time, but—"

"No! I love the house. The house has nothing to do with . . . with her. The house was there long before, and it will be there long after. Houses are like . . . mountains. They last longer than people. You can't blame houses for what people do! We just have to find out what happened. So long as we've done everything we can do to solve this thing, I can be perfectly happy there."

Another, very impatient bark from outside the garage door.

"Well, we people aren't going to live to find out anything if we don't feed Bela. His ancestors were wolves, and he's obviously deciding to revert to type."

Which brought a wan smile, at least.

By the time we had the household settled and ourselves bathed and relaxed in my big bed with glasses of wine on the bedside table, she seemed to have forgotten the passing anxiety and I didn't raise the question. I was as troubled as she was, but I didn't want her to know that. When she'd said, "Maybe there are more," I'd had one of those "by the pricking of my thumbs" moments, one of those absolutely certain "by God that's it" moments. The words came from her mouth, they resonated, and I recognized what she said as true. Yes. It is one man. Yes, there may be more.

Talking with Kate Mills had reminded me that it had been some time since I'd visited Nellie Arpels. I drove over to the shopping center to pick up a box of candies and then went through the back gate across the alley from the shop and knocked on her door. Nellie, in her eighties, lives in a converted garage at the rear of her daughter's house, so she can get out into the sun.

"Well, stranger," she said, head cocked to one side and resting more or less on the belly of the white cat, Perky, who was draped around Nellie's neck like a stole. "What brings you over?"

"Guilty conscience," I told her. "I haven't been over to see you since Grace and I got back."

Perky opened one eye, decided I wasn't important, and went back to sleep.

"And you sent only three postcards," she said grumpily. "I call that mean."

"You came to the wedding," I pointed out. "One of the few." We'd had a very small, private ceremony, with only my grandmother and aunt and a few friends invited, and we'd left immediately thereafter.

"That's true," she said, trying to see what I was holding behind me. "Is that for me?"

"Chocolates with orange creme centers." They were her favorites, and I'd bought her a pound of them. "Don't spend them all in one place."

"You do have a guilty conscience." She wrenched open the box and pounced on a candy with a little cry of delight. "Meant to tell you, you've got a look-alike."

"Me?"

"I was watching the movie critics. That newest James Bond. He looks just like you."

"Nellie, he does not. He's dark. My hair's red."

"Except for that. Built like you, too. When he was being Remington Steele, I always thought he was a little weedy, but he's filled out some. Acts like you. Those eyebrows, like now."

Self-consciously I lowered my eyebrows. I had always thought the actor in question was a little precious and supercilious. Me?

"So," she said, happy at having totally upset my apple-cart. "Tell me what's going on. I can tell something's bothering you. You look all washed out around the eyes."

So, while Nellie munched orange-filled chocolates, I sat down and told her about the new house and the body we'd found, and the other body that was like it four years ago, and one thing and another.

"You think they did it? Some of those Monmouths?"

"I've no reason to think so, Nellie. No more than the carpenters might have done it. Or any delivery man who drove in and saw the porch being built. Or anyone the carpenters or the Monmouths might have mentioned it to."

"The way you tell about the place, you couldn't see the porch from the street."

"Maybe it could have been seen then. The trees and bushes have grown up some in twenty-one years."

"Umph," she said, picking out another orange creme. "I think it was a Monmouth."

"Any particular one?"

"You haven't told me about any of them yet," she said. "Just the one, Matthew, and not much about him. There was his mother and his father and two sisters and a brother. That's five more. Plus the cook, and the maid, and this yardman. That's eight. And you said something about a foreign family . . . ?"

"That was later."

"Well, eight then. Eight people you have to find out about and tell me about." She grinned in satisfaction, rocking herself back and forth. "You will be busy."

"And you want to hear about each and every one of them, don't you?"

"That's what I've got you for, Jason. Excitement. It's just amazing how little excitement there is in an old woman's life when she's stuck in a chair behind a fence. I swear, I saw more when I was living upstairs in the attic."

"I could get you a really tall periscope," I suggested.

"Tssh." She rocked happily back and forth. "When are you going to see the Monmouth brother and sister?"

"Soon."

"Today?"

"I'll call them today and see when they can meet with me."

"Umm. Is Grace pregnant yet?"

"Nellie!"

"Well, she's old enough. Better get a move on."

I hadn't intended to tell anyone, but there I was, suddenly spilling everything to Nellie: how Grace had been affected by the child's body, how weepy she'd been.

"Right now isn't the time to talk to Grace about babies," I concluded. "She's feeling a little fragile."

She gave me a strange look, as though she'd decided not to say something that was on the tip of her tongue. What came out was, "Fine. Just don't put it off until exactly the right time, that's all I'm saying."

"I should think exactly the right time would be when one should have a child."

"Nope. If people did that, nobody would ever have a baby. There's wrong times, no doubt, but there just isn't any right time. Oh, being married makes it more right, of course, and it helps if you're healthy, but beyond that . . ." She rocked again, putting the lid back on her chocolates. "Thank you, Jason. What was it you said this Matthew man does?"

"He's a lawyer."

"That's what he is, what does he do?"

I'm sure my face was blank, and I felt a little stupid. "I don't know. He's not in a law office, so I guess he works for the M.M.A. Corporation."

"And what is it?"

I laughed. "I'll find out, Nellie. Silly of me not to have done that already."

I left as I often did after talking to Nellie, rejuvenated. Old ladies have that effect on me. They make me feel boyish, and enthusiastic. Thank God for old ladies, I thought, then spoiled it by wondering if James Bond liked old ladies. With all those women, how could he take the time?

I had little luck locating Nash and Joanna. Nash had an unlisted home number, and the one J. Monmouth in the book was disconnected. I finally resorted to calling Matthew's very efficient secretary and telling her I'd found some snapshots of Joanna in the demolished kitchen, could she give me Joanna's address, so I could send them to her. She remembered my previous visit well enough to decide I wasn't a mad bomber.

I was about to hang up after getting the address when I thought of Nellie's question.

"Just curious," I said, "but what does M.M.A. Corporation do?"

"The company was started sixty years ago by Mr. Monmouth's grandfather, Meridew Monmouth," she said. "It was first called Monmouth Construction. His son Matthew Sr. changed it to Matthew Monmouth and Sons, and this Mr. Monmouth, Matthew Jr., changed it again, to M. Monmouth and Associates. Though the firm still does some construction, most of Mr. Monmouth's work is in land acquisition and development, property management and leasing, environmental impact, union negotiations, all the legal and regulatory requirements that need to be met before building can be done."

"Some guy who wants to build an apartment house hires you to take care of the legal stuff?"

She laughed. "Well, providing the apartment house is forty stories high. More likely someone who wants to build a big mall or a tech center or a hotel convention complex."

I thanked her graciously and got out the city directory to see what phone number was attached to Joanna's address. No phone. Well, and well. There was not much doing at the shop, so I dug the photos out of the drawer, got into the car, and drove to the address mentioned, a big old house in the Capitol Hill area, not five minutes from my own. It was a conversion, one apartment per floor. The foyer listed three tenants, K. Winters, Morris Silver, and J. Watson. I took a chance on Watson and pressed the button.

A tinny, perhaps female voice barked an impatient, "Yes?"

"Joanna?" I asked.

"Yes?" again, not quite so short.

"My name is Jason Lynx. My wife and I just bought the house in north Denver where you grew up. We found some old photos, and I brought them by, on the off chance you might want them."

Long, very long silence. Then, "Bring them up," said the tinny box.

I brought them up. One flight. Door opening into a big room, pleasant and sunny, full of houseplants and one very large green and yellow parrot, who fixed me with a knowledgeable eye for all of ten seconds, then ignored me. It was my day for being ignored by animals.

I'd been expecting a female version of Matthew Monmouth, so Joanna came as a surprise. He had been rather prissily groomed and barbered, but she was very lovely in a natural, unmade-up way. She looked to be in her mid-to-late thirties, with her fair hair braided down the back in a long, thick plait tied with blue ribbon that matched her jeans. Her loose white shirt was paint smeared, and on an easel near the north window was a painting in progress; the parrot perched beside a teal-blue bowl full of limes, lemons, and oranges. Some of the same colors were smeared on her hands.

"What's this about the house?" she asked. "You bought the place? Thank God for that."

"It's a lovely house," I said. "We feel very fortunate to have it."

She was distracted, looking from me to the painting to

the parrot, then back at me as she muttered, "That house was Mom's Garden of Eden. Complete with snake."

"Who was the snake?"

This surprised her into awareness. "My father." She dropped the brush she was holding into a jar of clear liquid, swished it around until the liquid turned bright green, then dried the brush on a scrap of cloth she had tucked into her waistband. "He had her penned up out there like a rabbit in a cage. Wall all around the place, so nobody could get in or out without the guards seeing them . . ."

"The guards?"

She laughed. "The yardman and the cook. Steve and Helga. Mom couldn't take a deep breath without one of them reporting on her. And as for having company, or going anywhere . . . Well, if she went, Steve drove her, and she'd rather have died than been alone in a car with Steve. Sadistic bastard." She took a deep breath and dropped into a chair, gesturing at the one across the table from her.

I sat down with an audible thump. "One of the neighbors, Mrs. Mills, had a totally different impression of your mother."

"I can imagine," she said, getting up again to throw a cover over the painting. "You want some coffee? Or a beer?"

"Coffee would be fine, thank you."

She went into the adjacent kitchen. In a moment I heard the whirring scream of a coffee grinder. It upset the macaw, and he shrieked an accompaniment. Rustle rustle, clank clang, shriek shriek, and she was back, murmuring to the bird, offering him a handful of unshelled peanuts.

"Photos," she said, when she had the bird quiet.

"Oh, right." I dug them out of my inside front pocket. "I thought they must be of you and your brothers."

She took them, leafed through them, nodding slowly. "This one is of Lucia and me. She was twelve, I was eleven. And this one is all four of us, taken about that same time. That's Steve in the background. He'd just been hired."

"How do you remember that?"

"He's wearing a chauffeur's cap. He wore it for only a few weeks. He hated it, and Dad didn't make him wear it." She shook her head and went on to another picture. "These others are the Kettinger kids. The German side of Mother's family. These were taken after I left for college, or even later. I think Trina was six when they came, and she looks about nine or ten in this picture, around the time of the divorce, maybe. Mom was lonely and sick. None of us knew how sick she really was. Maybe even she didn't know it. Anyhow, she invited the Kettingers to come stay for a while, and they did. Him and her and the four kids. They were there for several years. Bratty kids, but no worse than we'd been, I suppose."

She threw the snapshots down on the table and went to fetch the coffee. I picked them up and looked at them with new eyes. The girls, Lucia and Joanna, alone together in jeans and sweaters and broad-brimmed hats that hid their hair and shadowed their faces: Joanna relaxed, smiling, eyes sparkling; her older sister grave, eyes watchful. The sibling group. Joanna, at twelve, her mouth pinched into a painful line, in school uniform. Next to her, with his arm tight around her, Matt at sixteen, already handsome and muscular, smiling confidently. Nash next to him, shorter but even sturdier, equally blond, a year or so younger, looking superior and remote. And then Lucia, thirteen, a little space between herself and the others, her eyes watchful, her mouth gravely quiet, her face seeming remote, uninvolved. She also wore a school uniform. It was as Grace had said. The boys were happy. The girls weren't. From what Joanna had just said, I could guess why. If Mama was a prisoner, probably the girls were too, right up to and including private school, and there in the background was their jailor, Steve. He had a lean, vulpine face, and a noticeable sneer. The uniform cap was tilted back on his head, and a cigarette protruded from one corner of his mouth. Not my idea of a proper chauffeur.

Joanne brought in a tray and poured coffee.

"Is your dad still alive?" I asked.

She shrugged, her mouth twisted into an unpleasant grin. "Technically, I suppose you'd say so. Alzheimer's. He's been in a nursing home for almost four years now. He still has the occasional lucid moment, few and far between."

"And Nash? In banking, isn't he?"

"*In* banking is about it. He has a so-called VP job that Matt got for him a couple of years ago. I'm surprised he's lasted this long. He never keeps jobs long. Actually, Nash's real career is being a victim. He's got a good mind and general good health, and what he does with it is figure out who's wounded him lately or who he's mad at, then he spends his whole life getting even. Sometimes he files lawsuits. At last count, he had about six of them going. He makes his living being a poor, pitiable, misunderstood baby. People pay him off just to get rid of him."

"What started him on that?"

"God knows. Maybe Dad did. Nash was his favorite.

Not Matt, which always surprised the heck out of me. Matt had to obey, but Nash had to be made allowances for. Matt had to work summers in the business, but Nash got a free ride. When a teacher let Matt have it, that was discipline, but if a teacher yelled at Nash, that was abuse. It took me years to figure it out. What was going on was that whenever Nash didn't get his way, he'd do something absolutely outrageous and he'd let it be known if he didn't get his way, he'd go on doing whatever the outrageous thing was. . . ."

"Like what?"

"Oh, anything dangerous or hurtful. Shutting himself up in his room without eating for a week, or making an appointment with the family lawyer to discuss the fact he was being abused, or threatening to jump off the roof, something like that. He simply made it so costly for anyone to try to discipline him that people gave up trying. Even my father, who usually welcomed a fight. Nash had him whipped. Nash never cared anything about the rest of us. Matt and I had to sue to get him to sell the house so we could have our share. Nash said Dad told him he wanted it to stay in the family, that he mustn't ever sell it, but hell, I need the money. I'm starting a gallery."

"I thought it was Matt who didn't want to sell. The real-estate agent said the oldest boy."

"Well, she got it wrong. It was whiny Nash. He claims Dad made him promise never to sell it. He claims it's his spiritual home. Hell, he never turned his hand over in that house; he never even mowed the lawn! California was his spiritual home, if anyplace ever was. Sun, sand, and risking his neck. Jumping out of planes, surfing. The only reason he came back here was that he got into some kind of trouble out there. Not that it was his fault. Nothing is ever his fault. He gets mad, then he talks to one of his therapists about it, getting madder and madder every time he tells the story, making it worse each time, then he ends up suing somebody. This time it'll be Matt and me, just wait. He's got a perfect bitch of a little wife, and she eggs him on."

"You're not married?"

She shivered. It was a shiver of revulsion, very clear, very plain, and I pretended not to notice it.

"Not anymore," she murmured.

Maybe she was lesbian. Maybe her parents' example didn't set well with her. In either case, I moved on.

"The little mudroom added onto the back of the house, do you remember anything about that?"

"I remember it ruined the look of the house and made the kitchen even darker. Helga said either keep Steve out of her kitchen or she'd quit. She hated him almost as much as Mother did."

"Her fellow guard?"

"They weren't friends. They weren't like . . . conspirators. They were . . . what should I say, independently evil! No. Steve was evil, but Helga was just a toady who pretended she was concerned about us. Steve was out-and-out sadistic. I mean it. He'd say things that would ruin your day, and he'd laugh. You know kids. How self-conscious they are. If I had a zit on my chin, depend on it, Steve would notice and remark on it and how awful it looked. He'd say, 'Gee, that's awful, Jo. It ruins your whole face.' And if I broke down and cried, oh, he loved that."

"What was his last name?" I asked.

"McHenry," she said. "With the emphasis on the *Mc*.

The only way we could get Steve's goat was by mispronouncing his name. We'd call him mcHENry, and he'd go blue." She laughed, a silly and rather joyous laugh. "I hope the bastard's dead."

"Sounds like there were several snakes in that garden."

She grinned a rueful acknowledgment.

"Mrs. Mills says your sister disappeared."

Volatile as fire, her face changed, her eyes narrowed and flooded with tears. "Lucy. Damn."

"Sorry," I murmured. "Didn't mean to raise a sore issue."

"It still hurts," she cried. "I loved her! She had no business doing that without telling me, going off that way. I still wake up in the night wondering what happened to her. Damn."

"Didn't she contact your mother after she left?"

She looked away from me. "Matthew says so now, but I never heard Mother say so then. Not that I blamed Lucia for going. She was so . . . tender. No defenses. She couldn't handle conflict. Dad, Mom, the boys, anybody could push her around. Poor Luce."

Part of that had been a lie. Her expression told me so. The big bird finished grooming himself and sidled along the table in Joanna's direction. She put out an absent-minded finger and scratched his neck. He craned, separating the feathers so she could do a more thorough job, and made an almost purring sound.

I pushed for the truth. "You think Matthew's lying about her having contacted your mother?"

It was the wrong question. She stiffened. "What in hell am I doing? Here I am, talking to a perfect stranger about my family. This has nothing to do with the house!"

"Sorry," I murmured. "I'm an inveterate snoop. I love hearing about people."

"Who are you, anyhow?"

I got out a card, one of the engraved ones, Jason Lynx Interiors, small print, very dignified. "My wife, Grace Willis, is a policewoman. My associates are very respectable. I'm not a newsman or anything of that kind."

She stared at the card, then at me, then at the card again. "So, you're entirely too nosy for a house buyer. What's this really about?"

I liked her. I hadn't liked Matthew at all, but I liked her. Without stopping to consider Grace's prohibitions, I opted for the truth. "We really are house buyers. We tore down the little mudroom on the back of the house." I kept my eyes on hers. Did she stiffen a little? I couldn't tell. "We found a body."

"No!" she cried. "Oh, no. How awful." Her eyes filled and she turned away, wiping her tears. When she turned back she said in a strangled voice, "Maybe it was Lucia."

Her tone was odd. I said, "No. It wasn't Lucia. This body has been there since the mudroom was built." I took her lax hand in mine, squeezing it. She jerked it away as if she'd been burned. Immediately, she began fishing for a tissue in the pocket of her shirt, wiping her streaming eyes.

I said again, "It wasn't Lucia. It never occurred to me that you might think so. The body was of an eleven-year-old girl. It had been there ever since the room was built."

"That bastard," she said. "Oh, that bastard."

"Who?"

Her eyes darted. She was deciding what to tell me. "Steve. Sadistic bastard. He . . . he was always touching us, Lucia and me. Never enough so you could say he meant to, you know. And he liked looking at little girls. We told Mother. It's one reason she hated him. Dad said it was nonsense, that she'd put it into our heads. It wasn't nonsense. We knew what he was like."

"Would you have any ideas about the little girl? Who she might have been?"

She stared past me, out the window. "When they built the mudroom? When was that?"

"About 1975."

She said, "I was a freshman in high school, Lucia was a sophomore. Parochial school, not that we're Catholic, but Dad preferred it. We didn't know any kids in the neighborhood, never got to. When Dad built that wall, he meant it. He kept the whole world out. He told us who we could see and when and where we could go, and we couldn't go anywhere alone. Steve always drove us. There were never any children there but us."

"When your parents were divorced, Steve left?"

"Dad wanted him to stay on the place. We all knew why, to spy on us. Mother said she wouldn't have him. I think Dad may have kept him on, but not as a chauffeur, I'd have known that. In the business, maybe. That was the big push, back then, when Grandpa died and Dad was taking over the business."

"It's three generations, then?"

"Oh, yes, and all three of them are big deals so far as Matt's concerned. Grandpa had a little construction business. Dad took it over and made it a bigger one. Then Matt went to law school, and he was Dad's vice president in charge of paperwork, I guess. It was Monmouth and Sons, then, but Nash wasn't interested in being a son. Every now and then he would come home, demanding a 'share' in the family business, Dad would give him a job, and he'd fool with it for a few weeks, then he'd run off to California to risk his neck again. Over and over, for almost ten years . . ."

"You said he had a wife?"

"Yeah. If you can call her that. She's from an old Denver family. They got married shortly after Mom died."

"Children?"

"You're kidding." She laughed harshly. "Nita wouldn't ruin her figure getting pregnant. She brags about wearing a size four."

"Tell me more about the business."

"Oh. Let's see. Matthew was VP and Dad was president. Then, about 1990, when Dad couldn't function anymore, Matt took over and turned the business into something else that was bigger yet. I should be glad. We all own shares. So far, they haven't paid us much. They will, when and if Matt stops putting all the income back into the business."

"And that's what Nash lives on?"

"Some. Some from his so-called job."

"You don't know if Steve's still around?"

"I haven't seen him since the divorce." She got up to throw the wadded tissue away, turning to ask, "Is it a secret? About the body?"

"The police haven't released the address where it was found," I said, realizing I was going to have to confess to Grace that I'd transgressed her rules of engagement. "Can you keep quiet about that?"

"Who would I tell?"

It was an interesting question. I would have thought she would tell her brothers. Evidently, she thought not.

I thanked her for her time. She thanked me for telling her. She got up to escort me to the door.

"I get the feeling you're going to go on snooping around, and you say your wife is a cop. If you find out anything about . . . will you tell me?" she begged. "Please. I'd like to know."

"Did your sister confide in you?"

"I think so. How do any of us know whether other people really tell us things?"

"Can you think of anyone else she might have confided in?"

"She had a friend at school. Clare. Clare who? I can't remember. If I think of it, I'll call you." She patted her shirt pocket, where she'd put my card. Her face was still streaked with tears as she shut the door behind me.

First thing back at the shop, I checked the phone book. No S. McHenry. No Steven McHenry. I got out the time-line chart and added the information Joanna had given me. Matthew joined the business after graduating law school, say around '81, and took over the business five years ago, say '91. He'd worked for his father for eleven years. Steve was definitely a factor, so I entered him. He'd been at the house, living over the garage when the girls were teens, from around 1970 until Mr. Monmouth left, which was around 1975. Even after that he may have worked for Matthew Monmouth Sr.

Was he also a child molester, murderer of young girls? Had he, by any chance, killed another little girl four years ago? The police could ask that question. Neither Grace nor Lieutenant Martinelli would thank me for intruding on that particular ground.

* * *

Grace arrived home reasonably ravenous. We put together a huge omelet with a green salad, and I defrosted a frozen dessert. Grace ate most of it, and I was delighted that her appetite had returned. When everything had been cleaned up, the animals fed and tended to, and no duty called, we sat in front of our gas fire—wood fires strictly prohibited in Denver—toasting our toes while I told Grace all about Joanna Monmouth.

"Steve McHenry," she mused, seeming quite relaxed about it, with no evidence of the tension she'd been showing recently. "He would have had opportunity to dispose of the body. If he was a pedophile, and a sadist, as Joanne says, he may have hurt the child, then killed her to keep her from telling on him. That would give him motive. Certainly a big strong man like that would have had no trouble strangling a child that size. If we could establish she lived in that area . . ."

"You'd have to know who she was, Grace. I got through only half the newspapers on Saturday. I'll see if I can't get back down there tomorrow."

"I'll find out what Martinelli came up with. He was going to go through all the missing-persons reports."

She sipped at her wine and the phone rang. Speak of the devil: Martinelli. I handed her the phone and listened to her responses: a soft grunt, um, oh really, yeah, and a final okay. She was scowling when she sat down again.

"What?" I demanded.

"No missing-persons reports from that long ago. It was precomputer. Everything over twenty years old is buried in some basement somewhere. He says he'll try, but without a name it looks fairly hopeless." Her voice was crisp, businesslike, unwifely.

"Fine time of night to call," I grumped. His call had

ruined the mood we'd managed to establish. Now she was on the prod again.

"He just got home. I left word for him about the other little girl, and I guess that jostled him some." She made a face, saying angrily, "You know, Jason, I'd really like to forget this, just for a day or two. There have been a lot of changes in my life recently, if you've noticed. . . ."

"In mine, too," I said, being sympathetic.

She actually snarled at me. "Nothing has changed in your life, Jason. You are living in the same place. You are keeping to the same schedule. You are occupying the same bed. We are not sleeping together any more frequently. The only change, so far as I can see, is that we are eating together somewhat more often than previously."

I took a deep breath. "Quite right," I said, nodding in a calm, reasonable way. "I see what you mean."

"Also," she said, still snarling, "you have not missed three menstrual periods."

"Three?" I'm sure my voice squeaked. I couldn't get out any other words at all.

She stood up and stalked to the window, where she peered out at absolutely nothing, her back rigid. "One toward the end of September, in the Bahamas. One toward the end of October, just when we were buying the house. Both of which I ascribed to stress or change or excitement. And one right about now. Which I cannot ascribe to anything but . . . being stupid."

All kinds of thoughts jostled in my head, things I wanted to say or ask or suggest. What I did, without thinking, was get up and remove her wineglass from her hand, at which point she burst into tears.

"You shouldn't . . . ," I mumbled.

"Oh, hell, Jason. French women and Italian women drink wine with their meals while they're pregnant, and they don't have retarded children."

"Maybe they do," I said, stung. "Maybe that explains the entire French population."

She started giggling, through the tears, and in a moment we had a full-fledged hysteria going on. I fetched washcloths for the face and hot tea for the throat and furnished pats and hugs, all the time frantically trying to think how this could have happened. We had been, according to Grace, very very careful. She didn't want to have a baby until we were settled. She had said so, very firmly, over and over!

"When?" I blurted, finally, when I'd thought of everything and nothing fit.

"That night after the beach party . . ."

The hotel threw weekly beach parties, much food and champagne and entertainment. Come to think of it, Grace and I had ended up in the surf, at the edge of the sand, after everyone else had gone away. . . .

I decided not to rehash the matter. If that had been the time, we had both been at fault. Both. I reminded myself sternly of this.

"How do you feel?" I asked. "Physically, I mean."

"I feel sick in the morning. I throw up. I feel weepy and cross. I can't get the waistband of my trousers buttoned."

"Already?"

"I'm retaining water," she said loftily. There was a look of grim determination on her face. "I'll have to cut down on salt."

I asked the fatal question. "How do you feel about it, mentally? Emotionally."

"I am very, very annoyed." Then the tears burst out again. We went through the patting, hugging, washcloth-for-the-face business a second time.

"Sweetheart, it isn't a tragedy."

"I wanted to be settled," she wailed.

"We'll *be* settled. I promise."

"We haven't even designed the kitchen yet."

"We'll do it."

"And we need a nursery."

"We'll do one. Pink and blue and green and yellow. Whatever."

"And . . . I ought to see the doctor."

"Grace! You mean you haven't?"

"We've been so busy. . . ." More tears, though not so copious and not so sorrowful.

"You'll see your doctor. Tomorrow."

"She's off on Wednesdays."

"Then on Thursday, you'll see her. I'll take you."

"I'm not crippled," she snapped. "I'm just pregnant."

"Right," I said, nodding furiously. "Whatever you say."

"You don't mind?"

I hugged her yet again and fell back on an old friend. "You know, sweets, when I saw Nellie Arpels this morning, she asked if you were pregnant. And I said no, it wasn't the right time yet. And she said there wasn't any right time to have a baby. There could be wrong times, she said, but no absolutely right times. So, as far as I can tell, this is as good a time as any."

She gave me a doubtful, slightly sulky look.

"And," I went on at full tilt, "we should be extremely thankful. When I think of all the people our age who are having fertility problems. Lord, Grace, how lucky we are. Think how thrilled Nellie will be."

"The nearest thing we've got to a grandma," she said, with a three-cornered little smile.

I hadn't thought about it, but she was right. This baby would have no grandparents. A great-grandmother, yes, and a great-aunt, but no grandma or grandpa.

"He or she will manage," I said.

"Should I change my name?"

"To what?"

"To your name. The baby will have your name, won't it?"

"He," I said firmly. "Or she. Not it."

"Well!" she challenged.

"The child," I said in my most lofty manner, "will be so-and-so Willis-Lynx or Lynx-Willis, depending on whether you want him or her in the middle of or at the end of the alphabet."

"It's rotten at the end," she said, with a giggle.

"It's not much better in the middle," I confided. "Grace, I'm happy for us. I know it isn't the way you planned it, but I'm happy for us."

"All that rolling around in the sand," she murmured in my ear.

What with one thing and another, we didn't have any further conversation that evening. And, to make sure that we didn't repeat the tears and the agonies, I resolved not to mention Janey Doe for some time. This did not mean I was giving up on her, I just wasn't going on with the charge of the Light Brigade.

Thursday Grace saw her doctor. Pregnancy confirmed. Alcohol to be strictly eschewed. She told her doctor about women in France and Italy, and the doctor said maybe the French and Italians have a racial tolerance built up over centuries of wine drinking, and did Grace want to experiment on her unborn child? Grace did not.

Thursday I also ran across the alley and told Nellie. She offered me a chocolate and her congratulations.

It was now getting to the tail end of November, the baby would be born mid-June, and that gave me around six months maximum to work on the new house. No, say five and a half. We'd have to be moved in well before the baby came, and all the fuss and mess should be over by then.

I told Mark and Eugenia all about it, soliciting their help. I explained to Grace what had to be done first— kitchen—and suggested she work on it with Mark, thereby avoiding familial conflict. We couldn't order cabinets until the layout was done. Meantime, however, we could get someone in to repair the plaster and start painting. We would buy baby furniture, but except for that, I suggested we use what furnishings we already had. That would do for the time being, and as we lived in the new house, we would get a better idea of how we wanted it to look and feel.

"Neither of us have any dining-room furniture," she remembered.

"When the kitchen is under way, we'll shop," I promised her. If she settled on a style for the kitchen, and colors she liked, then we could carry them into the rest of the house.

"I want that kind of paint you put in Valerie's bedroom."

I had to think for a moment. "Rag rolled?"

"Yes."

"Grace, we didn't do that. She did that herself, after we'd painted."

"Doesn't anyone do it professionally?"

"Sure. I can hire a painter to do it, but he'll charge an arm and a leg and may or may not do it well. That's the most labor intensive finish you can get. Valerie did it only on one wall."

"Fine," she said with a sunny smile. "If she did it after you painted, then you go ahead and have our house painted, and I'll do what Valerie did. While I'm baby tending."

The more I thought about it, the better I liked the idea. The mottled effect one achieves with rag rolling looks aged and mellow, like a natural surface. Since one starts with two coats of satin finish paint, that could be done now and the surface work could be done anytime thereafter, just so long as it was before the paint got dirty.

"How do you do it?" Grace wanted to know.

"You paint your walls a base color, either gloss or semigloss. The glazing will be either lighter or darker than the walls. When your walls are painted and thoroughly dry, you mix up some glazing compound, some paint, some paint thinner, and pigment, how thick or how thin, depending on the finish you want. You put on rubber gloves, and you dip a rag in the mixture and roll it across the painted wall, starting in a top corner and working across and down. Depending on how runny your mixture is, you get a mottled effect or a marbled effect or a drippy effect. If you don't want to rag roll it, you can use a sponge for a speckled effect, or a brush. You can striate it or false grain it. When you're all finished, and it's dry, you cover it with two coats of flat urethane varnish. That makes it washable."

"Wow," she said, eyes shining. "I want to, Jason. I want to paint the walls the color of the floor tile. . . ."

"Which color?"

"The color of the floor tile."

"Saltillo tile is natural clay. It varies from ocher to red, through tangerine and melon and apricot and blush rose."

"You're teasing."

"I'm not. Look at any six. Pick the color you want the walls. It'll be in there somewhere. Rosy maybe. Or more tannish. Or more tannish for the base coat and rosy for the glazing. I'll have Mark pick up some sample paints and you can experiment."

And with no more than that, five minutes of how to paint a wall, all of a sudden she was nest building. Den digging? Lair decorating? The weeps were over, the snappishness was gone, and she was bubbling around like a little pot, boiling over with happiness.

Friday of that week, I had a half day with nothing happening in it, so I decided to finish up the newspaper search for a missing child. Grace hadn't heard from Martinelli, and she hadn't called him, either, almost as if she'd decided to let matters lie for now. Valerie and Mark and Eugenia had joined us for Thanksgiving dinner—my family was out of town, Grace had none, the other three happened to be at loose ends—after which Grace and Valerie had spent the evening down in the basement workroom, experimenting with wall finishes. That morning I had furnished several big sheets of cardboard and suggested to Grace that she tape them to the wall so they'd be vertical when painted as drip finishes won't drip on a horizontal sheet. I suggested she finish each one differently. They got it down to a choice among four that they'd take over to the new house and see how they looked against the tile.

Grace went off to work Friday morning. The cop shop, unlike my office, was not closed for the long weekend. I went down to the library and picked up the newspaper files where I'd left off the week before.

The library was mind-numbingly quiet. I got sleepier and sleepier. The files clicked past, and I almost missed it. Page eight. *Rocky Mountain News*. April 11, 1975. Eleven-year-old missing from her home at 45th and Zuni. Left school at 3:30, never arrived home. Wearing . . . pink dress, pink sweater . . . Maria Luisa Montoya.

I made a copy of the page, then drove over to North Denver precinct, where Martinelli worked. He wasn't there, but his partner was. Martinelli was home, he said, installing a new water heater. I got the address, only about eighteen blocks from our new place.

When I arrived, he was out in front, breaking apart some large cartons to be carried off by what looked like a whole busload of kids. He came over to the car.

"Jason. What's up?"

I handed him the photocopy. He read it through, and I saw his eyes cloud a little, not really weeping, just sad. "Damn," he said. "Well, at least I've got a name and a date. That'll help me find the file. Not that there's necessarily anything helpful in it."

"Will you let me see it?"

"Sure. I can call Grace. . . ."

"Grace is pregnant," I said. "So just call me, okay? She's just settling into a new . . . what should we say. Role? Thinking of herself as mama? Children being hurt upsets her a lot right now. It happening at our new house is particularly upsetting."

He put his hand on my shoulder and squeezed. "The first one is always the hardest."

"How many do you have?" I asked, looking at the mob on the lawn.

"Only four of those are mine. I wanted to stop after two, but Celia's very, very religious. We have stopped after four. I've confessed to having a vasectomy and have been forgiven. Very understanding priest. Please, don't mention it in front of Celia. Seal of the confessional and all that."

He grinned me away, and I turned for home. Grace and I would definitely stop at two. We'd already talked about that.

Monday following, Martinelli dropped by the shop with a copy of the file. We went through it together, all the notes, all the interviews. One of them stopped me. "What's this?" I asked.

"Interview with the girl's aunt. She lived next door."

"No, the name. I can't read the name."

"Jones. Rosabel Jones."

"That's the name of the maid at the Monmouth house," I told him. "Kate Mills told me she used to talk to Rosabel Jones. I assumed she was black, though. The victim had a Hispanic last name."

"The victim's father was Hispanic," he said, referring to the notes. "Alberto Montoya. The mother's maiden name isn't given. She could be part black, or all black. Mom and Dad could both still be around. At least it's a place to start."

I couldn't keep the news from Grace. Tuesday morning it was in the newspaper. Girl's body identified. Interviews with the parents, now people in their late fifties, recalling the day Maria had disappeared.

"Oh, Jason," Grace wept over her breakfast cereal. "Oh, poor thing."

She got over it before she left for work. I told her Martinelli had been in touch, that we hadn't wanted to upset her just now. She didn't get angry, which I'd been afraid she might, but did become rather thoughtful.

"I think I'm all right," she said after half a cup more of coffee. "I was a little weepy there for a while, but I think I'm all right. So, whatever you find out, you can tell me, Jason. I just won't take time to do any digging with you right now. Not unless it's something you can't get at otherwise."

We left it like that. The Maria Montoya case was in my court.

three

WEDNESDAY AND THURSDAY went by in a bumpy blur. The weather had turned suddenly cold, and people were starting to shop for Christmas. Jason Lynx Interiors did what I would call, for us, a booming business. We sold majolica and brass, a few fancy mirrors, and several decorative tables, some chairs and étagères. One of our old customers decided on a marvelous breakfront he'd been looking at for four months, and I accepted an order for two Gothic Revival chairs, if we could find some that were, in the customer's words, intricate, vertical, and amusing. I called Myron in New York, and he said he'd look. The customer, an artist, wanted them for a hallway in a turn-of-the-century fake Gothic church he had converted into a studio. He was also in the market for quasi-religious artifacts, fake fonts, and so forth. I supposed he would use the font as a wine cooler, but restrained myself from asking.

On Friday, Joanna called. She had remembered the name of her sister's best friend, and had I learned anything new? I told her I had not, and she told me the name: Clare Simmons. Of course, Clare Simmons was probably someone else by now, and there were lots of Simmonses in the phone book.

"Joanna, do parochial schools have yearbooks? Might there be a teacher or administrator who remembers her?"

"St. Ursula's closed, Jason. Remember, back in the seventies and eighties, when all the busing was going on, and the parochial schools made a real effort to be color-blind and a lot of anglos moved to the suburbs? And there weren't as many nuns to teach? The diocese couldn't afford all those schools once they had to pay teachers, and they closed a lot of them. St. Ursula's was closed in the mid-eighties, I think."

"Okay, so that's a dead end. How about where she lived? In your neighborhood?"

"I don't think so. As I told you, there were no children there but us. We had no neighborhood friends. Dad seemed determined to keep us away from the whole world, and except for school, he pretty well managed it. Clare and Lucia were friends only at school. I used to see them having lunch together and sitting together in study hall and in chapel. I think they talked on the phone sometimes, but Lucia never went to her house, and she never came to ours."

I thanked her. After a few minutes' cogitation, I wrote out an ad and placed it in the personals column of both daily papers. "Friend of Lucia Monmouth wishes to locate Clare Simmons, student at St. Ursula's, 1975." I had the newspaper give it a box number rather than printing my phone number. Phone numbers in ads are second only to Yellow Pages ads as an invitation to every nut in the world. I placed the ad for a week, beginning Saturday.

Midafternoon on Friday, Mark stuck his head in the door and said I had a visitor, Nash Monmouth. I'd been going through sales catalogs, trying to find a few items our customers were interested in—including the amusing Gothic chairs—and I set them aside to welcome him. I would have known him from the photograph. He was strongly built, as fair as his older brother, his eyes were deeply blue, and he had that sulky, "Look at me, I'm important and you're not admiring me" expression that he'd worn in the snapshot.

"Mr. Monmouth," I said. "It's very nice to meet you."

"I don't think so," he said, with a slight sneer. "I don't intend that it shall be."

"Oh?" I felt my eyebrows ascending, à la the new James Bond, and quickly lowered them to half-mast. "Then what can I do for you?"

"You can stop pushing yourself in where you're not wanted. You can stop fiddling around with things that are none of your business."

"Such as what, Nash?"

"Mr. Monmouth to you, Jason."

I laughed, partly to annoy him, and partly because he was funny. Like a puppy, growling at a shoe. "Such as what, Mr. Monmouth?"

The laughter upset him. Across his shoulder, I saw Mark hovering, and I gave him the merest hint of a nod. He stayed where he was, just in case.

"Just because you've bought a house we once lived in, doesn't give you the right to poke around in our family."

I was fascinated by his eyes. His mouth was being nasty in the here and now, but his eyes were the eyes of someone in another room, listening, weighing, judging. I asked, "Have I poked around in your family?"

"You've been talking to Joanna." He said it as though it were an indictment. Talking to Joanna was a sin, a crime, something that was not done. Interesting.

"She's not a minor child, you know. It's up to her whether she talks to me or not, and she and I have been talking about a body we found at the house you once lived in, a body that was put there *while* you lived there. The police are also talking about that body, and I've told them everything Joanna told me."

"You have no right to . . ."

"To what? Be interested in a corpse we find under our floor? Back in 1975 an eleven-year-old girl named Maria Montoya disappeared, and a few weeks ago her body turned up under the floor of our new house. The way you're acting, one would think you had something to do with her death."

His nose pinched, his jaws tensed, he turned white. "We did not! We had nothing to do with it!"

We. Now that was interesting. "Someone did," I said in my most reasonable voice. "And according to Joanna, no one but family and servants got inside that wall."

He made a spitting sound, like an ill-tempered cat. "Anybody could get over that wall. Matthew and I got over that wall all the time, from the time we were seven or eight years old."

"So your idea is that someone climbed over the wall, with a body, in order to hide it, maybe? And then the person saw the room under construction and decided to hide it there?"

"That's no doubt what happened."

"What do you remember about Steve?" I asked, changing the subject, trying to throw him off balance.

He went ashen, though he didn't move or change expression. If I hadn't been watching his face, I wouldn't have noticed that he went into stasis, like a cornered animal, absolutely still, hoping no one would notice him.

"Steve?" I prodded. "Your dad's chauffeur? Do you know where he is now?"

"How would I know?"

"Do you know if your father kept him on the payroll after your parents were divorced?"

"He was on the company payroll as a driver, yes. He could drive anything with an engine. I used to see him at the yard."

"Yard?"

"The construction yard. Where we keep the heavy machinery the company uses for site preparation. That's what I was supposed to be, a site supervisor." He sneered again. "Work my way up from the bottom."

"But you didn't want to do that?"

"Hell, no. That's damned dirty hard work, and I've got just as much right as Matt has to sit on my ass and play with paper. Besides, we don't do that much construction anymore. It's a minor part of our business."

He took a deep breath and glared at me. "But that's none of your business, either. Matt and I, we just want you to stop fooling around in our lives."

"Well, Nash, you can tell your brother that I'm not interested in him or you, but I am interested in that little girl's body. The police are also interested. And if you want me and the police to quit asking questions and digging around, then maybe you could help us find out who put her there. Like maybe you could help us find Steve?"

"I'm not going to help you with anything," he said, getting up from his chair, putting both hands on the desk, leaning forward until his face was only inches from my own. "I'm telling you to leave our family completely alone. If you don't, you'll be very sorry. Bad things can happen to people who upset me, Mr. Lynx. Very bad things."

"A threat?" I said in my prissiest voice, letting the eyebrows go where they would. "Oh, gracious me, a threat."

He slammed out of the office. I heard him mutter something nasty to Mark, then the sound of his feet hammering down the stairs.

"What was that all about?" Mark asked.

"Damned if I know," I replied. "Guilty conscience, maybe. If not about the dead child, then about something else he's afraid we might uncover."

"How old was he when the child was murdered?"

"Seventeen. Thereabouts. I don't know their exact birthdays, but he's a year or so younger than Matthew Monmouth and Matthew was a freshman in college the year the girl was killed."

"What does this one do now?"

"Banking, says his brother. His sister says it won't last long. Matthew got him the job, but he won't hold on to it."

"Not with that personality, he won't."

Mark went back to whatever he'd been doing, and I went back to my catalogs, but my heart wasn't in it. Now that I'd met all three extant Monmouths, I was possessed with curiosity about their parents. They would have been a generation older than I. They had money, not a fortune, but a comfortable amount. The kids, though not Catholic, had been in parochial school. Someone, somewhere, had to have known them.

I decided to ask Mark's family friend, the redoubtable Amelia Wirtz, who either knew everyone or knew people who did. I hadn't seen her since shortly before Grace and I were married, at which time she'd gone off on a trip to forget a recent unpleasantness in which Grace and I had been unintentionally involved. Now she was back, said Mark, and I was back, so I gave her a call.

"Monmouth?" she questioned, after we'd exchanged greetings and congratulations. "Monmouth. That rings a bell. Now where . . ."

I filled her in on a few more details. The location of the house, the parochial school bit, M.M.A. Corporation.

"Of course," she said. "Virginia Ransome. She married him."

"You knew her?"

"I knew her mother, first. When I met Virginia I thought she was very sweet, very young, and utterly unblemished. She had that kind of wide-eyed innocence that's impervious to unpleasantness. Her mother took part in several good causes, and that's the context for my meeting with Virginia. At the moment I can't remember which good cause it was. Library, maybe. Or raising money for the symphony; the Ransomes were quite musical, great Wagner and Strauss fans. I remember Virginia as friendly and sweet, and totally unsophisticated. Then she married Matthew Monmouth, a carpenter's son from God knows where, and became Rapunzel."

After a pregnant silence, I asked, "Can you explain that? I'm afraid I don't get it."

"Oh, my dear, of course. Matthew Monmouth was simply not 'acceptable.' " Her voice put quotes around the word. "He was very much in the rough, more cubic zirconium than diamond, more an unyielding chunk of fieldstone than either. First generation off the factory floor, and no polish to him at all. All of us, her mother's friends, were kind to her—the way we are with people we think have made a fatal mistake—but I'm afraid we patronized him with the utmost politeness. People assumed he'd be impervious to nuance, but he was not at all thick. In fact, he was quite the opposite, very proud and thin-skinned, and his self-esteem wasn't up to dealing with ironic civility.

"I always thought he decided if Virginia's family and friends would not accept him, then she should have no family or friends. He simply locked her up in the tower, figuratively speaking. He blamed her, I'm certain, though she was the last person in the world to hurt anyone."

"Rapunzel fits," I said.

"Indeed. I think it was Francine Strange who first likened Virginia to Rapunzel, with Monmouth as the witch. Francine is gone now, of course, but she was frightfully perceptive about people, and Virginia's mésalliance was a favorite topic for gossip. After her new husband moved her to north Denver, we saw Virginia maybe once or twice a year, and when her children came along, they, too, were protected from friendship. Dreadfully incestuous, I thought, all moiled up like that. Still, except for the younger boy and the girl who disappeared . . ."

"Lucia," I offered.

"Lucia. Lucia Diane, I seem to remember. Except for her and the younger brother . . . Well, that is half of them, isn't it? Half a family's children turning out well is about par for the course. One of mine is all right and the other one's an idiot. According to my friends, that's the way it goes."

"Then the kids had no social life at all."

"My guess would be none until they went away to school. And their escape was no help to poor Virginia."

"How is a woman supposed to exist like that?" I demanded.

"Well, if they'd married, the children I mean, and settled down here in town, presumably Virginia would have been allowed to visit back and forth among them. But the children did not marry and settle down. I seem to think Joanna is dedicated to art, and Matthew to making money."

"How did Virginia get up the nerve to get a divorce?" I asked.

"One of life's mysteries, Jason. A brother or uncle showed up from the East Coast and retained a colleague of mine to handle a separation for her, very tight-lipped about it. None of us could figure that out, not even Francine. It was all very quiet. Later, when they were divorced, he gave her the house and adequate alimony, and she already had some relatives living with her. At the time I thought it was because she was afraid of being alone."

"Matt was in college, Nash in college, Lucia missing, and Joanna also in high school?"

"I think so, by the time of the divorce, though I wouldn't swear to where Nash was. He was always the troublesome one."

"Why did she marry Monmouth in the first place?"

"Why does anyone marry anyone, Jason? All of us marry because we think we're in love or to escape from our previous lives or to fulfill expectations we've been programmed with, or perhaps because of some biological attractant too subtle to be consciously detected. I read something lately about human pheromones being most attractive between persons genetically unlike. If true, it would explain some very strange relationships."

All of which served to reduce my curiosity without bringing me any closer to solving the puzzle of Maria

Montoya's death. Or that of the other little girl, the one who had turned up more recently.

All such thoughts and worries were driven from my mind by the arrival of an actual emergency on Saturday morning.

Lloyd and Helen Baldridge had hired me a few years before to do their Denver house. Neither of them was the least bit interested in decor. They were color-blind; so far as I could tell, they didn't know a Shaker bench from a Louis XIV sofa, but they had a lot of money and did want to make a good appearance before their friends and business associates. Lloyd was the inheritor of a fairly large fortune and president of a rather large brokerage firm, and in between handling money, he skied, water-skied, raced cars, jumped out of airplanes, climbed mountains, and hang . . . What is the past tense of glide? If it's ride, rode, ridden, shouldn't it be hang-glide, hang-glode, hang-glidden?

Whatever any lethal but lawful activity might be called, if it was lethal enough, Lloyd did it, and Helen accompanied him on his escapades. By my accounting, both of them should have been killed off several times over, but the Baldridges led a charmed life, continuously high on danger. Though he was now in his late forties and she was not too much younger, they still lived, so far as I could tell, entirely for the rush. The more tension and terror, the better they liked it. Whenever I saw them, I was reminded of cats: big, lazy-looking cats, who could move like lightning if they wanted to. Both of them had the same slumberous, languid manner that could change in a moment to alert, agile movement.

They had no children. They lived between three houses, the one in Acapulco that they'd bought fully furnished, the one in Vail that I had done for them, and the one in town that I had done for them. On Friday night, the house in town caught fire. Lloyd called at eight on Saturday morning, Helen took the phone away from him to yowl in my ear: they were both excited and agitated, having barely escaped with their lives by jumping from the attic, so they said. And, as they also said, they needed the house fixed, and new furniture put in it, because everything was, according to Helen, "Charred, like an old leftover campfire, Jason. Just awful. And it stinks, too."

"What's the hurry?" I demanded. "Move into the Vail house. Or rent yourselves a town house. You can afford it."

Oh, yes they could afford it, but they were hosting this international committee that was coming to Denver in mid-January to discuss the establishment of stock markets in previously socialist economies, and several of the men were to be houseguests, and oh, Jason, help, help!

Mark ordinarily doesn't work on Saturdays, but I called him and we went over to see what we could do. It was a disaster. The old stone facade was solid enough, though it looked like a hot dog left on the coals for too long, blistered and blackened. The inside had been accurately described by Helen. It was charred. What wasn't burned was soaking wet. Everything stank to high heaven of smoke and burned plastic.

Helen led me through the mess. They had been awakened, she said, by the smoke alarm that had been installed only two days before outside their bedroom on the second floor. I looked at the bedroom. The windows had bars on them, fastened to the outside wall.

"You couldn't have gotten out here," I said. "The grills don't have emergency releases on them!"

She laughed, almost hysterically. "I know. I never thought of that. We put them on to foil burglars, Jason, I wasn't planning to leap from them. And to top everything, the phone was out. We couldn't even call nine-one-one."

"So how did you get out?"

She took me out into the hall. "We started out this way, then the stairs went up in flames, right in our faces, and the only thing we could think of was to go up. The attic opens above our closet, so we went back in there." Suiting action to words, she led me back into her room, flung open the closet door, and disclosed the small, hatch-like opening in the ceiling.

"There are no windows up there," I said.

"No. But there's a ventilator grill. Lloyd kicked it out, and we crawled out onto the roof."

From which point they had crawled over onto a slightly lower roof and dropped to the ground. Not too dangerous for people who risked their lives almost daily for fun.

Helen seemed to be talking to herself when she murmured, "If I die, it should be in the open air, not in a house fire!" She sounded very angry. If it had been me, I'd have rejoiced at escaping!

Mark got on the phone to Bill Vetter, a guy we know who does cleanup after fires, and he joined us at the building.

"I think you can save the Persian rugs in the front hall and the den," quoth he, "but all the downstairs carpet is shot."

I made a note.

"The drapes in the dining room might be okay after cleaning; it's worth trying, at least. Both the front windows in the living room are burned, including everything around them. What's under?"

"Basement," I said.

"Original wood floor?"

"Right."

"Well, hey, Jason, you know the answer on that one. In these three rooms, pull it up and lay a new one. It'll never lie flat after the soaking it had, even if the joists were okay, which they're not. Now the kitchen's okay except for deodorizing and repainting and matching two cabinets that got singed. And the back bedrooms, upstairs, they're smelly, but they'll be all right. Servants' quarters are over the garage, and they weren't touched. Basically, what you need is everything done over in the living room, the dining room, and the den, starting with floor joists and including the walls and window frames. . . ." He went on with the dispiriting list, ending with scrubbing or maybe sandblasting the facade. The fire had started in the basement, and had burned upward along the front wall of the house. The rooms at the back were not as badly damaged.

Obviously, this was more than mere decor. I referred to our files and started matching fabrics and colors and mailing orders for immediate shipment. Bill Vetter's people started cleaning the upstairs. Meantime, Mark found and Lloyd hired one of our favorite contractors who was available to remove burned floor joists and subfloors and put in new ones to bridge the burned areas, and to take out the burned window frames, broken and cracked plaster and cabinets and replace them all. Bill Vetter pulled out all the curtains and fabrics in the place, including upholstered furniture, and sent them to be deodorized and cleaned while he cleaned everything unremovable on site, including the upstairs carpets. I thought they still smelled, but Bill assured me I was smelling the downstairs, which had not yet been thoroughly deodorized.

When it has taken several months, or in some cases, several years, to bring a house together into one unified look and feel, one does not walk out into the shopping mall and buy something comparable. All I could do was find pieces that resembled the burned ones, here and there, some in catalogs, some in stores, some, I hoped, by calling Myron, which I'd do on Monday. The woman who made our drapes would also be available to meet with me on Monday, though it would probably be some time before she could start the replacements. She was good, she was fast, and she was busy.

I put in a couple of fairly long days, and on Sunday night, while Grace was happily soaking in the tub, Lloyd and Helen came to the shop where we sat in the downstairs office going over the plan. They needed the figures to report to their insurers, but they were already bored by the whole thing. It was no longer exciting.

"I really liked the way it looked before, Jason," said Helen in a languid tone. "Just make it look like that."

I had already explained three times that I couldn't make it look exactly like that. I smiled and told her I'd do my best. For the first time, I gave thanks they were color-blind and aesthetically challenged.

I offered them a drink. They invited us to supper. I went upstairs and asked Grace, who said sure, that would be nice. While she got dressed, we had drinks downstairs and somehow the subject turned to banking. I mentioned Matt Monmouth, and Lloyd looked up alertly.

"You know him?" I asked.

"I know of the family," he said.

"Did you by any chance know the grandfather?" I asked.

"I've met members of all three generations. My father decided I needed some general experience before coming into the firm, so I worked for a while in banks and other brokerage houses. One of my early jobs was as a loan officer at the bank where Grandfather Monmouth got his construction loans. That was twenty-five years ago. Way before Helen and I were married . . ."

"You had no life before we were married," she purred at him.

"Right, honey cake. I didn't live till I met you." He gave her a smoldering look that covered his face like a mask and made me shift uncomfortably. The lecherous mask departed as quickly as it had come, and he was himself. "Anyhow, I admired the old rooster. His first name on the documents was Meridew, but everyone called him Doozy. He'd strut like a bullfighter, he had dirt under his fingernails, every other word was fuckin' this or fuckin' that, but he'd take no sass from anyone, and he always paid his loans on time."

"Do you know Nash?"

He shrugged, noncommittal.

"How did he get his job, then?"

Lloyd shrugged, then grinned. "Don't say I told you, Jason, but I was having a few drinks with a certain banker who confided that he'd been offered the M.M.A. account, a very large account, need I say, provided he could create a job for Nash. So Nash sits at a desk in a neat little office, and he checks figures on loan documents that have already been checked by someone else, and once in a while, they feed him an applicant they're going to approve anyhow."

"Doesn't Nash want to be in the family business?"

Lloyd leaned back, sipped his neat scotch, and grinned his lopsided grin at me.

"He's outspoken about refusing to work for his brother, one of those sibling rivalry things."

"You knew his dad?"

"Matthew Sr. was running the business by the time old man Doozy died in the late seventies. Matt Sr. was a client of our firm and a friend of my father's, so I knew him to say good morning to. His wife divorced him, and it made Matt pretty mad, so he set out to prove to the world how important he was. He started putting twenty-four hours a day into the business, buying property and adding equipment and rolling his loans. By the early eighties, Denver was boomtown, everybody was into oil, oil shale, we were putting up office buildings like crazy. You remember, Jason."

I said I remembered.

He went on, "Well, the mid-eighties came. The oil boom collapsed like a punctured condom. Nobody was building anything. Matthew Sr. began to lose it, and he went a little crazy."

"He has Alzheimer's," I said.

"Well, maybe he had the start of it back then. Anyhow, to make a long story short, when Matthew Jr. took over the business, it was in trouble. He preferred not to get his hands dirty and it was a bad time for building anyhow. So he sold off some of the equipment and most of the real estate, and he became a legal-technical construction consultant, free to go where business was good, even if it was lousy here. M.M.A. does everything from land acquisition to zoning changes. Matt's a lot smarter than I ever gave him credit for. We don't socialize; I see Nash around town more than I do Matt; but everybody knows his business is bigger than ever."

I got up and refilled his drink. "I met Matt Monmouth recently," I offered, "and Nash paid me a visit. He sure seems to have a chip on his shoulder about something."

The Baldridges exchanged meaningful looks. "Oh, Nash spends a good deal of time being mad at most anybody," said Helen. She said it almost fondly, as though Nash's attributes were not only memorable but acceptable. "Jason, why are you so interested in the Monmouth family?"

I told them we'd just bought a house in north Denver that had once been owned by the Monmouth family, and we were naturally curious about people who'd lived there before.

At which point, Grace came down the stairs, and we all went out to dinner. It was not a comfortable dinner. The Baldridges drank a good deal more than I did, and Grace wasn't drinking at all. The more they drank, the more insistent they became that Grace and I join them in their sports. Skiing would be fine, or failing that, scuba diving for depth records in Mexico, or, failing that, sky diving. I said no, and no, and no thank you, which seemed only to redouble their efforts until Grace said we were still on our honeymoon, and we wanted some time just to be together. She did this in her cooing voice, totally unlike herself, which I thought totally believable to anyone who did not know us at all well.

At this, they let up. The evening ended with an invitation, by the Baldridges, for us to join their "We were burned out" party on New Year's Eve. Though I had the feeling Grace didn't really want to go, neither of us was quick-thinking enough to invent an excuse.

Any retail business that isn't busy in the few weeks before Christmas probably hasn't a chance of survival. Ours, thankfully, seemed to be a survivor. It felt like almost every customer we'd ever had called or dropped in during the next three weeks. Sometimes it was he, coming by in the A.M. to find something for her, and then it was she, coming by in the P.M. to find something for him. A lot of Mark's friends did their shopping with us. Back during the summer, Eugenia and I had ordered a great many smallish things that would make good gifts without requiring a major cash outlay, and she did a brisk business in these. There's an Italian pottery, Deruta, that makes marvelous cachepots, canisters, and plates, hand decorated all over with geometrics and flourishes, gorgeous deep blues and aquas, bright yellows and reds. I'd first seen them at a shop in Santa Fe. They're fairly expensive, as such things go, but they make wonderful gifts. One canister by itself is great on a desk, holding cigars or what have you. One or two plates are perfect on a short wall between windows. We sold a pile of them.

People who come to us are not usually in a hurry. They like to sit and have a cup of coffee or eggnog, they like to nibble a cookie (which we buy tons of two or three times a week from Sweet Soiree), and they like to chat with Mark, or Eugenia, or me. Which means that during the weeks before Christmas I did not do anything more about Maria Luisa Montoya. I had called Martinelli and told him everything I knew or surmised, so strictly speaking my duty was done. He didn't call me back saying the case was solved, however, so I imagined he was as busy as I was.

Grace and I went over to the new house half a dozen times in the evenings, inspecting the work done by the plasterers and the painters. The kitchen cabinets we had ordered would be in sometime in January, so we were assured, and Grace had picked out her countertop material and one pattern of tile for the floor and another for the backsplash. My own kitchen, over the shop, is high tech. A lot of plastic and metal. Grace's, at her apartment house, is country. The new one would be halfway between: light wood instead of plastic, clay tile instead of metal around the stove, clay tile instead of vinyl on the floor. I suggested to her that we also tile the breakfast area, the lower wall, at least. It would be cheerful, and I recalled having a baby who threw food amazing distances.

We put up our first tree together, in the living room over the shop, a little one, more personal than the decorations downstairs. Eugenia turned Christmas Eve afternoon into a baby shower when a dozen people arrived bearing gifts for the baby.

"That's what Christmas is about, isn't it?" she demanded, when I said she shouldn't have. "Gifts for a baby."

Put like that, one had to be gracious. Besides, Grace loved it. Amelia was one of the guests. I cornered her in the kitchen and asked if Virginia Ransome Monmouth had any close family, siblings, parents, whatever.

"The elder Ransomes are both gone," Amelia said. "Virginia had a sister and a brother. The brother was considerably older, and no longer living here. I met the sister a few times before Virginia married. She was quite a bit younger, and to tell you the truth, Jason, I can't remember a thing about her, not even her name."

"How would I find out?"

"The way you always find things out, dear boy. I'm sure her name was mentioned in the paper when her sister got married. Early fifties, I think. She'd have been a teenager then."

And we went back to the party.

Christmas morning, Grace and I exchanged gifts. I bought her a heavy gold chain and three pendants she could hang from it, alone or together, including a red-gold cat with emerald eyes who somewhat resembled Critter. Grace loved jewelry, but she never bought it for herself. I also provided a Santa Claus gift certificate at the best maternity-clothing shop in town—or so I was assured by several friends who were supposed to know. That afternoon, just to get out of the house, we drove over to the Baldridge place to see if the fire damage was repaired.

The building is an old mansion, near downtown, set on a large lot with a wrought-iron fence around it. We went up the stone steps to the pillared porch, and I unlocked the door and turned on the lights to see if we could safely go in by that route. For a wonder, the floors were down and finished. The plastering was done. The paint job was half done. The place no longer smelled of anything but fresh paint, though it reeked of that. Now if the furniture arrived on time, and the drapery fabrics arrived on time, the Baldridges could host their conference with tranquility.

"I didn't like them much that night we had dinner with them," Grace confided as we wandered through the house, checking one thing and another.

"I didn't either, that much," I said. "I was a little surprised by that. I'd always considered them pleasant enough people."

"They're the first couple I've ever met who actually live for excitement. Oh, I know there are people like that. Some of my colleagues are like that, but the Baldridges seem to spend most of their time and money getting high on danger. Like they never grew up."

I thought about this for a time, reflecting on my own adolescence. "A lot of us probably wouldn't grow up unless we had to. I mean, the day comes when in order to live, you have to make money for the grocer and the rent and the utilities. Lloyd and Helen never had that reality to worry about. The money was always there."

We walked through the dressing-room suite into the master bedroom with its huge, tester-draped bed. I showed her the hatch to the attic and explained how the Baldridges had escaped the night of the fire.

She shuddered. "The house must have been at least a third destroyed! It would have been cheaper to build a new one."

"It wasn't that bad, actually. And I'm sure insurance paid for a good part of the renovation. Besides, Lloyd does have a very highly paid job."

"His life seems so wasteful!" she exclaimed.

"You'd rather see him feeding the poor?"

"Something like that. Maybe. I don't know!"

"Well, in a sense, he does feed the poor. When he and Helen go down a white-water river, they're paying the guy who built the boat and the guide and the men who packaged the field rations, and so on and so on. It's like NASA. Every now and then I hear people complaining about 'spending all that money in space,' as though there were some kind of celestial piggy bank between us and the moon where the money got deposited forever, but the money is spent right here on Earth. Some of it pays salaries for scientists and engineers, and they use their money to pay rent to someone else, and to buy groceries from someone else, and to pay baby-sitters, and to pay the people who mow their lawns. Some of the money buys material, which pays the people who dig ore or manufacture things, and they use their money to pay medical bills for their kids or the school fees or the gas bill. It's the same with the Baldridges. They spread a lot of their money around. The guy you want to hate for economic reasons is the one who hoards it under his mattress. People who put their money into circulation are actually creating jobs."

"All right," she said, snuggling. "I won't hate them. But I still don't like them. We'll go to their New Year's Eve party, but I'd just as soon not get buddy-buddy with them. I hope when I'm fiftyish I have something better to do than chasing thrills and pretending I'm twenty-nine, like she does. There's something creepy about them."

I'd never thought of Lloyd or Helen as creepy, so I put this down to cattiness, which I shouldn't have. "Some people thrive on tension."

"Not me," she said drowsily. "I like things relaxed."

Then why, my dear, I asked myself silently, did you become a cop? Surely one can't call that profession relaxed. Unless, perhaps, you're chasing down art fraud or something equally esoteric, something done in museums or libraries. But Grace spent very little time in museums or libraries. Instead, she chased down robbers and burglars and drive-by shooters. She investigated murders and arsons and half a hundred other kinds of unhappy and dangerous events. She sometimes risked her life, though as she repeatedly assured me, hardly ever. Now she was asleep on my shoulder, head rolling gently whenever we turned a corner. She liked things relaxed.

Maybe, to Grace, her job was relaxed because it was at arm's length. The evil events weren't happening to her, or to people she loved. I knew for a fact that if something happened to me, she would be anything but relaxed. Presumably, if anything happened to our child . . .

And perhaps that's why she'd been so attracted to the place in north Denver. Perhaps she, like Matthew Monmouth Sr., saw that place as a haven from the world. An enclosed Eden. A walled enclave. A place to which one could retreat whenever one needed renewal.

Her head rolled again, and she took a little sighing breath. I felt a wave of that almost unbearable tenderness that sneaks up on me from time to time. I'm never sure it's a healthy feeling. It could become an obsession, that overwhelming desire to protect someone or something. Some beautiful, unique artifacts make me feel that way. I'd felt that way about my poor boy, with reason. I felt it for Grace sometimes, that desire to wrap her in cotton batting, without good reason. Grace, as she has frequently pointed out, can take care of herself.

I wondered if Matthew Monmouth Sr. had felt this fierce protectiveness? Had he, too, wanted to keep his love safe from any harm? Or had his motive been what Amelia suggested, bruised ego, dog in the manger, if your friends don't like me, then you can't associate with them.

Neither idea had the right ring to it. Not from what Amelia had said. That wasn't the way he would think. It wasn't protection, and it wasn't ego. Monmouth would have thought of it in terms of loyalty: You married me; I require you to be loyal to me. I require that your loyalty be measured in my terms, that my friends be your friends and my enemies be your enemies.

He would have thought of it in terms of a family standing together. The friend of one is the friend of all, or he is no friend of any. That had the right ring to it. An almost Sicilian attitude, a stance that proclaimed, "I do not associate with those people, and you are my wife, therefore you do not associate with them either." And because she was weak, because she was generous, he built a wall around her and provided a chauffeur to keep her under control, just to be sure she complied.

Poor Virginia.

We arrived home. Grace woke, all rosy cheeked and drifty from her little sleep. She gave me a strangely analytical glance and said accusingly, "You've been working on something!"

"Oh, just ruminating," I said, half pulling, half lifting her from the car.

"Tell me!"

"Tomorrow, over breakfast. If you still want to know."

Over breakfast she did want to know, and I filled her in on my conversations with Joanna and Amelia and the Baldridges, and my ruminations about what kind of person Matt Sr. had actually been.

"That poor woman!" she cried through a mouthful of toast, scattering crumbs. "Mph." She chewed, sipped, swallowed. "What a rotten man. Do you think any of that has anything to do with the little girl's death?"

I didn't know. "Maybe. Maybe not. You know me,

Grace. I just get in and thrash around, asking questions, until something seems to make sense."

She went off to work, as did I. Mark brought in the mail, which included a brown envelope from one of the daily papers. It contained a single letter, in the original envelope, a response to the box number at the paper. This was the first and only response I'd received.

The envelope was plain, white, the kind you buy in boxes at the office-supply place, three blue lines in the upper left-hand corner for the return address, left blank. It carried an ordinary stamp and was postmarked somewhere unreadable in New Mexico. I slit it carefully with my letter opener, taking out the single sheet inside. Block letters, printed, not a clue as to age, sex, anything.

To whom it may concern:
Twenty-one years ago death came to innocents. Death in life pays for death of life. The accounts will be closed. Let it be.

I leaned back in my chair, staring at the words. Twenty-one years ago a little girl died. Twenty-one years ago Lucia disappeared. Death in life pays for death of life. What was death in life? Imprisonment? Or were both victim and killer dead? If that were true, then why let it be?

Was this from Clare Simmons? If not, who else could have sent it?

The only other person I could think of was the other one mentioned in the ad. Lucia Monmouth. Up until this moment I'd assumed she was dead.

Of course the letter could be from someone else who knew Lucia, or had known her. I walked out of my office and handed the letter to Mark, watching him puzzle over it. He, too, looked at the postmark.

"Is this genuine? Or is someone playing games?"

"Was there any report outside Denver of the discovery of the body? If there wasn't, how did this person know when the child died?"

"This person may not be talking about the child," Mark replied. "Maybe he or she is talking about Lucia."

"Why New Mexico?"

"Nash or Matt or Joanna could have driven down there and dropped this in the mail, just to confuse the issue."

"Why? What point would there be? They've all met me. Surely they're smart enough to know this won't make me back off."

"Who do you think wrote it?"

"I think Lucia Monmouth could have written it."

"Why?!"

"I have no logical reason for thinking so. But I do think so."

I stalked back into my own office in high dudgeon, angry at the person who'd done this. Angry at Lucia if she had done it. Peevish at this muddying of the waters. The one person I had been able to eliminate was Lucia. Now her ball was back in play, bouncing around all over the place.

If Lucia was still alive, then she really had run away. Why would she have done that?

There were so many possible reasons: Because home was intolerable. Because she was failing school. Because someone had threatened her. Because she was in love, and it was hopeless. Because she was in love and ran away to be with him. Or her.

I jotted the possible reasons down, one by one, seeing where they led.

Intolerable home: This might have meant fights, abuse, a nasty chauffeur who spied on her. It was only a year or so after Lucia left that her mother divorced her father. Maybe Lucia's departure was one of the reasons. Or one of the symptoms of the underlying trouble.

Failing school: One could find out. Joanna would know.

Someone threatened her: Who? The same list. Father. Steve. About what? About the little girl buried under the floor. Assume Lucia knew about it. Assume Lucia was threatened: Keep your mouth shut or you'll be there, too.

In love: Joanna might have known about a love affair and simply not told me. Or, someone else might have known. A teacher. A counselor.

The archdiocese would be bound to have records of St. Ursula's school. They would know who had taught there. Or who the principal was. I could ask there.

I wadded up the paper, then smoothed it out again. Death pays for death.

Damn it, not always, it doesn't.

I drafted another ad. "Attempting to locate missing family member. Anyone who taught at St. Ursula's school 1974–1976 please contact Box Number————."

That was general enough. Possibly too general to be useful, but people loved sticking their noses in, loved thinking they might have some information that would solve a mystery.

The archdiocese would know. Why in hell didn't I just go ask them?

Because, said my scarred inner self, my burned child self, that frightened small person who still occasionally disrupts my life, the church bore some responsibility for screwing up my life before I was ever born. Or if not the church, people who did things in its name!

My more adult self demanded that I stop being silly. You're not going to church to convert, it harangued me. You're just going to an office to ask some questions.

In the end, the naggy adult Jason won. I went down to the archdiocese and asked if they had records of St. Ursula's school, and could they tell me, please, the names of teachers or administrators? Pretty please.

The nice young woman behind the counter looked up a file on her computer, copied down something in a firm hand, and handed me a slip of paper. Pearl Cope, with an address in Lakewood.

"Retired," said the woman behind the counter. "She was the principal for twenty years, until the school closed."

"Not a nun," I said.

"No, just a very good administrator. People still speak very highly of her."

I smiled my thanks and drove to the address in Lakewood. A pleasant little house, rather overgrown with leggy shrubs on a grassy corner, just now rather dim and drear in the winter light. I knocked, which caused something inside to go bump, and then bump again. A small dog yapped, eager-ferocious, and footsteps approached the door, with murmurings.

The murmurer turned out to be a gray-haired woman escorted by a small dog who ran at the screen door, scrabbled his way up it two or three feet, then bounced off to land with another bump.

"Don't mind Sinbad," she said cheerily, a smile re-arranging her sags and wrinkles, like bunting being hoisted into place. "I used to have students just like him, always bouncing off the walls."

The dog, a wiry little fuzz-faced terrier of some indeterminate kind, made another run at the door, bounced off it once again, then circled his mistress and told me to be off, go away, what did I mean, bothering people.

"Shush, Sinbad," said the woman. "What can I do for you?"

"I'm trying to find someone who knew a student at St. Ursula's, back in the seventies. . . ."

"Come in, come in," she gestured me in, Sinbad circling, me following. She dropped into a comfortable chair, Sinbad hitting her lap before it was fully formed. "St. Ursula's, is it? Now I wonder who it is you're looking for."

"Lucia Monmouth."

She frowned, remembering. "Such a sweet girl. She really belonged in a convent, you know. That kind is just born to be in a convent. But she ran away."

"So everyone thought. Yes. But right now it's important we figure out whether she really did or not. You remembered her right off the bat."

She made a humphing sound, a kind of muffled snort. "Well, she's one of the ones I would remember even if I hadn't had the police in my office for days on end. They interviewed every teacher the children had had, back to first grade. You think I wouldn't remember!"

"You mean the Monmouth children?"

"The children who disappeared. Lucia Monmouth, and Maria Montoya. Of course they thought Lucia had run off and Maria had been kidnapped. . . ."

"Maria Montoya was a student at St. Ursula's?" The paper hadn't said so. The case file hadn't said so. But the police must have known, if the woman before me had been questioned about them both. "The police came to you about both children?"

"No, no." She shook her head at me, and Sinbad gave me a dirty look. "The police came late one afternoon to talk about Lucia and her friends and who might know her. She was missing from her home. And I told them, while they were looking for Lucia, they must look for Maria, too. Her mother had called me that morning to say Maria had never come home from school the day before."

"Why did she wait so long to call?"

"She'd talked to some of the children on the bus, who said Maria was on the bus, so she never thought to call me until the next day."

"Let me get this straight. Maria's mother calls you and says Maria was on the bus the day before, but she never came home."

"Right."

"And coincident with this, the police come to tell you that Lucia Monmouth has disappeared from her home."

"Right."

This was all entirely too coincidental. Unless, as Grace often says, the co-incidence is because it co-happened. "How did the school get involved with Maria Montoya? Surely her family couldn't have afforded a private school."

"The school had a certain number of scholarships. We had a scholarship committee that considered nominations from our student body or their parents, and I think it was one of the Monmouth children who nominated the little Montoya girl."

As Grace says, not coincidental at all. "She was the

niece of the Monmouth maid, Rosabel Jones," I said. "The Monmouths either heard about her from Rosabel or met her through Rosabel." I got up and stalked around. "The police questioned everyone about Lucia?"

"Everyone we could think of."

"You had another student named Clare Simmons."

"That's right."

"Was she questioned?"

"I don't remember. I think I'd remember if it happened at school. And I do remember that Clare had a lengthy bout with mononucleosis. She might have been absent then."

"So Clare might never have been asked?"

She shrugged, cocking her head. "I just don't know. At the time, I guess I presumed the police talked to her at home, but I don't recall their telling me so. What is all this?"

I sat back down and told her, beginning with the fact that Maria had been found. When I finished, she was crying. Though she was quiet about it, it set Sinbad into a mournful whine, a high-pitched little screech that set my nerves on edge.

"Poor child. Oh, poor child," she mourned, to Sinbad's accompaniment. "And Lucia, too . . ."

"I think both girls are part of the same thing. There are too many connections for them not to be linked."

"I can see that." She dried her eyes. "Would you join me in a cup of tea? I'm going to put the kettle on."

Her kitchen was warm, brightly colored, neat, and efficient. Kettle, tea, and pot were all within easy reach. She made the tea, put some cookies on a plate, and we sat at the kitchen table.

"I've been trying to remember anything else that might

help," she said, holding her warm cup with a little sigh of comfort. "There was simply nothing. Lucia was there one day, gone the next, and there was nothing to tell anyone where she'd gone. I don't think I'd have connected the two disappearances because of the age difference. I mean, the kind of awful person who would be interested in an eleven-year-old probably wouldn't bother a fifteen-year-old, would they?"

I made an acknowledging sound around a mouthful of cookie.

She shook her head. "I thought the police were probably right. The littler girl had been kidnapped and the older one had run away. Well, girls do run away."

"But you, personally, don't know of any reason why Lucia would have run away."

She stared at her cup, her face turning pink.

"What is it?" I asked gently. She looked very distressed.

"That was so long ago," she said. "The laws were different. We considered our duties differently. . . ."

"What?"

"She, Lucia, sometimes she was . . . oh, if it were now, we'd have to call the police."

"She was injured? Bruised?"

"Bruised sometimes. On her arms. Sometimes on her face. I asked the gym teacher to take a peek, and she said yes, on her legs and back, too."

"Who would she have told?"

"Clare. She'd have told Clare, if she told anyone. And you'll be asking next where Clare is."

I nodded. She just sat there, shaking her head.

"Well," I said, trying for a patient tone.

"Well, I don't know," she replied. "I wasn't particularly interested in Clare. One has girls like Clare all the time. She was shifty. She told a great many lies. She was one of that sort of girl who is always at the center of trouble, not always actively involved, but somehow causative. The seed planter. The rumormonger. You know?"

I did know. "How can I find out where she is?"

"Well, we had yearbooks. I've got a complete set in the other room. There's a section at the back where we included news of alums. I should say certain kinds of news, people getting married, having babies, dying. If they went to jail, we didn't report on that. One wouldn't want prospective students thinking we turned out jail-birds. I think Clare would have graduated in 1977, so let's start with 1978."

I fetched 1978 and '79 for her and '80 and '81 for myself. The alum section wasn't huge, the names of former students were in bold type, it took only a few minutes to scan the pages. No luck. I fetched later books, and in 1983, we found it. Clare Simmons married to well-known sculptor Alfredo Lujan of Taos, New Mexico. She would have been twenty-three. She would be in her late thirties now. And if still married to Alfredo, she might still be living in New Mexico, where the anonymous letter came from.

"Would Clare have been the kind of girl to send anonymous letters?" I asked.

Pearl Cope nodded. "Just the kind of girl to do that. Don't misunderstand me, please. I've always thought that people like Clare are the way they are because they have to be, to survive at home. If telling the truth gets you a smack on the face, you learn not to tell the truth. If you need something and can't ask for what you need, you try to get it other ways. I never blamed Clare; it was just that her style made her unlikable. One of the things about Lucia that intrigued me was that she liked Clare, or pitied her, or something." She laughed. "But then, as I said earlier, Lucia belonged in a convent. She had that absolutely incorruptible purity. She was simply too good for her own good."

I thanked my hostess. I asked her to call me if she thought of anything else that might help.

Sinbad accompanied us to the door, silently, watchfully, making sure that I left and the door was shut behind me. When the latch clicked, he gave one short, satisfied bark, and I heard the click click of his toenails along the floor.

As soon as I got back to the shop, I would call New Mexico directory assistance and find out if there was a phone for Alfredo Lujan. When I got to the shop, however, I learned from Mark that there were two gentlemen from the police waiting to see me. I found them in my office, one round, one angular, one mild-rosy, one savage-dark.

"Lieutenant Morrow," the round one introduced himself. "This is Detective Miller. We're investigating a suspected arson, Mr. Lynx."

"Arson?" I'm sure my jaw dropped. "The Baldridge place?"

"Why would you say their place?" This was savage-dark, jumping like a spider.

"Because it's the only fire I'm aware of having happened recently. Certainly it's the only one I've been involved in."

"Involved?"

"Fixing the mess," I said, dropping into my chair. "I had no idea it was arson. Is that definite? Or just a suspicion?"

"We'll ask—"

I laughed. "I know. You'll ask the questions. How can I help you?"

We went over my involvement with the Baldridges since day one. I asked Mark for the customer file and made that available to them, including the billings. I showed them the lists of materials and job bids I had on the restoration.

"How come this carpet was only forty a yard when you put it in and now it's over sixty?" demanded Miller.

"Because the original carpet is no longer available, and this is the closest I can get. Because when I did it originally, I got a quantity discount. Because of inflation. Any or all of those."

"You mean they're all true," said Morrow. "More or less."

"Exactly. Is there some suspicion of insurance fraud?"

"We'll ask—" blurted Miller.

"No, I don't mind telling you," interjected Morrow. "Arson is arson, whether there's insurance fraud or not. Firemen risk their lives, equipment is used, the city is at considerable expense. If there's insurance fraud, it may be easier to convict, that's all."

"The Baldridges don't need money," I said, puzzled.

"We know," said Miller. Then he sat there looking at me for a long time while I puzzled.

When their silence began to pall, I said sarcastically, "Well, if you're looking for a motive, I can swear it wasn't just an excuse for redecorating. They're not changing anything, and they don't care enough about it one way or the other."

"What do you mean?" asked Miller.

I explained that they wanted their place to look expensive and well done, but they themselves had no ideas on the matter. "So," I concluded, "if it was arson, and they have no reason, then somebody else did it."

"Any ideas why someone else might have?" Morrow asked, suddenly relaxed.

Miller gave him a look, wolfhound to bloodhound.

"It's okay, Guy." Morrow grinned at his colleague. "Mr. Lynx is practically a member of the force."

"Have we met?" I asked. "I mean, before?"

"Don't think so. But I've worked with Grace a couple times. I saw her downtown the other day, and she told me you're expecting."

I accepted this olive branch. "I don't have a clue why anyone would want to burn the Baldridge place. I've been with Lloyd and Helen on a purely social basis exactly once, and that was a few weeks back when they asked Grace and me to join them for dinner, spur-of-the-moment kind of thing. Other than that, I've met them only on the job, and that file you're looking at has a record of all such meetings."

"Grace tells me you've got a kind of mind that puts two and two together to get seventeen," Morrow said. "Let me give you two and two, and you see what it comes to. Here's this wealthy couple. Three times lately one or the other of them have come close to getting themselves killed. I mean, that's just recently. The guy came close to getting buried in an avalanche last spring. When he was rock climbing this last summer, a rope broke, and he damn near fell five hundred feet which would have been what you might say, definitively fatal."

"They told you this?"

"Nah. I had a little talk with their insurance guy. The avalanche resulted in a claim for destroyed ski stuff. Then when the rope failed, he broke a leg bone. He's got what you'd call an astronomical deductible, something around ten thousand per year, so these were just claims against his deductible. The insurance company isn't worried. He dies doing any of this risky stuff, he's not insured."

"Why does he have insurance at all?"

"He carries a million against accidental death, except for the stuff he does for fun. He jumps out of a plane, no insurance. He skis an avalanche, no insurance. But if his house catches fire and he burns up, he's insured."

"Which would involve Helen. Was he the only one who had near misses?" I asked.

Morrow shook his head. "Nope. She's come close, too. She did a balloon thing in Albuquerque last year where she missed a power line by this much." He held up thumb and forefinger, a crack apart.

"You're not going to tell me who the beneficiary of the insurance is, are you?"

Miller shrugged. "Let's just say, they both die, his business gets a lot richer."

"You're sure this was arson? Positive?"

"Positive," he replied. "Set in a basement storage room that's very seldom entered, much less used. With an accelerant. And a simple but effective incendiary device. Now, does that tell you anything?"

"At the moment, nothing," I said. "If the house burned, both their lives were at risk. If the only other beneficiary is the business, then I'd want to know who at the business could profit. Otherwise . . . it seems pointless. Unless . . ."

"Yeah?"

"Unless it isn't for profit. Maybe somebody just hates him, or her, or both."

"I had considered that," said Morrow, getting his round self out of the chair. "Nice meeting you, Mr. Lynx . . ."

"Jason."

"Right, Jason."

They drifted out, savage-dark turning to stare at me warningly as they went. These guys didn't need to play bad cop–good cop, they were built for the job.

Mark said, "What was that about?"

I told him. We agreed it was odd. Lloyd had never struck me as the kind of man who would make enemies, and Helen was past the age when females are hated most. Young women can be hated by rivals, by cast-off lovers or would-be lovers, by ex-husbands. Older women are hated mostly by family, I should think. Misunderstood sons and daughters, or ones who like to think they are. Maybe ex-husbands who are paying alimony, but Helen had never been married before. She called Lloyd "my first husband." "Now, my first husband," she would say, "he preferred this or that." Then she'd grin at him threateningly.

When Grace got home, I filled her in on the day and we sat late over our supper, talking about the Baldridges.

"You know," she said, sipping at the cranberry juice cocktail we pregnant people were substituting for wine, "people don't really need much reason to hate other people. Sometimes people come all unglued for some little thing, like somebody's cat digging up their petunias, or somebody playing the stereo too late or too loud. Half the murders we get now are because someone dissed someone else, which just means a person says something wrong at the wrong time, when the other guy was too drunk or too angry to control himself."

"But that kind of murder is sudden," I objected. "Arson is planned. Somebody had to get into the house, which has at least two live-in servants, into the basement, into that room, which isn't used, and then someone had to get out again, leaving whatever device they'd come up with. And they had to carry the stuff in with them."

She nodded. "So, he pretended to be a deliveryman. Or a meter reader. He wore a uniform, and he told the maid he'd only need a minute. It isn't that hard, Jason."

"You'd still need a reason."

"Well, that's what I was saying. The reason some people do things might not seem like reason at all to you or me."

The visit of the arson investigators had put Clare Simmons out of my mind, but the following morning I called directory assistance and found that there were several A. Lujans in the general vicinity of Taos. I hung up and sat back in my chair, trying to decide whether to call on the phone or not. If I got Clare on the phone, even if she had sent me the anonymous letter, she might not admit to having done so. If she was defensive, as Pearl Cope had indicated, she would probably not open up to that extent. If, as Ms. Cope had also indicated, it was in her nature to prevaricate or shy away from threat, getting anything out of her on the phone might be impossible. All of which gave me a good excuse for going to Taos myself.

I broached the subject to Grace. She didn't want to go. She wanted to sleep all weekend. If I would go away, that would be very nice, because then she could sleep all weekend without worrying about me.

It's so nice to feel needed. I was very slightly rueful and very slightly amused by thinking it was a good thing I didn't take myself too seriously, because Grace certainly didn't.

It was ski season, and the Taos ski area was presumably pulling in people by the thousands, so I called ahead for reservations. I started with the Sagebrush, for old time's sake. I'd spent a memorable weekend there once with neither of my wives, between my two marriages, in a chilly room over the laundry, where we'd been separated from the soft chatter of the Spanish-speaking maids by only a plank floor and where a good fire in the fireplace almost, but not quite, took the chill off the room. The only way to stay warm had been to stay in bed and drink champagne, and we'd managed that. If Grace had gone with me this time, we'd have definitely stayed somewhere else, but since my bride was quite willing to send me off on my own, why not indulge nostalgia.

Though Christmas week was busy, the Sagebrush had had a cancellation. I reserved for three nights, just in case.

"I think you're in love with New Mexico," Grace challenged, as I packed my bag. "You never go to Utah, or Kansas, or Wyoming."

"Why would I go to Kansas? Kansas is just a spacer holding Colorado and Missouri apart. The wind never stops blowing in Wyoming, and Utah is too self-righteous."

"I like Kansas," she said stoutly. "Nice people come from there."

"Aha! Precisely my point. Nice people *come* from there. Even Dorothy Gale left Kansas."

"I just meant, you always seem to end up in New Mexico."

"It's where good Coloradoans go when they pass on, and if they're very, very good, they don't have to wait until they pass on. Very little snow, a relaxed lifestyle, and fewer holier-than-thous."

"Colorado doesn't have that many holier-than-thous."

"Where've you been lately, sweetheart? Hmmm? Driven through Colorado Springs lately? That's Rush Limbaugh's spiritual home. The cradle of militias and militant creationism, boobus über alles."

"Maybe you'd better not stop there."

"I don't, when I can help it." I gave her a hug, took my bag down to the car, came back to get my wallet, went down to the car, came back to get my car keys.

"You're in a state," said my bride.

"Not really, just not totally with it. I keep thinking I've forgotten something."

"Possibly because you have forgotten something. Get going, Jason. I have to get ready for work."

I patted all my pockets once more and departed. Just outside Pueblo I realized what I'd forgotten. I'd been going to suggest to Grace that she talk to Martinelli about finding any or all of the three Monmouth servants who'd been around when Maria disappeared: Helga Jensen, Rosabel Jones, and Steve, whatever his name was. I was quite eager to meet Steve.

It's about a five-and-a-half-hour drive from Denver to Taos. I stopped a couple of times to admire the view or stretch my legs. When I got to my room in the Sagebrush Inn, I lay down for a moment and woke up two hours later. Grace wasn't the only one who needed some extra sleep. It was close to four-thirty, time when stores closed, and I wanted to call a couple of art galleries to find out about the local noted sculptor.

It turned out I didn't need more than one phone call. I'd passed Alfredo Lujan's studio on my way into town. It was a few miles north of Taos, a well-known landmark, and it was open to the public from eleven to five daily, evenings by appointment.

Tomorrow was soon enough. I ate a satisfactory supper, had some wine since Grace wasn't there to feel deprived, called her up to see how she was, exchanged no news for no news, forgot once more to mention the Monmouth servants, and fell into bed by nine. The place had been remodeled since I'd been there last. There were no more cracks between the floorboards, no soft Spanish voices insinuating murmurings into my ears. Even if there had been, no amount of nostalgia could have kept me awake.

four

I SLEPT LATE, breakfasted in town on a scrambled-egg-and-cheese burrito with green chile salsa, wandered around looking at art both real and unreal. You can always tell that a town or city has a reputation for being "arty," when it has at least one gallery dedicated to the ugly. I don't mean just plain stuff that misses being either beautiful or meaningful by a mile. I mean stuff that is so purposefully and grossly unattractive that one instinctively turns one's eyes away. Human figures disgusting to look at. Constructions made of materials that create an aversive reaction, a sort of "whoops, don't step in that" feeling. Other galleries come and go, but the galleries dedicated to ugly go on forever, claiming to represent "artists," selling "art," consulting on "art." Walking through one of these places with eyes open and other senses operative is equivalent to being seasick.

I have known for years that there is a secret international cartel that handles ugly, rather as De Beers handles diamonds, sort of a UPEC. The cartel sets up outlets in various cities and releases a predetermined amount of ugly to the public, like drugs, gradually desensitizing people and building a demand for the product. UPEC sponsors ugly movies and appallingly ugly TV shows—

daytime talk shows with ugly participants blatting about doing ugly things to other ugly people, or sitcoms where mouthy, uncivil persons put down other mouthy, uncivil people. If there's a beautiful view from the highway, UPEC arranges for an ugly billboard to be put up. It arranges for ugly buildings to be built in ugly cities, and often UPEC is able to accomplish miles and miles of continuous ugly along the approaches to those cities. UPEC also owns fashion houses where it distributes clothing no sane woman would wear. And the more ugly that is spread around, the fewer and fewer people realize it is, indeed, very ugly; the fewer people demand something better, until, at last, no one cares anymore.

Suffice it to say that Taos had its share of ugly, just as Santa Fe had its share, just as Denver and San Franciso and New York have their shares. It's possible that ugly is already the majority influence. Around ten to eleven, I wearied of the tour, got back in the car, and drove north along the highway to the small sign identifying Lujan's studio. It hung on a stretch of coyote fence behind a parking area. The rickety gate opened onto a graveled path that curved through squatty piñons around a low hill to the right.

As I passed between two trees, I felt someone watching me and turned to meet the gaze of a shawled woman, realizing she was sculpture and yet, in the same moment, saying "Good morning" as I would to someone living. Despite its stillness the figure seemed vibrantly alive. Further off, slightly up the hill, a group of blanketed young men stood speaking to one another. As I moved along, other lifesize figures were disclosed, singly or in groups, populating this arid hillside with thought and conversation and meaning and intent, giving me to understand that I was not alone in the place.

The studio appeared below me when I came around the hill, a long, low, adobe building with a sloped metal roof. Beyond the studio a driveway approached from down the valley, and beyond the driveway a small house crouched into a curve of the land, looking both sheltered and supplicant. The path ended at the top of a long flight of rough stairs that I descended one slow step at a time, each step accompanied by the measured clang of a hammer and the muted roar of a torch.

The studio was open to the air through three overhead doors. The area outside was scattered with old fifty-gallon drums, chunks of I-beam, and oddly shaped slabs of heavy sheet steel. Inside the central bay, face-masked figures moved among fiery smokes and radiating showers of sparks. The metal casting from which the smokes and sparks rose was massive, almost monstrous, a grieving woman, every line of her body sagging, her brooding gaze falling upon the dead child in her lap. It was an ethnic pietà, a shawl-covered Indian or Hispanic mother grieving for her lost child.

One worker shouted, and another moved forward, both made squat and troll-like by heavy aprons and leather gauntlets. Tools changed hands. A grinding wheel shrieked along the edge of the bronze mantle, removing the burrs of metal that had remained when the sculpture came out of the cast. One troll's faceplate caught the light as it turned in my direction, then that one moved toward me while the sparks went on.

I waited where I was. Only when the face mask was hinged back did I realize the helper was a woman, olive skinned, dark haired. I had not asked Ms. Cope what Clare Simmons looked like, but I tried anyhow.

"Clare? Clare Simmons?"

"Limpia Montaño Lujan," she said, pulling off her gauntlet and offering her hand. "Who were you looking for?"

"I'm looking for a woman who was, I'm told, married to Alfredo Lujan around fifteen years ago. Her name was Clare Simmons."

She gave me a grave look, her head slightly cocked. "His first wife. Yes. I'm sorry. She left Alfredo some years ago. He divorced her before he married me." She smiled. "Just in case, you know. He thinks she's gone forever, but I worry she may come back."

"Damn," I said, feelingly.

"Something urgent?"

"Oh, something important, yes. This case seems to be full of disappearing women!"

"Someone else?"

"A woman in Denver whose name was Lucia Monmouth. Clare was her friend. I thought Clare might know something about her. Do you think your husband . . . might know something?"

"Wait until he's finished, and you can ask him. It won't be much longer." She dropped her faceplate, resumed her gauntlet, and went back to her husband, handing him this, picking up that. They moved smoothly together, obviously from long practice.

When the grinding wheel reached the bottom of the long, flowing line of the mantle, the troll-king turned it off, set it down, threw back his faceplate, and immediately lit a cigarette. His wife spoke softly to him, and he turned toward me, regarding me thoughtfully for some moments before he came toward me, a stocky, dark-haired man with a long braid down his back.

We shook hands. I introduced myself and gave him my card. He asked, "You're looking for Clare?"

"I'm looking for some information I thought she might have. Did she ever talk about a school friend of hers named Lucia Monmouth?"

"The girl who ran away?"

"The girl people assumed ran away, yes."

He settled himself atop an empty drum, enjoying his cigarette. "Clare used to say that the only person she'd ever known who'd had a worse life than Clare herself was her friend Lucia, and Lucia got out of her rotten life by running away. Then she'd say, maybe that's what she ought to do to get away from her own rotten life, run away." He smiled through his cigarette smoke. "One morning I woke up, and she'd done it."

"Run away?"

"Well, she was gone. Her clothes were gone. A few little things of hers around the house had been broken and thrown in the trash, like she'd burned her bridges. I never saw Clare again. I got no gripe coming. She wasn't the easiest woman to live with."

"You divorced her?"

"After I began to know Limpia."

"And you have no idea where she went?"

"So far as I'm concerned, she went into the nothing. She used to say she wished she had the guts to follow Lucia's example, but she didn't. She said Lucia had the right idea."

"And what idea was that?"

He grinned, dropped his cigarette, got down from his

perch to step on it firmly, grinding it into the ground. "To vanish from the world."

"Suicide?"

He shrugged, not saying.

I stared at the ground he had trampled, wondering where to go next. The question came out without consideration.

"Why was Clare's life miserable?"

I met his suddenly angry eyes, and said, "Sorry. Is that a personal question I shouldn't have asked?"

"Why did you?"

"I guess I was wondering what her definition of miserable was. Nobody else seems to know Lucia's life was miserable, or why she left."

He was silent for a long moment, so long I thought I'd lost any contact with him. Then he murmured, almost to himself, "Clare talked sometimes. She'd sit out on the porch with a drink, talking. She knew I was just inside the window. She knew I could hear, but she wasn't talking to me. Maybe she was talking to God. She went to parochial school, she was very religious—or maybe I should say very frightened—and her religion made her miserable.

"To me, a person's religion should make him happy, you know?" He gestured into the studio, where Limpia busied herself around the massive casting. "That's my religion, my work. It makes me joyous. Every day I discover something, learn something, like a revelation. Clare's religion didn't make her joyous. Every day for her was a war between what she thought she was supposed to feel or think and what she actually felt or thought. She was so tied up, anytime she felt happy, she was sure it was a sin she'd have to pay for in hell. I told her to forget hell, men create hell, not God, but she couldn't do that."

"But you never overheard anything that might help me find Lucia?"

He shook his head, a peculiar expression on his face. "Not really. From what little I heard, or paid attention to, I gathered it was a family thing. Count on it, if it was a family thing, then Lucia's family know perfectly well why Lucia left. They probably don't want to admit it."

I thanked him for his time. He walked with me up the long stairs and back along the path as he introduced me to the sculptures along the way. "This is Talking Woman. I met her at a powwow in Gallup. This is Black Bear. He's a rodeo rider. That little girl over there, that's Yellow Bird. She died. Leukemia. Her mother comes here every now and then, to visit with her."

The figures were stylized, and yet I knew that any of them would be instantly recognizable to anyone who had known them. Not caricature. Not portraiture. Art that went beyond portraiture to the essence. I had come a long way for absolutely no help with Lucia, but seeing this collection made it worthwhile.

We stopped beside my car.

"Forgive me for being presumptuous," I said. "But anything you can tell me may help. How and when did you meet Clare?"

"Back in the early eighties. I was on a panel in Santa Fe, some art dealers' convention, I've forgotten exactly what. She was in the audience. Afterward, she asked me for a job."

"Did she say what she was doing in Santa Fe?"

For the first time he seemed uncomfortable. "She said

she'd come to New Mexico to be with a friend of hers."
He lit another cigarette.

Blowing smoke, I told myself. In more ways than one,
the man is blowing smoke.

"Could that friend have been Lucia?"

"I suppose it could have been."

"And you hired her?"

He got that slightly uncomfortable look again. "Not
exactly. She didn't have any place to stay. . . ."

"So you told her she could stay with you."

"She said she was afraid of being alone, that she was a
good cook and could keep house. It's safe out here. I told
her she could stay for a few days, yes."

"And?"

"And she stayed longer than that."

"And you ended up marrying her."

He grinned fiercely. "Respectability mattered to her.
She was scared to death of committing a sin. She said
she'd been bad when she was a little girl, that she couldn't
commit any more sins or God wouldn't forgive her. Now
respectability doesn't matter a damn to me. The fact she
lived here was her business, nobody else's. But after
she'd been here about a year, she started telling people we
were married. I never told anyone we were, but I never
contradicted her, either."

"But you got a divorce."

"After she'd been gone for a long while, yes. In
Mexico. A quickie. Just to avoid any possible legal
hassles that might arise later, any possible claims she
might make. Unhappy people spread it, you know? They
can't be content until they've made other people as
unhappy as possible."

"And you married Limpia."

"Right. Limpia and me, we got married in 1986. License and everything. We have three kids, two boys and a girl. And we have happiness. I let Clare live here because I pitied her, because she had no happiness. I didn't marry her legally because I couldn't marry a woman like that, sad all the time, miserable all the time. I sure wouldn't have children with a woman like that, her kids would be the same way."

I mused on this. He seemed in no hurry to depart. "She said she came to be with a friend," I said. "Did she ever go somewhere without you, where the friend might be?"

"She went places without me most of the time. She wasn't helpful, like Limpia. When I was working, she'd be anywhere. She'd go for long walks out on the desert, even when the weather was lousy. She went to church, different ones, sometimes two or three times a week. She was Catholic, but she went to other churches, too. She went to town, shopping for the stuff we needed here, groceries, household stuff. I paid her for housekeeping, enough so she didn't need to feel dependent. I told her she was free to come or go anytime."

He dropped his cigarette and stamped it out. "Look, I pitied her. I cared for her. I didn't love her, but I did for her, charitably. You hear what I'm saying?"

I did. I heard what he was saying, but I also heard the echo of things not said. I retrieved the anonymous letter, in its original envelope, from my breast pocket and handed it to him. He puzzled over the envelope, then took out the letter and unfolded it.

After staring at it for a lengthy time, he said flatly, "This is why you're here."

"Right."

"You think Clare sent this."

"She could have. Or, if she's alive, Lucia could have."

"Who was it who died twenty-two years ago?"

"A little girl named Maria Montoya was murdered. Lucia vanished that same time, so maybe she died, too. We don't know."

"If Lucia was dead, then Clare would have had no reason to come here to be with her, several years later."

"That's true."

He handed me the letter. "That's addressed to the *Rocky Mountain News* in Denver. Did you run an ad?"

"In both the Denver dailies, yes."

"We don't see those papers much down here," he said significantly. "Whoever answered your ad had to see it first. They weren't likely to see it in New Mexico. I'd look closer to home, if I were you."

He took my hand and said his good-byes, still with that significant look. I got in my car and left, somewhat chagrined, somewhat annoyed. I was convinced Lujan could have helped me more if he'd been willing to do so. He had considered telling me whatever he knew, but he had decided not to. It wasn't out of any concern for himself, I was sure of that. Maybe he felt the story wasn't his to tell. Maybe he knew something significant about Clare, or Lucia, something personal or painful, something told to him in confidence. I knew one thing for certain. In his work as in his life, the man simply breathed integrity. If Lujan had sworn not to tell anyone, he wouldn't tell anyone.

The family knows, he'd as much as said. They just don't want to admit it. In other words, find out somewhere else.

I would get nothing out of Nash, nothing out of Matthew. Maybe Joanna would talk to me honestly, if I indicated I knew some of it. What was it Pearl Cope had said about Lucia's being bruised? "That was another time, we saw our duty differently. . . ." In the nineties, Ms. Cope would have been required to report suspected abuse. Back in the seventies, probably not. What would she have done instead, considering that the school was a parochial school and most of the families belonged to the parish? Maybe talk to the priest? Ask him to call on the family? Or call the mother in for a little conference? If the former, I could guess what welcome the priest would have had from Matthew Sr. If the latter, poor Virginia/Rapunzel wouldn't have been allowed to confer with teacher or priest.

And once again, where were Rosabel Jones, Helga Jensen, and Steve McHenry in all this? If Lucia had been abused at home, all three of them probably had known about it.

I made half a dozen mental notes and got back to the Sagebrush before check-out time. I could not think of an excuse to hang around Taos any longer. I called home, got the machine, and left a message for Grace; I'd eat on the road and be home about nine.

Best laid plans of mice and men, and all that. It began snowing when I was north of Taos about twenty miles and snowed harder the farther north I went. I got halfway up La Veta pass, visibility was down to nothing, the road was icy, a flatbed truck coming toward me slid across the road and I went off the side, luckily not where it was straight down. Even so, there would be no getting back onto the road without a tow truck.

The truck driver got himself straightened out, stopped for me, and we went together into Fort Garland, which is

a wide spot in the road with a couple of truck stops in it. I
called Grace and told her where I was, not to worry.
Then, while I waited for a tow truck and the truck driver
waited for a break in the weather, we had bad coffee and
fairly decent sandwiches and very good peach pie. The
skinny woman behind the counter said home-canned
peaches, and I believed it. Pity she couldn't grow her
own coffee.

The truck driver was a native of Saguache, pro-
nounced sah-watch, not sa-goo-atch-ey, and he'd been
driving hay trucks all his life, so he said. He had just
dropped twenty tons of barn-stored small bales at a stable
up north of Colorado Springs, and he was coming back
empty. I told him I'd been in Taos, and he mentioned his
sister worked near there.

"Not that I see her all that often," he said. "Since she's
vanished from the world."

I guess my mouth dropped open. "Somebody else used
those words to me recently. What do they mean?"

He laughed comfortably. "It's what they say at the
retreat house where Jennie lives. People come there who
need to vanish from the world."

I probed and questioned and got some idea about the
place. It was run by a lay group, not a church. It provided
very spartan room and board out in the desert, in return
for either cash or labor. The group had some funding
from a benefactor or benefactors, enough to keep the
place going. They had meditation at different times
during the day and night, and everyone was required to
keep silence at all times. The only person allowed to talk
was the person in the gatehouse, where visitors came, or
the person directing the meditation.

"Your sister lives there?"

"For the last six years. She works in the garden in the summertime, and in the kitchen. They have a dozen or so permanent people. The others are all visitors."

"And what's it called?"

"The Well of Silence. At least, that's what Jennie says it's called. I've heard it called other things. 'That nut house,' for one. Actually, she's happy there. There was always a lot of fighting in our house when we were growing up. I think she likes the peace and quiet."

"And when people go there, they vanish from the world."

"Yeah. That's what the folder says, 'Come if you want to vanish from the world.' No TV, no fax, no phone. Just the wind and the birds and the coyotes, I guess."

"And where exactly is this place?"

"North of Taos. Here, I'll show you on the map."

And he showed me, a place not three miles as the crow flies from Alfredo Lujan's studio. The map wasn't a topographical one, so I couldn't tell if the distance between was easily walkable, but I recalled it as mostly flat.

Several hours later, when the tow truck took me up the pass and extricated me from the snowdrift, I turned the car around and followed it back into Fort Garland. Grace got yet another call advising her of a change of plans. I spent the night where I was.

The following morning, I was on my way back to Taos, the snow keeping pace with me as I moved south. The lady with the stick on the TV had pointed to a high and a low and a satellite picture full of white swirls that were swinging south and east, across New Mexico, Oklahoma, and parts of Texas.

In Colorado and New Mexico our "hidden places" tend to be in the mountains. Much of the land in both states is flat, arid, and treeless, and you can't hide anything very successfully. Old wrecked cars stand out like monuments. Somebody's cast-off bedspring becomes a landmark. Get back into the canyons, however, or into the mountains among the pines and spruces and firs, and you can lose most anything, including yourself. The Well of Silence had lost itself in a wide, wooded canyon with a little stream that wandered along the bottom into a scooped-out pond. The cottonwoods told me the stream was there, and dried cattails told me the pond was there. Both were either dry or frozen, in either case invisible under a light coating of snow.

There was, as I'd been told, a gatehouse, a sturdy little log house with a smoking stovepipe out the top next to a counterweighted barrier that reached across the road. As I drove up, a woman came out, pulling a poncho around herself and stamping her feet into low boots. The sign on the side of the gatehouse said, "Come, if you would vanish from the world."

I stopped and got out. It's harder to tell someone to scat if they've already dismounted.

"Can I help you?" she asked. She was like a stored walnut, dried and wrinkled and hard as a rock. Forty, maybe. Or thirty or seventy. It was hard to tell how much was age and how much was going barefoot in the boonies for some decades.

"I hope so," I said in my best Jason-Lynx-being-ingratiating manner. "I'm searching for two women. Their names are Clare Simmons and Lucia Monmouth. One or both of them might have stayed here for a while, Lucia anytime after 1975 and Clare maybe during the last fifteen years."

"What do you want with them?"

I thought about it. "Well, if I find Lucia, I don't want Clare at all. But if I can't find Lucia, I thought Clare might know where she is. And I want Lucia to tell me anything she knows about a little girl who was murdered twenty-two years ago in Denver."

"My, oh, my," she said. "What a load of trouble you're carrying."

"Not for Lucia. I don't think Lucia did it, but she may know who did."

"And if she does, will that bring that little girl back?"

There was something self-satisfied in her voice, that "I know the right way and you'd better listen, buster" tone that aggravated me.

"No, but we may be able to stop more little girls being murdered. Whoever did it may still be doing it. There's at least one additional and more recent body."

That stopped her. She actually flushed. "I'm sorry," she said. "I shouldn't have presumed. You wouldn't have come all this way unless it was important. Come in and sit down."

I went in. The one-room hut was very clean and furnished sparingly. Wide plank floor. Log walls. Two chairs. One narrow bed, neatly made up. One table, big enough for one person. A shelf of books. A dry sink with a bucket and pan set in it. No running water, obviously. I hadn't noticed a privy out back, but I was sure there'd be one.

She sat in one chair, gesturing me into the other. She sat primly, knees together, feet aligned, hands folded in lap, eyes slightly downcast. "The first thing you need to know is that people here don't use names and don't know one another's names. For instance, I'm the Gatekeeper. That's what I'm called. There's a Visitors Manager and a

Meals Manager. There's a Meditation Leader and a Disciplinarian. There are Visitors. Anyone who comes here, comes silently. He or she gets through the gate, they go on down to the retreat house, they're given a private cell where they will stay while with us, except during walks or group meditation or meals. Arrangements to stay here have to be made by mail, in advance. On the wall of each cell, there's a schedule posted, and people are supposed to keep to the schedule, signaled by the bells. No one wears a watch. There are no clocks. There is no phone, or TV, or fax. Nothing electrical.

"We are vegetarian. We grow a lot of our own food. We have a building program going on. We have periods of study, work, relaxation, and meditation every day. We have a small group of well-to-do benefactors who support us, some of them come here from time to time, but I don't know their names either. We don't get to know one another, we don't ask about one another, we don't exchange names or addresses. We do consider labels to be improper, so I can't say if Clare or Lucia were ever here."

I sighed. "If arrangements are made in advance, by mail, then mail must be sent to people. It has to be addressed to them, by name."

"The Visitors Manager does that. She—or sometimes he—does all that. When she writes to them, after they've paid or agreed to do so much labor, she gives them a code word to use when they arrive, so the Gatekeeper knows to let them in. Like after breakfast she'll beckon me into her office, and she'll give me a note saying, expect wind and snow today, and I know two people are coming who will give me a little card with the word wind or snow on it."

"So you don't need to talk either."

"Just when someone unexpected arrives. Like now."

"And the only person who would know about Clare or Lucia is the Visitors Manager."

"She wouldn't know. She's only been Visitors Manager for a few weeks. Whenever a visitor leaves, all the paper that mentions him or her is burned. It's called the Immolation. No record is kept that the world may ever see, for we're vanished from the world."

"You elect a new manager how often?"

"We don't elect anyone. We take turns. Everyone gets to be a manager and Gatekeeper and all of it. It wouldn't be fair to expect me to be Gatekeeper all the time."

"Don't you have to speak to teach new people what to do?"

"It's all written down. Each thing is written down, in the book. Here's the Gatekeeper's book." And she reached it down from a sparsely populated shelf, a loose-leaf binder with a dozen closely typed pages inside and a label reading GATEKEEPER'S BOOK.

I flipped through. Routines for everything. What to do when you have to leave the gate to go to the bathroom. What to do if someone falls ill on the road and comes for help. What to do if someone inside the retreat falls ill. What to do if some rowdy person insists on getting in. What to do when a bona fide visitor arrives. What to do during meditation while remaining in the gatehouse. What to do at night if someone arrives. And so on, and so on.

"There are Visitors' books," she said. "And Meditation Leader's books, and so on."

"Is it a religious organization?" I asked, handing her back her set of instructions.

"We are forbidden to mention religion. Sometimes, in emergencies, we have to talk, like when there was an avalanche and water backed up in the canyon and it endangered the retreat house, but when that happens, we have to stick to the topic, we're not allowed to speak of anything divisive. No religion, no sex, no politics, no philosophy. Nothing that divides people according to their beliefs or nature."

"So," I said. "I'm at a dead end."

She shook her head. "I am sorry. It seems very important to you, but I simply have no way of helping you."

"What if I had a picture of Clare or Lucia?"

She looked interested. "Do you?"

"No. I don't know if any exist. But if I had one, could you or someone show it to the people here?"

"I suppose I could put pictures on the bulletin board with a note asking anyone who knows whether they were here at some former time to write to you."

"How many people are there?" I asked. "Here, now."

"Fifteen who're here all the time, twelve now-and-thens, six visitors."

"Do children come?"

"No. People come to get away from children. Children can't be quiet." She said it firmly.

"May I see, inside?"

She turned the book and pointed to a paragraph. What to do if someone wants to see inside. If the person seems sober and well motivated, ring bell for escort. She stepped outside and rang the bell, using a long-handled striker. The tone went off somewhere and returned. After a moment, another bell sounded, twice.

"It'll be a minute," she said, pointing to a bench beside

the path. "Remember, don't talk to him. He can't answer you."

It was more than a minute. It was perhaps fifteen minutes before a young man with a straggly beard came quietly along the path, touched me on the shoulder, and led the way. We went past an adobe building under construction, stacks of adobe bricks ready to use, no one working on it in the cold. Adobe needs soft mud as mortar, and it's definitely a warm-weather method of construction. We went past an outdoor assembly place, arranged rather like a Greek theater. We went into a long building divided by a central hall and six short cross halls into groups of four cells, rooms about six by seven, each with a few pegs on the wall, a cot, a chair, and either a skylight or a window. I counted them. The far end of the building was one large room in which cushions were placed in rows. Probably they meditated outside in good weather, inside in bad. We went through a dining room, six tables for eight, arranged like the cells. I assumed every room had a specific seat in the dining room. We went past what smelled like a kitchen, onion and basil and garlic and fresh-baked bread. No meat smells. There was a chicken house, and someone was going along the nest boxes with a basket, so evidently eggs were allowed.

My escort squinted at the sky and walked faster. We climbed a small hill and looked into a kind of gazebo or teahouse where several people sat cross legged, blankets wrapped around them. There didn't seem to be any uniform dress. Everyone was wearing jeans or sweats or miscellaneous grunge. The view below was of a very large vegetable garden with several people working in it. Since it was far too cold to be gardening, I peered through the light snowfall, trying to figure out what they were doing. When one of the figures turned, laden down, I realized they'd been digging up a trench full of carrots. I hadn't known they could be stored that way.

During the tour I heard the wind. I heard a bird, maybe a chickadee, rattling away somewhere. I heard chickens talking. There wasn't a people noise anywhere. The people walked quietly, moved quietly. Even the diggers down in the garden were going about their work slowly, methodically, without noise. There wasn't an ugly anywhere, sight nor sound nor smell.

A hand on my shoulder, again. My escort led me at a brisk pace back the way we'd come. When we arrived beside my car, he held out his hand, giving me a brochure. When I took it, the hand turned up. I put a twenty into it. He bowed slightly and returned more quickly than he had come, stopping only long enough to drop the money into a box outside the gatehouse door.

The brochure had the mailing address of the place. I put it in my breast pocket and got into the car. As I was getting out my keys I heard the bell again, three soft dongs, evenly spaced. Time for something my escort hadn't wanted to miss. I wondered if the bell ringer was allowed to have a watch.

Once again I started for home. This time the storm had gone on without me. The pass was a little icy, but not too bad. I made good time and was home by dark. Grace had saved me some supper, and I crawled into bed beside her with the feeling I'd been gone for weeks.

"So," she murmured. "What did you find out?"

"I found us a place to go when the baby drives us crazy," I said. "I found the quietest place on earth."

* * *

Next day was New Year's Eve. Grace and I would be going to the Baldridge party at a downtown hotel where they'd taken over part of the top floor or some such nonsense. What with getting ready and all, that would more or less take care of the afternoon and evening. Mark and Eugenia were off, the phone was switched to the U.S. West message service. I slept late, and then called Pearl Cope while I was having coffee. She said I could come over and pick up a couple of her yearbooks from St. Ursula's. Only the seniors had individual pictures in the books, but of course, Clare had graduated. Also, there were other, group shots, which might show Lucia in the background. She said she'd take a look.

Sinbad greeted me when I arrived, smelled me all the way around, and decided I'd been there before so probably didn't warrant biting.

"I found Clare," Pearl said. "But I can't find Lucia."

She handed me the book with a marker in it, and I opened it to confront Clare Simmons. She had acne and a simper. She wore glasses. Her hair was dark, cut way too short. Her face was unremarkable.

"When I saw this picture, I realized that I'd seen her a time or two after she left school," Pearl told me. "Before I retired. She got better looking. Her face cleared up, and she wore contacts and someone gave her a really good haircut."

"So between graduating in '77 and meeting Lujan in '83, she still may have been here in town."

"It's possible."

"Which means she might have heard from Lucia during that time, or even during the preceding two years after Lucia disappeared."

"I suppose she might have. Can't you find this Lujan

man and ask him? If he's a well-known artist, he shouldn't be hard to find."

I sat down and told her about Lujan and the Well of Silence. Her eyes sparkled and she asked questions. "So the reason you want a picture is to see if Clare was ever there."

"Clare or Lucia. I can make a case for Lucia being there. So, I'll send this picture to the Gatekeeper, and I guess I'll ask Joanna if she has a picture of Lucia."

"Joanna was Lucia's sister, wasn't she? I always liked her. She was a year younger than Lucia, but she was a lot more grown-up. Practical, you know? Sensible. Figured out what was right and then held her ground. Lucia was always off with the fairies, or maybe the angels."

"One more thing," I said. "Clare's family. I didn't ask the other day, because I thought we'd find her in New Mexico, but since we didn't, how about my asking her parents about her."

"Much luck to you," she snorted. "One of the few things I remember about Clare was that it was impossible to get her family to do anything. They wouldn't keep appointments for school visits, they wouldn't conference with the teacher, they wouldn't help with disciplinary problems. However, you give it a try. They lived six blocks from the school, I think it was on Pike."

There were two Simmonses on Pike, but only one six blocks from where St. Ursula's had stood, where now a set of elegant and expensive town houses were placed, within walking distance of the church. The Simmons house was another thing altogether, narrow, dark, squeezed in, with a neglected patch in front, partly grass, mostly bare dirt. Clare would be thirty-six or -seven by now, so I anticipated that Clare's parents would be in their late fifties or sixties, if not older.

The slattern who answered the door wasn't old enough to be Mrs. Simmons. I introduced myself, provided a card, and said I'd like to talk with either of the Simmonses.

"Dad's dead," she said, trying to tie her wrapper around herself to hide several feet of dirty nightgown. "Ma's still here, if you wanna come in."

I didn't wanna, but I did. "Are you Clare's sister?" I asked.

"Was," she grunted at me. "Clare's dead."

"She is not!" blurted a voice from the hall. Mrs. Simmons, no doubt, sharp as a whetted knife, stiff as an icicle, starched housedress faded by a hundred washings, crisp, iron-gray hair set like concrete in those tight little waves no one sees anymore.

"Clare's not dead. She's just left home."

"Yeah, well she left it a hell of a long time ago," said the slattern, slip-slopping back through the living room to the remoter regions of the house.

"Mrs. Simmons," I said, producing another card. "I'm searching for a childhood friend of your daughter's. Perhaps you met her? Lucia Monmouth?"

She turned on me, fire eyed. "Them Monmouths! Too good for us. Way, way too good for us. Clare invited her over, for a sleep-over, like kids do, but oh, no, Lucia couldn't stay anyplace but home. Like they was afraid she'd catch something."

Her voice rose and fell in accustomed phrases, as though I'd pressed a Start button. This was an old grievance, long rehearsed, remembered not as an event but as a plaint in the mouth, like the words of an old song.

"How old was she then?"

Silence. Mrs. Simmons couldn't remember. "High school," she said at last. "They was in high school."

"Well, Lucia disappeared in her sophomore year. She was fifteen. So it had to be before that."

She shrugged, bored with the subject. "So?"

"So, do you remember whether Clare was ever in touch with Lucia after they were sophomores? After Lucia went missing?"

Her attempt at concentration was pitiful to watch. Her face mirrored the effort, chasing thoughts from one place to another, settling on none.

"That Lucy called Clare," said the slattern from the doorway. Now she was wearing jeans and a sweater. "Long distance. Collect. Remember?"

"Thas right!" Mama crowed. "She did that. Called here collect. Like I'd have paid for two kids to talk long distance. Crazy."

"When was that?"

"Day Clare graduated," said the slattern. "Because Clare thought that's why she called, to say congrats."

"Where did she call from, do you remember?"

They didn't remember. This was leading nowhere useful.

"Do I understand that you don't know where Clare is now?"

"Ran off, got married to some foreigner, we said, all right, you made your bed, now you lie in it." Mama gritted her teeth in satisfaction.

"You said that, or you wrote that to her, or what?"

"Said it, right to her face. She brings him here, to the house, says he's her husband. He don't say boo, yes or no, but I figured they wasn't really married. She didn't have no ring, and you know those people, they don't get married. They just live together, have ten or twelve kids, then he runs off with somebody else. Far's I know, that's what happened to Clare."

"I don't think so. They didn't have any children, and she left him, not the other way around."

"Well what did she go and do that for! Of all the dumb stunts."

"When did she come back here with the man?"

"I got married that year," said the slattern. "It was '83."

"And you got unmarried mighty quick, too, missy," said her mother. "You and your bratty kids."

"And you don't remember anything about Lucia Monmouth, or about Clare's seeing her or hearing from her, or anything." I looked from mother to sister and back again, trying to solicit any information either of them might have. If their blank, unresponsive faces were any indicators, they had none on this or any other topic.

I thanked them. Mother stalked away, back rigid, daughter accompanied me to the door.

"She called here," said daughter, in a whisper. "Last year."

"Who?" I asked. "Clare?"

"Yes. It was right after Dad died. She read it in the paper, and she asked if Ma was all right, and I said she was. She's got her social security and I've got the welfare, so we make out all right."

"You didn't tell your mother that Clare called?"

"Nah. Why get her all inna upset. She was already fussed enough over Dad being dead. Don't know why.

He wasn't no good for anything since the stroke, just laid there, like a log."

"Were you living here when Clare and Lucia were in school together?"

"Where else would I be? I'm two years younger than Clare."

"So you knew they were friends?"

"I knew they tried to be friends. Nobody could be friends with her folks and my folks. I don't know anybody hates more people than my folks except maybe her folks. Ma always wanted to know why Clare run off, well gees, anybody knew that! Same reason Lucy run off, for cripes' sake."

"Why was that?"

"Family at her all the time. With Clare it was Dad. With Lucy, it was her brother. He wouldn't let up on her, you know. He said she was younger, she had to do what he said."

"Nasty."

"Lucia had to run off from him, and I know about that. I used to eat lunch with them at school. They'd talk, like I wasn't even there. I tell you, I'da run off, too, if I'da had a chance."

I thanked her and departed, considerably depressed. I now knew why Clare and Lucia had tried to be friends. They shared equally miserable family lives and probably understood one another completely.

I also knew that the Monmouths hadn't told me all they might have. One of the brothers knew a lot more than he was telling. It was the wrong time to talk to Joanna, but when the New Year's revelry was over, I'd do it. This time, I'd ask Grace to come along. Between the two of us, maybe we could come up with something.

* * *

I had promised Grace that we would show up at the party, have dinner, dance a time or two, then depart early if she liked. She said she thought she would like, though she would know better after we got there. The Baldridges had said "festive dress," and festive we became. Grace's favorite party dress wouldn't quite go around her. She wasn't showing yet, but her waist had definitely widened. She treated herself to a new dress, nonmaternity, she said, just cut differently, to give her a bit more room. She looked like a silver gilt rose in it, with petals around the hem and the sleeves. My bow to festivity was a fancy vest with gold threads and bright colors.

On arrival we were immediately surrounded by Lloyd and Helen and their close friends. We were introduced to the Phillipses, Bret and Barbara; to the Dahlbergs, Beatrice and John; then very quickly to a James and a Jackie, a Cornell and a Bibsie, at which point I lost count. Dinner was served at round tables, each seating eight. There were ten of them in the room, every seat filled, a considerable party. Grace and I were at a table with the Phillipses, the Dahlbergs, and the Baldridges. The other two couples we had met when we first arrived were at an adjacent table, and there was a good deal of joshing back and forth.

Grace had told me to have a few drinks and enjoy myself, she'd drive us home, so I had a very few drinks. I'm not much of a drinker; it's not a talent I've ever managed to acquire. Jacob, my foster father, had been abstemious in the Jewish fashion, which meant wine with meals and a little schnapps now and then, always accompanied, if I was around, by semistern admonitions about moderation. I never saw him drunk. In my navy days, I managed to overdo it a few times, more through inadvertence than intention, and the result was unpleasant enough to make Jacob's admonitions come forcibly to mind. So, let it be understood that by the time dinner was well along, I was pleasantly warmed by wine and predinner drinks, but I was not high.

Dinner was over except for dessert. We were drinking champagne. Grace excused herself to go to the ladies' room. I escorted her partway and was standing, exchanging small talk with a man seated at an adjacent table. Mr. Dahlberg, John, said something that I didn't catch, and the two couples at the adjacent table turned toward him. All those at our table took up their champagne glasses, as did the two couples at the adjacent table. "The Carlyles," said John Dahlberg, lifting his glass. Bret Phillips then said, "To the Benedicts." A waiter passed in front of me, and I missed the next bit. Then one of the men, Cornell somebody, at the adjacent table said, "To departed friends," and they all drank.

Grace returned, and she and I resumed our seats. I did so with a slightly queasy feeling that made me think, at least momentarily, I might be drunk. Then I realized it was the expression on Lloyd's face that made me uneasy. There for a moment, during the toasting, he had shared with Helen an expression which I recognized but could not identify. It was not a comforting expression, and a shadow of it lingered in his face as he spoke jovially to us, welcoming us back.

The dancing started almost immediately thereafter, giving me an excuse to escape. Grace and I danced twice. Then Grace and a couple of other women got involved in a long, laughing conversation in one corner. I wandered about, saying hello to the people I knew and introducing myself to the ones I didn't. At one point I made a trip to the bar, and while I waited for my drink, I saw that Grace's group had been joined by two couples we'd met earlier, James and Jackie somebody, Cornell and Bibsie somebody.

An acquaintance spoke to me, and we sat at another table talking for a while. When he left, I realized that Grace and I had been separated for half an hour or so, that she might be feeling abandoned or might want to leave. I got up and moved toward the table where she was sitting with the two couples, the other women having departed somewhere. As I approached, she excused herself to the seated quartet, smiled gaily at them and me, attached herself firmly to my right arm, and muttered into my ear, "Let's dance, Jason."

It was not a sexy invitation. It was not an invitation at all. It was a command performance got up to look like newlyweds canoodling, which I suppose was believable. The music being slow, we danced, perhaps more closely than was consonant with good taste, while she, smiling the while, told me there was something rotten going on.

"Smile, damn it, Jason. I don't want them to know I've caught on."

I smiled, turned, dipped, danced her away from that side of the floor to the other, where we were less exposed to the gaze of the people she'd been with.

"Just what have you caught on to?" I asked, grinning like an idiot.

"I'm not sure. It's just . . . the people at the table where I was, they're old friends and drinking buddies of Lloyd and Helen. All the time I was talking to them, I felt like they were talking to each other over my head, using code words, you know."

"Rude," I suggested.

"Not just rude. You see the screen inside the door over there?"

I glanced over. A tall, five-panel velvet screen had been set just inside the door, to allow access without making the party visible to people passing in the corridor. When we'd entered the room, a sign set against it had identified BALDRIDGE NEW YEAR'S EVE PARTY.

Grace went on, "We were at the table against the inside of the screen. When I got tired of all the talking over my head, I said I had to go to the ladies' room. When I came back, I was putting my wallet back in my purse—from when I tipped the attendant in there—and I was standing right behind the screen trying to get my purse fastened. And I heard them."

Spin, reverse, spin again, and end up with her facing away from them. "Heard them what?"

"The four people at that table. Jackie said it was hard luck that they'd drawn the Baldridges. And James, her husband, said another five minutes, he'd have won because both routes out were blocked. And then his wife said, it was Lloyd and Helen's turn now, and she wondered who they'd draw, and then she gave this kind of hysterical little laugh."

"I am not following this," I said, smiling romantically into her eyes.

"I didn't either, Jason, just listen! And then her husband said, well, one chance in five it's you and me, babe, let's be sure there's no bars on our windows. And the other man, Cornell, said it beat free fall, and Bibsie, his wife, said, hush, don't talk about it here, the little blonde will be coming back any minute after her tinkle. And they all laughed again. So I sneaked back down the hall, and came in again with a group of other people, and joined them like I hadn't heard a thing."

"Which you didn't, really."

"Well it's some kind of game they play, Jason. And that laughter! It was really nasty, creepy laughter."

"Who are these people?"

"The Slades, Cornell and Bibsie, and the Rodales, James and Jackie. And I figure there must be two more couples. . . ."

"What would make you think that?"

"One chance out of five, the man said. So, there'll be four couples besides Lloyd and Helen. And the other two are probably the ones at our table tonight, the Phillipses and the Dahlbergs."

"Couples who do what?"

"I don't know! Play this nasty danger game, whatever it is. Maybe like kids, daring each other to do stupid, dangerous things. Or gambling on who's going to have the next accident. And if they get injured, you win a point or something."

I made a face. "I'm guessing you've had enough of this festivity."

"Let's stay just a few minutes more. Maybe we can figure out what they're up to." She had that look she sometimes gets, that "Aha, the truth is within my grasp" look.

I swallowed my apprehension and agreed, reminding myself that we were just dancing, partying, having fun. We danced a bit more, then wandered in the direction of the table where Lloyd and Helen were sitting. If we were leaving early, we'd need to say good-bye.

They were with the Phillipses and the Dahlbergs once again, along with a younger couple I hadn't met, talking about free climbing a particular rock face on a particular mountain I'd never heard of. I quickly gathered that a lot of this climb had to be done under an overhang while dangling from one finger or toe. I listened. I watched. Of the eight people gathered around the table, six of them had made this climb. The ones who hadn't were a younger couple, the Fieldses. He, Paul Fields, was eager to make the effort, his wife Caetlin didn't want to, so all the other people at the table were focused on her pale and frightened face.

They wore the same expression I had seen on Lloyd's and Helen's faces earlier. This time I recognized it. I had seen those glittering eyes, those avid looks, those exposed teeth on nature documentaries. Wild dogs chasing down a gazelle. Hyenas gathering around a kill. Caetlin Fields was the gazelle; the others were the hyenas. "We'll get you into training," Paul yammered at her. "I can't wait."

They were all a little drunk. I thought at the time they would have been more responsive to Caetlin's obvious distress if they'd been sober. But they were a little drunk and I'm sure they assumed we were, too, if they thought of it at all. Lloyd turned toward me, slightly bleary eyed:

"And you two! You don't know what fun is. Done any rock climbing at all, Jason?"

If he'd been sober, he'd have remembered that I hadn't. He'd talked about his sports at obsessive length the time we'd had supper together, trying to get me involved. I said something noncommittal, told the assembled group that we two were keeping early evenings, that it had been a great party. I slurred a little. "Don't know when I've had as great a time. But we've got to take off, you know, get the little bride home in time for curfew."

Grace played the little bride quite well, and we were fulsomely petted and hugged and bid to get together soon. The party was in full cry when we went quietly out and away, down into the depths where the car was parked. We got into it rather like two small animals escaping into our burrow, not moving for a long moment, just relishing the safety of it.

"Okay," Grace whispered. "Did you figure something out?"

"Nothing beyond the fact that I feel more than slightly queasy. I'm coming to agree with you, love. I don't much like the Baldridges, and I'm not fond of their friends, either. Have you got your notebook with you? Let me borrow a page to jot down the names of the people we met, the ones you overheard, the ones at the table when we said good night."

"My notebook's in my purse."

I dug it out and found a clean page.

"Five couples," she said, backing us slowly out of the parking slot. "Baldridges, of course. Then the Phillipses and Dahlbergs. The Slades and the Rodales."

I wrote them down. "That last bunch, there were James and Jackie Rodale, Cornell and what's his wife's name? I was introduced, but I've forgotten."

"Bibsie," she said. "What about the younger ones, the Fieldses?"

"They aren't part of it." Then it came to me. "Unless they're recruits."

"Are they set on recruiting us, too? Is that why we were invited to dinner, and to the party tonight?"

"Possibly. Though they may get kicks out of showing off their adventures in front of other people."

"How do they decide who to recruit?"

"They no doubt focus on people who demonstrate a complete lack of common sense over a period of time. Those they can inveigle into going rock climbing or hang gliding or sky jumping with them. Something. I think I misled Lloyd one time when I told him what I'd done in the navy. He assumed I'd picked my military career when in fact it just happened to me."

"The odds are going to catch up to them," she said soberly. "Somebody's going to get killed."

"Maybe someone already has," I said. "I'm writing two more names down: the Carlyles and the Benedicts. When you and I left the table during dinner, as I was coming back, the Baldridges and the others at our table, plus the ones at the adjacent table, were toasting departed friends. I picked up on those two names."

"You think?" she asked, hushed. "You think the Carlyles and the Benedicts died in these adventures of theirs?"

"I don't know," I said. "I haven't any idea."

"My God," she said. "Well, at least we can find out if people by those names have died recently."

"They may not be local. Remember, the Baldridges have a house in Mexico, and one in Vail."

"And, to hear Helen tell it, they also spend time flitting about in France and Argentina and several other countries." She thought about this for a moment, then said, "Though if it's a game they're playing it would only be fun if the whole group was around. They wouldn't play the danger somewhere else unless they're all there."

"Betts and Bitts," I said.

"What?"

"Betts and Bitts Sullivan. The society-page writers. 'News Who?'"

"Your antique buddies?"

"Well, in a manner of speaking. They know everyone, Grace. They know who goes, who comes, who sleeps with whom. They know who people were back in the primordial ooze."

"They'll know who the Baldridges hang out with?"

"They will. And who they travel with, if anyone. And maybe even who the Carlyles and the Benedicts are. Or were."

New Year's Day we slept in, lazed around, and watched the Rose Parade on TV, what we could see of it. When are the networks going to figure out that we like seeing the floats and hearing the bands, not seeing the faces and hearing the voices of their garrulous, trivial damned commentators! By judicious use of the remote, we managed to see most of the parade and avoid the mind-numbing chatter. Next day was January 2, and real life reasserted itself. There was the matter of inventory, which we always take the first week in January because business is dead that week anyhow. The job takes several days and on this occasion it had all three of us, plus temporary help, at each other's throats.

It seems to be some corollary of Murphy's Law that stuff gets moved. Try as we will to keep track of it, it gets moved! The colonial breakfront that should be in the little display room somehow ends up in Mark's office. The little rococo-revival side chair that used to sit at an equally charming desk in the back display room has somehow gravitated to Eugenia's desk, because, as it turned out, her own chair had sprung a castor. Multiply this by several hundred, and we were all fagged by the time each item had been tracked down and the inventory had been more or less reconciled with the sales ticket numbers.

Part of the complexity was my fault. In order to check inventory, everything had to be numbered and fed into our computer program. I hadn't listed the stuff we'd brought from Colorado Springs, so there were no numbers in the program except for the few items already sold. Selling something requires a number, but moving something requires nothing but inattention and momentary stupidity.

At any rate, we sorted and fiddled and assigned numbers and we cursed a lot, and accused one another of insanity, and cried eureka at intervals. As usual, we ended up with half a dozen items on the inventory list that we couldn't find. They had disappeared. We entered an MP, misplaced, next to each item, hoping they might turn up during the year. One time we found six matched fiddle-back chairs in the elevator, covered with moving mats, and nobody remembered putting them there. Our accountant says that we would need to be audited only once to convince us this slight inconvenience is worthwhile. If he calls inventory a slight inconvenience, I'd prefer to take his word for the rest of it.

While I was up to my neck in inventory, the kitchen cabinets for the new house arrived and were installed. Grace went over alone to see how they looked and returned smiling quietly. That night she asked me what we should do next about Maria Montoya; she wouldn't feel right about moving in unless we'd done our best for her.

I reminded her of the next item on my mental list, finding Helga Jensen, Rosabel Jones, and Steve McHenry. She said she'd do that if I called Betts and Bitts and picked their brains about the Baldridges. I felt like a general with a war on three fronts.

However, by the end of the week the inventory was done and the computer did its thing so we could provide figures for the past year to the tax man. We looked at the bottom line and toasted one another because we had, once again, come out in the black. Then, as she does every year at this time, Eugenia left for vacation, peace and quiet descended, and I could think again.

I called Bitts/Betts and asked if I could treat them to lunch. They burbled at me—positively, I think. At any rate, when I drove up to the chosen restaurant the following day, they were both there, waiting.

A friend of mine owns the place, and I'd asked him for a quiet table somewhere in a corner. When we were all seated, provided with drinks, and had ordered food, I said in my most mysterious voice, "I need your help."

Immediate attention, twitters, trills, chittering. "Oh, Jasey, what, anything, dear, you know that, what can we do."

"Do you know anyone named Carlyle and anyone named Benedict, and if you do, do you know of a connection between the two?"

"Benny Carlyle, do you suppose dear, but he's been dead an age, must be his son . . ."

"The son hasn't been in the good old U. S. of A. for years. . . ."

"Then I'm thinking of the wrong Carlyle, I meant Oswald."

"B.O.? That's what they called him in school!"

"Oh, shattering. So bad when children are cruel. It sticks for years. I still remember things people said to you and me. Could it be the Wilson Carlyles?"

I sat and listened while this went on for some time
before we were served, while we were served, while we
were eating, until, at last—after disqualifying about ten
Benedicts, Bensons, and Bentons or Carlyles, Carltons,
and Carberrys—Betts or Bitts said, "Now if it's the
William Benedicts, then it must be the Carson Carlyles."

"Why?" I asked, the first word I'd uttered in some time.

"Because they were so close!" cried Bitts, or Betts.
"Roommates in college, best men at one another's wed-
dings, godfathers to one another's children. . . ."

"They had children?"

"The Benedicts did, indeed, and so sad when the boat
blew up, all the Benedict family, gone at once, William
and Elaine and the two little ones, I've forgotten their
names. And then, for Carson and Eleanor to go the same
year!"

"The same year," I said.

"Just last year," they cried. "Sky diving. And his chute
didn't open, and she dived, you know, trying to catch
him before he fell. Right into the ground, they said. Right
into the ground." She wiped her eyes and fell to her meal
with increased energy.

"That was a real love match," said the other one.
"They were devoted to one another."

"I thought they had pressure releases on parachutes
now," I offered. "When you're too close to the ground,
they open automatically, don't they?"

"I don't know about that. All I know is Bibsie told me
that Eleanor Carlyle dove right into the ground trying to
catch Carson before he . . . well, splashed. Poor thing.
Maybe she tried to open her chute and it wouldn't."

"Bibsie Slade?" I asked.

"Yes. Mrs. Cornell Slade. Cornell and William were

fast friends, part of that crowd, you know. The Phillipses, and the Dahlbergs, and John Dahlberg's sister Anita and her husband. And the Rodales, and the Baldridges. That sporty crowd."

"They ski, and climb mountains," I offered. "Someone mentioned that."

"Oh, my dear, yes. And they have affairs back and forth among themselves, and they do speed-boat races and endurance riding and competitive motorcycle racing. There's absolutely nothing they don't do. And they've always been so fortunate! None of them has ever been hurt, right up until the Benedicts died. That seemed to change their luck. Next it was the Carlyles, and then the Slades had that close call during the cross-country-ski race, and then Lloyd and Helen Baldridge were almost caught in an avalanche, and there was a rope that broke when the Dahlbergs and the Baldridges were rock climbing. A miracle they made it! And then the Baldridges' house caught fire. . . ."

"But that's something else," said the other one. "That's not a sports accident. The others were all sports accidents."

"Tell me about the Slades' ski-race close call," I asked.

"Oh, it had something to do with the flags being misplaced," one of them said, the other continuing: "You know, the flags that mark the course. It was snowing, with very poor visibility, and they almost went over the edge of a cliff! They barely avoided it. Such bad luck now."

"Heaven knows where it will end."

"It's the pot of gold," said the other one. "Barbara Phillips blames it on the pot of gold. It's supposed to be a secret, but she was quite tiddly and she let it gush out. They each put in a million, you know. Lloyd has it invested at the bank. And the survivor takes all. Such a silly, adolescent thing to do. Barbara thinks the bad luck all started then."

I was dumbfounded. "But they're all very wealthy people. They don't need the money."

"They don't seem to," agreed Betts/Bitts. "They all live very well indeed, but I've heard things. About Lloyd's bank, for instance. And Dahlberg Oil isn't what it once was. Now, Jase dear, why did you want to know all this?"

I hadn't thought of an excuse for wanting to know, so I opted for candor. "Well, I'm fixing up Lloyd and Helen's house. The one that almost burned, you know. I heard about the Carlyles and the Benedicts, but it was all most mysterious. I was just curious."

They nodded like two mandarins. "You take current trends into account when you do that house over, Jason. You figure they're on a bad luck slide, because all the signs are there, my dear, believe us, they are. You put in a fire escape and a good security system. When you run into hard luck clients, you have to figure that into the equation. We always do."

And I realized with shock that they always did. A surprising number of their "News Who?" forecasts, both dire and delightful, turned out to be true. Obviously, they did it through an intimate knowledge of human nature.

"A good sprinkler system," I agreed, sober faced. "I'll certainly build that in."

They thanked me for lunch and went their happy way,

still chattering. I, more quietly, took myself back to the office. I would have much to tell Grace that night.

As it turned out, we had much to tell one another.

five

GRACE FOUND THE Monmouth cook, Helga Jensen, in the city directory. She was now in her late sixties, happily retired from any cookery except the annual dinners put on by her church. She would be happy to see us, said Grace, if we cared to drop by.

"That hardly accords with the way Joanna remembers her," I said. "Joanna seemed to think Helga was one of the jailers."

"She could have been. She could have been hired to be. That wouldn't necessarily make her a bad person."

"So, are we going to drop by?"

"This evening. After supper. She says she baked today, so don't have dessert."

We found Helga on the near east side in a middle-aged brick four-plex with a hipped roof, shutters, and a picket fence, everything about it as neat and freshly painted as a movie set. Helga herself answered the door, a stocky, red-cheeked woman, hair braided into a stiff tiara, a perfect stereotype of the cheerful mid-European housewife. Despite name and appearance, what came out of her mouth was pure American. She begged us to come in, said she'd been dying for some company, and what was this about the house in north Denver. A body? Her whole self oozed eager interest, not to say appetite.

We gave her our coats and sat ourselves down on the living-room sofa, upholstered in a fabric so immaculate that I knew she had removed the plastic covers only moments before. I told myself sternly not to spill anything. Helga did not waste a moment. She was forthright in her intentions and desires. We were to call her Helga (we wouldn't have dared argue), and she would call us Jason and Grace. We would be friendly. She liked being friendly. She then excused herself, returning momentarily with a laden tray bearing a lemon cake with walnuts, plus carrot cake (a particular fondness of mine, dating from days at The Home, when carrot cake after Friday supper signaled freedom for a whole weekend), plus tea and coffee.

The tray went on the dining-room table, and we were summoned to sit there. I wasn't the only one worried about spillage. Still, I carefully napkined myself before taking a slice of each kind of cake, together with what proved to be an excellent cup of coffee. My estimation of Helga Jensen went up in the instant.

"So," she said comfortably, sitting back. "Tell me!"

Grace did the telling, in between mouthfuls.

Helga's eyes filled up. "Oh, that poor baby. When did it happen?"

"1975," I said. "The same year Lucia left home."

"That was another poor baby," she said, with a sad shake of her head. "I told him he was doing the wrong thing."

"Who?" I asked.

"Mr. Monmouth. That man was just so pig stubborn about how he wanted his family protected. I told him you couldn't lock up young ones like that. Either they'd wither and die or they'd break loose."

"Joanna seemed to think you agreed with her dad?"

"Me! Not a chance. That man and me, we argued about it all the time, mostly over breakfast. She, the missus, never came down to breakfast, and all the kids did was grab a piece of toast and run, but he liked his breakfasts. I'd tell him to let up on those kids a little, and he'd tell me I worked for him, and if I valued my job, I'd obey his wishes. Well, I figured better me, at least trying to help them, than some other person who wouldn't."

"How did you help them?" Grace asked.

"Oh, the boys were over that wall all the time. Up the tree and over the wall, like a pair of squirrels. Rosabel said they'd been doing it since they were no higher than my knee. And the girls, making their little giggly phone calls when he said they couldn't use the phone. I never told on them and I blackmailed that Steve McHenry so he couldn't."

"Blackmailed?"

"Steve liked to pick up little things and forget to give them back. Money. And maybe a pair of earrings or cuff links or a nice little silver teapot. I told him he keep his mouth shut, I keep mine shut."

I swallowed another delicious mouthful. "What were the girls like?"

"Well, from the time she was tiny, Lucia just went off somewhere, you know. Dreamland. You could speak to her and she wouldn't even hear you. She lived somewhere else, off in her mind. Sometimes she . . ." Her voice dwindled, sadly. "Sometimes she would come to. Nash would say something nasty to her, and she'd look at him, like she really saw him, and her face . . ."

"What?" My fork remained poised. The expression on Helga's large, comfortable face was suddenly terrible in its play of sadness and anger. "What, Helga?"

"She'd look like a child whose toys all got smashed, sort of wondering and afraid and lost, as though she didn't even have words to say how she felt. Every time I saw that expression, I'd tell myself I had to do something, but I could never figure out what to do."

"What did you do?" Grace asked gently.

She laughed, guiltily. "Cookies. And eclairs. And cake. Anything sweet and good I could give the child."

"What did Nash say to her that upset her so?"

"I never knew. What he was saying wasn't what he was saying, you know? He'd say, 'Remember, Loos-ee-ya. You don't want to upset me, do you, Loos-ee-ya?'"

Grace said, "As though there were something between the two of them?"

We watched while Helga struggled to put into words something she had only felt.

"Something, yes. Something nasty. Me and Rosabel used to talk about it. Nash was . . . he was kind of rotten. Even when he was little. He'd lie. He never argued or fussed, he'd stand right there and listen to you, then he'd go off like you never said a word. Like words was just water, running off him. The only thing that mattered to Nash was getting his own way. He could be awful if he didn't get his own way. The rest of us were just the chorus, you know?"

"Like in a Greek play?"

"Or an opera. Like that. Just bystanders."

"What do you mean awful," I asked. "What kind of things did he do?"

"Oh, he'd destroy things, or he'd threaten people, or one time they had a pet rabbit, and he killed it. . . ."

"And his father stood for that?"

"Punishing him just made him do something worse! That boy had a will of iron, I tell you. No way could you make him do anything he didn't want to do. He'd have his way or he'd die trying."

"Was he like that all the time? Or just before Lucia went away?"

"Oh, it was all the time. Of course, I didn't start working for them until Nash was about twelve, so all I know about before then is what Rosabel told me, but he was teasing Lucia and making her life miserable when I first got there. I think he beat on her, too, but I could never prove it. I tried to tell the mister once, but he wouldn't listen to me. He said it was nonsense, Nash was just going through a phase, and all kids got banged up, playing. What kind of playing would that be, giving her bruises like that?"

"What about Matt?" I asked. "Was he unpleasant to the girls?"

"Matt? Not unpleasant, no, just . . . he took after his daddy. He was the watchdog on his family. If one of the girls tried to get away with something, not coming right home from school or sneaking out to visit a friend, Matt would come down like a cleaver. He didn't hit, he just threatened to tell his dad. But Matt never told on Nash. Nash got away with murder. Like the rules didn't apply to him. I remember . . ."

"What?"

"I shouldn't be talking like this. Mr. Monmouth was generous with me."

Grace said, "We've got to find out somewhere, Helga. What do you remember?"

"I remember the time Matt forged Nash's report card for him. Changed all those Ds to Bs. Their dad never caught on. He had blinders on where those boys were concerned, where the whole family was concerned. Matt always protected Nash."

"I understood you stayed after the divorce?"

"I was sorry for her. Mrs. Monmouth, Virginia, she was such a dishrag. No starch left in her. She was a lot like Lucia. There was nothing in either of them to . . . fight with. Like when white people came to this country and the Indians didn't have any resistance to measles or whooping cough, you know? They just laid down and died. That's the way she was. Just laid down and died."

Grace disagreed. "She must have had some fight in her. She got the divorce."

"Well, that's true. I hadn't thought of that. And I never did know the truth about it either. She had something she used over him or he'd never have let her divorce him. That whole ruckus started when Lucia left, about then, anyhow. One of the missus's relatives came, but I was off that week, so I didn't meet him. The mister moved out and took Nash with him, and that was a couple years before she ever filed for divorce, too, so it was something big. Matt was in school. The only ones left there were her and Joanna and Rosabel and me, and Rosabel didn't stay after Virginia's relatives came."

"From Germany. The Kettingers."

"Mrs. Kettinger, Olga, was her sister."

"She was?" Grace asked. "But she lived in Germany?"

"Olga and Virginia's mother was German. The girls grew up speaking German. Virginia used to speak it to me, what little I remember from home. Olga had married a German man, but he got into some kind of money trouble, and Virginia Monmouth was so lonely and so sick, she couldn't go to them to help, but she could bring them to her. And I'll give them credit, too. Whatever kind of trouble they were in over there, they were very good to her. Olga did massage, and Virginia really enjoyed that, and Olga kept the place clean, too, and her husband took care of the grounds, and their kids helped. They were real normal, noisy kids. It did Virginia good to hear them yelling and carrying on."

"What did she die of?"

"She had a cancer. Some slow, painful kind they couldn't do much for. Now, these days, they might cure it, but that was a long time ago."

"She died in 1982," Grace said. "What did you do then?"

"Well, I worked as cook for a sorority house right up until two years ago when I turned sixty-five. I'd been paying for this place right along, and now it's paid for and I've got the rents from the other three units coming in, and my social security and the money Mrs. Monmouth left me. I'm doing all right."

"Mrs. Monmouth left you some money?" I commented.

"She had the house from the divorce, and that went to her children. But she had some other money from her family, and she said one time she was splitting it four ways among her kids, but the way she left it was she left me Lucia's share and she left Nash's and Matt's shares to her sister, Mrs. Kettinger. And she left Joanna's share to Joanna."

"So she wrote off three of her children?" Grace set down her plate and finished the last of her tea.

"She was very unhappy with the boys from the time Lucia left."

"I thought Matt went on living there?" I said.

"Him? No. He kept a room there, but he was never in it. He knew she didn't want him there. He used it as a mailing address, though. Sometimes he'd stop by and pick up the mail. I think he was trying to pretend there was nothing wrong, trying to pretend he hadn't done anything wrong. I know for a fact he used to tell people he lived there."

"What had he done wrong?" I asked.

"Well, that's it, you see. I don't know. I just know she was unhappy with both those boys, and when Mr. Monmouth moved out, she told him to take Nash and Matt with him, she didn't want to see them ever again."

"So there was something," Grace murmured. "And the boys were responsible?"

Helga shrugged. "I guessed so. I never knew with either of those boys. They could be real sneaky."

"Would you happen to have a picture of Lucia?" I asked.

She shook her head, smiling. "She didn't like people taking her picture, especially not with her sister and brothers. She said they all looked like family and she didn't. She'd always stand off to one side. She was real self-conscious about it."

"Looked like family?" Grace questioned. "How do you mean?"

"Blond. They was all blond, him and her, and the kids, all but Lucia. They called her a throwback."

"She was dark?"

"It wasn't she was so dark, it was they was so light! She was just ordinary, but the rest of them was all silver hair and blue eyes, like they'd been bleached. Well, like you, my dear! Anyhow, she was embarrassed about it, so she didn't often have her picture taken."

I took a deep breath and asked the hard question. "Do you think she killed herself, Helga?"

"Her? No. Not on your life. Like I said, she always went off to fairyland, in her head. I think that's what she did. She just went off to fairyland in her head and found herself a new life without those rotten brothers in it."

"You wouldn't remember any special fairyland, would you?"

"Oh, she had a different one every week or so. She was always showing me articles in the paper or in magazines about some wonderful place. One time it was Tibet and the next time it was a place down in Mexico. And sometimes the school would send home information about retreat places, and she always looked at those, too."

"She was thinking about monasteries, then. Convents? Could she have run off and joined a convent somewhere?" I had no idea whether it was possible to do this at age fifteen, but it would explain a lot.

Helga shook her head, however. "Not a Catholic one. She didn't believe the religion. She and Joanna, they were little unbelievers. Many the time I heard them going on about something they'd been told in religion class at school, with Lucia telling Joanna how it upset her. She used to say the religion class was noisy, isn't that funny? Things she didn't like, they were noisy."

Grace asked, "Noisy? What do you mean?"

"Just noisy. Things that she liked, they were quiet, and things she didn't like, they were noisy. Like in her head."

Grace and I looked at each other, wondering if there were any other questions we could ask. Neither of us

could think of any, so we thanked our hostess, compli-
mented her on the cake and the coffee, and departed.

"This case is just full of old ladies," said Grace, on our
way home. "You must attract them like flies."

"Only three," I said. "Kate Mills, and Pearl Cope, and
Helga Jensen. A trio is not a plethora."

"You ought to sic Helga onto Kate Mills," said my
bride. "Helga needs something to do."

"What makes you think that?"

"Her house has been cleaned so often, it squeaks. And
I'll bet Kate Mills could use some help."

It was a thought. I'd been planning an old ladies' luncheon. Maybe I'd ask Helga.

As we neared home Grace said, "I've been putting off
telling you, but I heard from Lloyd Baldridge today." She
sounded depressed.

"You did? What in hell did he want?"

"He really wants us to take a few days to go snorkeling
with him and Helen, in Baja California."

"I wish he'd let up," I said angrily.

I stopped for a red light, and she reached over to stroke
my hand, which was clenched. "How about we tell him
we're pregnant. That would forestall him. None of his
bunch have children."

"That hasn't always been true, Grace." I gritted my
teeth remembering the Benedict boat explosion. The fact
that the Benedict children were along hadn't stopped
their taking risks. Since we were talking about the
Baldridges, it was time to tell Grace what I'd found out.
"Today I had lunch with Betts and Bitts. . . ."

I told her what Bitts and Betts had said about the Carlyles and the Benedicts, what they'd said about the
Slades' narrow escape while cross-country skiing, and

about the Dahlbergs' and Baldridges' near thing while rock climbing. "The arson investigators mentioned the Baldridges had had a couple of close calls. Lloyd encountered an avalanche, and he was with the Dahlbergs when the rope broke. Betts and Bitts think the whole group is on a hard-luck trail."

"Are they all trying to get killed!" she cried. "The whole bunch of them seem determined to commit suicide. And he asks us to go along! I think that stinks."

It was the word that made the connection for me. Something stinks. Helen had said it to me: It stinks. The stairs were blocked and there were bars on the upstairs windows. And it stinks, or did, before we deodorized it. The Baldridges' town house. I pulled over to the curb and stopped abruptly.

"Jason! What is it?"

"I'm having an irrational brainstorm," I confessed, wondering if it was, indeed, irrational.

"So? Tell me!" She leaned forward, peering into my face with her full attention.

"It was about thrill seekers," I muttered, pounding the steering wheel with a clenched fist, trying to think my way through it. "Suppose you're a thrill seeker, one who lives for excitement, for the rush, and you spend your life doing dangerous things. After a while, wouldn't you get to that 'been there, done that' point where all the excitement wears thin?"

"Probably. If you were that kind of person."

"Right. And when things got kind of boring, you'd talk with your thrill-seeker friends about it, and maybe you'd try to figure out something to jack up the tension a little. And at that point somebody says, hey, I know. Let's form a couples club, a secret society, a covert group. We'll draw straws, as couples, and the ones with the short straw have to try to murder one of the other couples."

It sounded weak and foolish and impossible as I said it.

"How did you come up with that?" she demanded.

I rubbed my head, trying to connect. "It was that conversation you overheard at the New Year's Eve party. The man mentioned the stairs being blocked and bars on the windows. Both those things matched what happened during the fire at the Baldridge place. The stairs were blocked. There are bars on the windows at the back. It was definitely arson. And they barely got out through the attic space, where they kicked out a ventilator grill and jumped. They were still all pumped up about it when they called the following morning. And when Helen showed me the damage she said something . . . something about she had planned on dying in the open air. . . . As though a non-sport-related accident didn't count. Maybe the rules specified a sporting accident. . . . Oh, this is ridiculous!"

Grace was staring through the windshield, furrows between her eyebrows, squinting a little. "I think you've got it wrong about drawing straws. They don't draw straws, they do it in turns. That's what Rodale said, it was Helen and Lloyd's *turn*. The couple whose turn it is, that couple draws a *name*. The Baldridges will draw one name from the hat, and they will try to kill that person."

"Couple," I corrected. "That couple. This is a married people's game. If we're right, it was the Rodales, either or both, who set fire to the Baldridges' house. Maybe she . . . what's her name? Jackie Rodale. Maybe she got Helen out of the house while her husband planted the device. And those close calls the Baldridges had! Avalanches can be triggered. Ropes can be frayed. And there's something else: Bitts and Betts say there's a poker pot, that each of the original couples put a million dollars into a pot that goes to the survivor. If we're right about the Benedicts and Carlyles being part of it, there's seven million dollars waiting for the last pair left standing."

Grace nodded, her face very concentrated and still. "It could be more than that. We don't know how many are dead. You heard only two names, but there could have been more of them to start with."

"True." I pulled out into the street once more, nervously checking traffic in all directions. "Though if there had been, I think the Sullivan sisters would have come up with the names."

Grace erupted angrily, "Why, though? That's what I can't figure out."

"Excitement, Grace. You're the one who said it's all Lloyd and Helen live for."

"I understand *that*, Jason. I know people like that, even down at the precinct there are more than a few of them. They're cops because they get a rush, being a cop. Forget all the protect-and-serve stuff, what they like are the dangerous arrests and the high-speed chases. You see tapes of cops beating on somebody, and it's all part of the same thing. You know, catch it! Catch it! Then kill it! Kill it! Like a dog with a rabbit. And as for this money bit, it's just another kind of high-stakes gambling. It adds to the rush. That part I get, believe me!

"What I *don't* get is why they're so determined to get us involved in their lives. Why keep after us the way they do? Is it to get more money into the pot? Or what?"

"Not more money. Lloyd is in a position to check

anybody's net worth if he wants to, so if money were it, he'd know his game is out of our league. That young Fields couple at the party, they didn't look like big money either. The only reason I can come up with is that Lloyd and Helen—or maybe the whole bunch—are looking for some herd immunity. They need to make their group bigger and more amorphous, to spread out the deaths or narrow escapes and make them look more accidental. Their in-group is too small, it shares too many characteristics, it's too identifiable."

"You mean, to outsiders?"

"Exactly. Betts and Bitts are complete outsiders. I tossed them the names Carlyle and Benedict, nothing else, just that. In just a few minutes of conversation, they came up with all the names we came up with, and they recognized all these people as belonging together. 'That sporty group,' they called it, and then they went on with all this business about the group being on a bad-luck binge."

"So you think Lloyd and Helen just want us as some kind of camouflage?"

"Like zebras," I said. "On the nature programs. All those stripes running in a herd confuse the lions. It makes it harder to single out any one of them."

I drove the rest of the way home in complete silence; neither of us said another word. We turned into our alleyway, thumbed the control to the garage door, drove in, and let the door go down behind us, sitting there in the dark, each of us lost in our own thoughts. I was thinking about danger, and the deadly attraction it has for some people. Grace was, as I might have guessed, thinking like a cop.

Eventually, she said, "I wonder what we could get them on. Assisted suicide?"

"Murder, I should think. Or conspiracy to commit murder."

"Is it murder if you conspire to do it to yourself? Weren't all of them expecting someone in their group to fool with their parachutes or blow up their boat?"

"The Benedict kids weren't," I said, regretting it immediately, for she gasped. She'd forgotten the children. I put my arm around her.

She murmured, "You're right, Jason. The kids weren't part of the group. They died in that boat explosion, along with their parents. If that wasn't an accident, if someone actually did that . . . well, if we can get any of them at all, it ought to be for murder."

As she left next morning, Grace said she'd have a private off-the-record talk with a friend in the DA's office. I suggested she also get in touch with Miller and Morrow, the two guys who were investigating the arson.

"It's all guesswork," she complained. "And you didn't think they were that sympathetic."

"It's up to you." I didn't want the two cops camping on our doorstep any more than she did.

"They'll laugh," she said.

"So? Is this the first time Jason and Grace, those amateur sleuths . . ."

"I'm not an amateur. I am a professional sleuth."

"So, is it the first time we've been laughed at?"

I very much wanted out of the middle of the Baldridge mess. If she could drop it in someone else's lap, I would cheer and we would thereafter stay clear of the Baldridges.

I crossed my fingers and made a very strong wish that somebody—besides Grace—would take it seriously.

The next few days were busy, a lot of little stuff, the tax man needing records we hadn't given him, a customer needing repairs on a two-hundred-year-old piece of furniture that her prize pair of Abyssinian cats had done their best to reduce to kindling, an insurance company needing valuation of some furniture we'd sold six or eight years ago for a fire claim. This last brought Lloyd to mind, and no sooner did I think of him than he called to suggest, yet again, that we join him and Helen in a scuba vacation in Baja. This time I was ready for him. I told him my leg had been acting up from an old gunshot wound, the doctor had forbidden me to use it any more than necessary until we had evaluated the possibility of doing some corrective surgery. Having thus established myself as a wimp, I figured he would put me down as a bad candidate and forget it.

Forlorn hope. A day later, early evening, Helen called Grace to renew the invitation and suggest that Grace could leave me at home if she liked.

Grace's cheeks were quite pink when she reported this conversation over supper. "I laughed a gay little laugh. I told her when we'd been married as long as she and Lloyd had, maybe we'd pall on each other and need outside excitement, but right at the moment, I didn't care to leave you behind, anywhere." Her eyes flashed and she thumped her fist on the table, an angry banty hen. "I used my sexy voice."

"Ouch," I cringed. "She wouldn't have liked that."

"I've tried being polite," she snapped. "Why should I care what she thinks? I told the whole Baldridge story to my assistant-DA friend, Jennifer Allen. I also told

Jennifer about the arson guys and the arson guys about her. Let them work together."

Bela, hearing dissension, put his massive head in my lap and whined. I told him everything was all right, Grace and I were fine, thank you. Schnitz, seeing the head in my lap, decided to contest for possession. I got up and found snacks for both of them. The sound of the refrigerator door brought Critter, who wandered in, tail high, ears flattened to the sides, staring haughtily at Schnitz. The food defused that situation, at least momentarily.

I sat back down by my bride, who was poking angrily at her plate.

"Once you started telling, you certainly told all and sundry," I commented.

"I'm trying to achieve a critical mass of suspicion, one that'll go off with a bang and obliterate them!"

"Please keep in mind they haven't paid all their bills yet. I think we'll bill them at intervals rather than waiting until the job is over. Can you arrange with the arson guys not to arrest them until they've paid up?"

"Very funny," she said in a snide voice. "Meantime, I'm going to find that young woman they were trying to recruit and drop a bug in her ear."

"You mean Caetlin Fields. Be careful," I warned her. "Slander, and all that."

"I won't do a thing but tell her what's already happened to people. I'll find a way to run into her somewhere, casually. As a cop, it's my duty."

"Do the Baldridges know you're a cop?" I'd been trying for several days to remember if we'd ever mentioned Grace's profession to Lloyd or Helen. Sometimes when we're with people we don't know well, we don't mention her job because it's amazing how uncomfortable some people get when a cop is around. Sometimes everyone has a better time if they think she's a clerk in the recorder's office. Of course it works both ways. Some of her cop colleagues are more comfortable if they think Jason Lynx sells cars. To some, decor is as suspect as ballet, or designing women's clothes.

"I think we've always said I work for the city," she said thoughtfully. "Why?"

"Just be careful, dear one. It was you who told me they were creepy."

"Right at the moment, I just want them both to go to Baja and leave us alone. I want to concentrate on Maria. I thought the other night we were really getting some-where, and then we had to get sidetracked with the damned Baldridges."

"Forget them," I said dismissively, waving my magic wand. "They're gone. What do we do next about Maria Montoya?"

"I thought what Helga had to say about Nash was interesting, that he had something he was holding over Lucia's head. I'm also interested in Helga's description of Nash as completely amoral, and Steve as no better."

"You lean toward someone in the house having killed the little girl."

"Jason, if that little girl had been killed yesterday, we'd look first at the people in the house, wouldn't we? It doesn't matter that the murder was twenty-two years ago, the same rule should apply."

"What about the other little girl they found four years ago?"

"Oh!" She looked startled. "I forgot to tell you. I did follow up on that. The place they found the other body was under construction, remember? It was a big, big development. Guess who the contractor was?"

"Not M.M.A.?"

"Yessir." She gave me a crooked little smile. "Do you believe that?"

"Steve worked for M.M.A.," I said. "After the divorce. Maybe he's still there?"

"Matt *is* M.M.A.," she returned. "And we know he's still there."

"Motive," I growled. "What was the motive?"

"Maybe one of the two of them is a sick, nasty bastard."

Who knew? Lucia, maybe, if that's what made her run away. Joanna, maybe, if Lucia confided in her. I tapped my fork on the table, a habit that irritated Grace enormously. I do it only when I'm frustrated.

Grace said in exasperation, "Jason, what would you do if I weren't around?"

"About Maria Montoya?"

"Yes. What would you do?"

"I'd go talk to Joanna."

"Then for heaven's sake, go talk to Joanna."

Accordingly, next afternoon I went back to talk to Joanna.

She was hard at work, and when I first came in she told me to sit down and be quiet for a few minutes while she finished some detail in the painting she was working on. A lot of her work was abstract. Sometimes I like abstract things, purely as designs, and sometimes I don't. Looking at those hanging on and standing around the walls, I liked some quite a bit. Most of the ones I liked would have made excellent fabric patterns. I liked her representational things better, particularly the ones depicting birds. I looked around for the big parrot and saw him in the corner, asleep on his perch, looking hung over. Maybe he'd been posing late.

After a bit, Joanna muttered, snarled, wiped at the canvas with a cloth and turned to me with a ferocious expression that was totally belied by her tear-filled eyes.

"You've come about Nash!"

I tried to look innocent and startled.

"Oh, come on," she growled, slopping turpentine into a jar and slapping her brushes into it. "He came over here before Christmas, having a tantrum. The minute he told me he went to see you, I knew you'd be back."

"Why?"

"Nash's actions almost always end up having an opposite effect from the one he intends." She dropped into a chair, wiping angry tears from her cheeks.

"He seemed very anxious that we not investigate the little girl's death. Both my wife and I feel very strongly about that."

"Well you don't have any monopoly on feelings, you know! Ever since you came, that first time, I've thought about her, wondered if she was afraid, if she was hurt. I talked to Matt about it and he said it had to be an outsider. What outsider? It has to have been one of us!"

"Why, Joanna?"

"Because of everything that happened in the family! I don't believe in coincidence! If that little girl was killed when the mudroom was being built, then it happened during spring vacation, when Matt was home from school and we were all there. It was almost the last time we were ever all there together. After that Lucia left home. Just went away, all by herself. Matt went back to school, and Dad moved out, taking Nash with him."

"I had wondered if Lucia had really left, or whether maybe she'd been killed, too," I said.

Joanna shook her head. "She called me several weeks after she left to tell me she was all right. She didn't say where she was. She told me not to let anyone know that she'd called, certainly not the boys or Dad. I told her Dad and Nash had moved out already and Matt was back at school. She said she was glad the boys were gone, but I still shouldn't tell Mom she'd called. She knew the boys or Dad wouldn't leave her in peace, and she knew Mom couldn't keep quiet about it. Poor Mom. She never could suffer in silence. If she was upset about something, everyone knew it."

"And you think she was upset about Maria Montoya's death?"

"I don't know if she ever knew about Maria Montoya. She never mentioned it to me. But she knew Lucia had gone, and she had to know there was a reason, that something bad had happened! Something Lucia couldn't . . . couldn't tolerate. Maybe Lucia saw the child killed, or saw the body? Maybe . . . Nash saw it and told her it was there? That would be typical of Nash."

"But you are prepared to swear that she left of her own volition and that she called you some weeks later?"

"Yes. And I kept my word to her, too. I didn't tell anyone until eight years later when . . . when Mother was dying. She was grieving over Lucia and I told her Lucia was all right. That was the only time I could trust her not to tell the boys, when she was dying." She wept, then got up and left the room. I heard water running. After a time she returned, not greatly improved, still teary.

"Joanna, forgive me for not understanding, but when Lucia called, didn't you ask her why she went?"

"Of course I asked. Lucia told me she went because she couldn't stay with us anymore. She had tried, she said, but she couldn't keep her mind quiet anymore."

"Meaning?"

"Meaning! Who the hell knows! Half the time I didn't know what Lucia was talking about! She didn't make it any clearer than that! She never did. She was always off somewhere. Fantasy. She lived in a dreamworld. She didn't connect."

I took a deep breath, wishing Grace were with me. "Okay, Joanna, bear with me, but I'm going to understand this or die trying. She went to school, right?"

"Of course."

"She had classes? She did homework? She got good grades?"

"She got good grades in some things. Things she could read and remember, she got good grades in. Things where she could express herself, like art, she got good grades in. She was talented in art. If she'd cared about it, she'd have been a lot better than I am."

She stood up, frowning. "She liked things where there were no conflicts, I mean, you know, like math or science. One and one always equal two. Stuff always falls down, not up. That kind of class Lucia enjoyed. She called them quiet classes."

"So she got good grades?"

"In math. In science. In art. But where she had to make a judgment that was subject to argument, like in social studies, or in English class, deciding who or what really caused the death of Romeo and Juliet, she couldn't do it. No, she *wouldn't* do it. In religion class—we had to take it even though we weren't Catholic—we'd talk about sin. Stealing, for instance. Stealing is a sin, and that's a rule, so Lucia ought to have accepted it. It ought to have fit in with her 'quiet' subjects. But Lucia said the rules themselves were noisy, they didn't make sense. She could come up with twenty cases in which stealing was the only thing that made sense. Stealing medicine for a dying child. Stealing food for a starving mother. Stealing a horse so you could take someone to a doctor or plow a field to plant food for a family. She was born to situational ethics."

She sounded so outraged that I laughed. "Now wait a minute. You're describing pragmatism. You're not describing someone who lives a fantasy life."

"When you absolutely refuse to make any kind of a judgment or choice about people, even when they do rotten things, when you float through life refusing to discriminate, accepting everyone, that's fantasy."

I commented, "Pearl Cope says she belonged in a convent."

"Well, hell." She fumed silently for a moment. "That's a kind of fantasy, too."

"What you're saying is that Lucia would not make judgments about people."

"That's part of what I'm saying, yes."

"So, even if she knew Steve had done something rotten, she wouldn't have judged him. Or if Nash had done something. She wouldn't have ratted on him."

She looked momentarily startled. "I suppose that's true."

"But if the person kept doing it, over and over, causing pain, causing agony that she, Lucia, could see and feel . . . what might she do? She wouldn't act? It would be distressing, unquiet. Right?"

"Right."

"So she might run? To find the quiet she'd lost?"

She shrugged. "Mr. Lynx . . ."

"Jason."

"Jason, I don't know. You're trying to figure her out. Hell, I was—am her sister. Maybe if I'd been a year older instead of a year younger, but I never could figure her out. Maybe Mrs. Cope was right. If Lucia had been in a convent, I wouldn't have tried to figure her out. I'd have just said, well, God's talking to her and maybe she's very holy or something." She turned away from me, the tears flowing again.

"When she ran, where would she have gone? Helga said she had fairylands."

"Not fairylands. Utopias. Gardens of Eden."

"You knew about them?"

"Tibet. I remember her talking about Tibet."

"But you don't honestly think she'd have gone there."

"Someplace like there. Someplace remote. And quiet. You're right about that. When she was troubled, she always said it was noise that was bothering her. She said it was jagged, with sharp points. Even when we were little, I understood that she meant noise inside her head. I always imagined it as a kind of mental static."

"Do you believe your brother was involved in the little girl's death?"

"Jason, I don't know what I believe except that something terrible happened twenty-one years ago, and the result was that my older sister went away and my father left home and my mother turned into a weepy, trembling invalid, years before she died. The little girl . . . she wasn't the only innocent who died then! So far as I am concerned, Lucia did, too!"

I patted her shoulder. I sympathized. I told her I

thought we'd wind up the whole thing very shortly. Then I asked her for a picture of Lucia. She had one, a studio portrait taken when Lucia was fourteen. The formal pose gave no hint of her personality. It was a pretty, neutral face, with nothing remarkable about it except the glowing, percipient eyes. They were large, slightly protuberant, and really did seem lit with an interior light. Strange, and memorable eyes. She was darker than her siblings, both in skin and hair, and she looked somewhat familiar. A glance at Joanna verified that they shared a family resemblance. The shape of the nose and jaw were very much alike.

I left Joanna with a few sympathetic words. That night, after supper, with the gas fire at our toes and Grace and me snuggled closely on the couch, I tried to synthesize the whole thing so it made sense.

"Putting what Helga said together with what Pearl Cope said with what Joanna said about Lucia, I get a picture of a girl who could not handle conflicting ideas or demands. She was bright enough, but incapable of decision—or perhaps, incapable of deciding between people. She couldn't hold out against a strong personality. She would give way. Some things she thought of as *quiet*, and those were the things that did not trouble her, happenings or studies with rules she could not only obey but agree with. Her utopias were all quiet places, remote places. Conflicting events or ideas were noisy. When she felt too much noise in her head, she couldn't handle it. Whatever happened in 1975 was too noisy for her."

Grace put her head on my shoulder. "That place you found in New Mexico. The Well of Silence. That sounds like a utopia for her."

"It came immediately to mind," I admitted. "There

must be a connection. If Clare went there, it wasn't by accident. And I don't believe either the sculptor or his wife is ignorant of the place. They're only three miles away from it, and places like that get talked about. Besides, Helga said Lucia had a clipping about a place in Mexico. It was probably New Mexico."

"Would she confuse the two?"

I laughed. "In 1996 the ticket sales office for the Atlanta Olympics turned down orders from New Mexico on the grounds that they didn't fill foreign orders."

"You're kidding." She curled sideways, giving me an indignant look.

"Honestly, Grace. Kids don't learn geography anymore. Lucia might have confused the two. Or Helga could have confused the two." I settled her more closely while engaging in lofty though fleeting thoughts about home schooling our own child, children.

"Do you have the feeling this is getting very weird?" Grace asked, somewhat petulantly. "I've done murder investigations, and I don't recall ever having one that seemed to spread out so. The damned thing is like an octopus."

"There aren't that many loose ends. Steve McHenry is one. . . ."

"Martinelli's looking for him. He told me he had a lead on him. He's going to call me tomorrow."

"Well, I've left one thing hanging. I never did send pictures of Clare and Lucia to the Gatekeeper at the Well. Now that I've got one of Lucia and one of Clare, I'll get that done."

"You've got one of Clare when she was seventeen and one of Lucia when she was fourteen. Clare and Lucia, assuming they're still alive, are now thirty-six or -seven years old. Do you really think the pictures will help?"

"Does the department have one of those computer programs that age pictures of faces?"

"I don't know. It's never come up. I have a hunch if we do, it will be expensive or it'll have to be cleared through some other office or something." She yawned enormously, like Critter, exposing a pink void surrounded by sharp little white teeth.

"All right." I made a mental note to cultivate someone who was into computers. Ridiculous not to have an aging program at one's fingertips. "I'll send copies of the pictures we have, you take the originals and either you or Martinelli can find out if they can be aged."

"Which will lead us where?" she asked sleepily. "I forget."

"To Clare, who might lead us to Lucia. Or to Lucia herself. And from Lucia, maybe to whoever killed Maria."

I was answered by an irascible little snore. Six months ago, Grace would have been at my throat to get this thing figured out. Six months ago, she would never have fallen asleep without an evening snack, or several. She had stopping being sick in the mornings. She was sleeping longer than usual. Pregnancy seemed to be calming her down. I wasn't sure I liked that. I'd always relied on Grace to keep me moving. It irked me to think I might have to apply my own self-discipline.

Nonetheless, come morning I had copies of the pictures made and sent them off together with a letter to the Gatekeeper, remembering, as I dropped the envelope into the mailbox, that my Gatekeeper might not be Gatekeeper anymore. She hadn't told me how often they changed jobs. Too often wouldn't be a good idea. No one would ever get good at their job that way. Maybe they switched often enough to avoid boredom but not so often as to assure incompetence.

I wandered around the shop, upstairs, downstairs. I fussed at Eugenia, who told me to go away and let her alone. I sat at my desk, trying to figure out why I was so nudgey. The tile layers were at work in the kitchen of the new house. Temporary repairs had been made to the roofs that leaked. Eventually the upstairs balconies would be enclosed, but not just yet. I didn't want to overextend us while the Maria Montoya business still hung fire. Grace and I had done a sketchy plan placing our furniture, hers and mine, when we moved into the new house. As time went by we'd add and subtract to make it look right. An added Grace note: one of her tenants had told her she'd be happy to manage the little apartment house for a slight decrease in rent. One minor concern removed.

So, plans for our future lives were moving along well; the business seemed in all respects to be prosperous and productive; Grace was having an uneventful pregnancy; and yet here I was, teetering uneasily, caught in mid-impulse like an ant in a chunk of amber, still trying to figure out what happened to Maria Montoya. It wasn't a throat-catching kind of anxiety, not one of those paralyzing or horrifying things. It was just a nagging worry, a disquieting itch, a something not right that needed to be fixed before one could allow oneself to be happy.

It did not help that, for some reason I could not fathom, Lloyd and Helen Baldridge called me, both of them on the phone simultaneously, renewing their assault, like ghosts of Christmases yet to come.

Lloyd said he had a marvelous orthopedic surgeon who could do wonders for my leg. Helen knew a wonderful trainer who did absolutely marvelous things in rehab. Lloyd thought stretching out in the Mexican sun would be good for me. Helen thought Grace was looking a little overworked, why didn't I insist on a vacation.

I finally decided enough was enough.

"You're very kind," I said in my most charming voice. "Though I'd love it if Grace left the police force and concentrated on me, she's not going to do it. She loves being a cop. And part of being a cop is that she plans her vacations way ahead, just like any other working stiff, right? Now she and I have our summer all planned. She's taking maternity leave a month before the baby is due, then we're taking a month's leave together. I don't think a quick trip to Acapulco fits in with our plans, thanks a lot."

Lloyd mumbled something about another call, and the line went dead. I waited. Neither of them came back. I smiled very slightly, and hung up the phone. Now what was it that got them? Cop-hood, or pregnancy? Or both?

I told Grace when she got home that night.

"It was my being a cop," she said, dropping into the chair across the desk from me. "I got a call from Lieutenant Morrow and Detective Miller. The Baldridge maid remembers a phone man coming into the house the day before the fire. He said he needed to trace a wire, and she remembers his carrying an aluminum can, like a soda can. They found the can lying in that basement room where the fire started; it was part of the incendiary apparatus. The fire burned up the wall, the can was below the fire line so it wasn't much damaged. They got fingerprints off it. I mentioned the Rodales' name along with all the others, the Slades, the Phillipses, the Dahlbergs. We've got a conference tomorrow so I can tell them the rest of it."

"Still guesswork, Grace."

"They know that. But if the fingerprints are Rodale's, it'll go a long way toward making it real."

"There might be some evidence for the boat explosion that killed the Benedicts," I muttered, wondering if the boat had been salvaged.

She agreed. "I called the sheriff's office and queried the sky-diving accident. The deputy was there at the time. He told me nobody ever looked at the parachutes that didn't open."

"That seems unlikely."

"They died in empty sky country, out northeast, where the plane took off from some little strip in a pasture, and the local sheriff's office did the investigation. According to the deputy, somebody from the sheriff's office asked the others in the party who had packed the chutes, and the witnesses all said Carlyle packed both of them. So, the conclusion was that either Carlyle did it wrong and it was an accident, or he did it right and it was murder-suicide. There was no insurance involved, so nobody looked any closer."

"It's still shoddy investigation."

She got up, took off her jacket, folded it neatly, and put it across her arm, saying crisply, "Well, it happens, Jason. Training offered to deputies isn't the greatest. And most law enforcement types, let's face it, are not in the top tenth percentile on the intelligence scale, or even the top twenty. They do tend to be a bit more physical than mental, and the larger forces try to make up in training what isn't there naturally, but even well-trained people

have off days. I've come in on cases where people have
been walking all over the evidence, where people have lost
the evidence, where people have interrupted the chain of
custody, where people have contaminated the evidence
or never even looked at it. . . ." Her voice had risen, and
now she cleared her throat, staring threateningly at the
wall. "Or where they had looked at it and didn't realize it
even *was* evidence."

"My, my, we are in a snit."

She snarled, "Well, it was a long day. The captain got
me to thinking about intelligence levels when he got
sniffy about my doing all this stuff which, as he put it,
nobody had assigned me. I told him when a body turns
up in my house, nobody has to assign me, and when
some guy tries to get me involved in a thrill club, nobody
has to assign me that, either. He told me he'd make
allowances since I was preggy. I told him not to bother."

She flung herself down in the chair once more, looking
very angry and silver-pink and adorable.

"How about dinner on the town?"

"I'd have to change."

"Yes. I think that would be in order."

"I'd have to bathe."

"That might also be in order. I could join you. We
could drink cranberry juice cocktail together. Or I picked
up some new raspberry-flavored stuff that tastes quite
nice."

"I want champagne."

"Um. You want Lucretia Willis-Lynx to be born with
a taste for the finer things of life?"

"Lucretia?" She giggled.

"Well, since at her stage of life, champagne is poison,
I thought of the Borgias, naturally."

"I didn't mean it. I mean, I meant it, but I didn't really mean it."

"I know. Why don't you get in the tub with a tall glass of raspberry and seltzer and pretend it's pink champagne. Why don't I join you in the tub. Why don't we steam and stew and think of all the nice things in the world there are to eat. And do. And think about."

She giggled again, slightly teary. "I never used to cry. Well, hardly ever."

"One of the few functions that husbands fulfill, now as in primitive times, is being cried at and upon. Most of the rules of life have changed, most gender roles are passé, but that one remains. Husbands are for crying on."

"The captain is a rat."

"Right. He has the longest tail of any rat in the world."

"And Martinelli is a tattletale."

"Martinelli is beneath contempt. His tail is almost as long as the captain's."

"Right."

Eventually we ended up having dinner in north Denver at Little Pepina's, one of the Italian places we had promised one another we would try. We then went over to the new house and spent a contented hour wandering through it and talking about what wonderful things we were going to do with it.

There is a certain light of which I've always been fond, a kind of old-master's light, as aged varnish on ancient paintings, a butterscotch glow, rich as amber. There were rooms in our house that had that light. The stairway had it, and the hall. The living room had it. It was a sunset glow that persisted throughout the day, due mostly to the light reflected from the floors and the overhanging eaves. Someone, at some time, had painted the eaves a rich coppery hue that reflected the Saltillo tiles.

The plasterer had suggested to me a type of plaster which finished naturally, without paint, in that same rosy amber. The house glowed with it. We walked hand in hand around it, loving it. We made no mention of Maria Montoya.

Four days later, I got the letter. Postmarked Albuquerque. Which doesn't mean anything except that it was mailed somewhere in New Mexico.

> Dear Mr. Lynx:
> Where I am is unimportant. What I could tell you might be important, but I have sworn never to tell anyone. I have written to those who must answer for what they have done, and you must look to them for the answer. Please. Leave me in quiet.

It was signed, "Lucia Monmouth."

The only thing I could assume from this is that the pictures sent to the Well of Silence had provoked the letter. Therefore, there was a connection. Either Lucia was there, at the place, or someone there knew where she was.

Please, she said. Please.

When I showed it to Grace, she said, "Damn!"

"There's definitely a connection with the retreat place."

"Of course there is. And she begs to be let alone. When I'm responsible for a case and somebody who's not a suspect says please, let me alone, it's damned hard to press, you know? I feel for them. I feel for her. It must have been a desperate situation to make her leave like that, all those years ago. One thing I'm convinced of, Matt and Nash, one or both, know all about it."

"You said Martinelli was looking for Steve. Did he find him?" I asked.

"Oh, right. Steve had a record, half a dozen arrests for this and that, breaking and entering, burglary, possession of stolen property, never anything really big."

"Had?"

"He was out on parole when he died about a year ago. He had AIDS. He was forty-seven. That means he was a young guy when he was working for Monmouth. Twenty-five, maybe."

My mouth dropped open. Whatever I had suspected about Steve, it had not included . . . well, what hadn't it included? "Was he gay?" I asked. "Did he use drugs?"

"Both, according to Martinelli, though the drug use started during an incarceration about five years ago, too late to have been the cause."

I said, "But if he was gay . . ."

"He's not likely to be the murderer of an eleven-year-old girl, right?"

She looked unhappy about that. Grace had rather liked Steve for the murder.

I said, "Not if sex was the motive, no."

"Which brings us back to the two boys. And I'll bet their father knew which."

"What makes you think so?"

She made an exasperated face. "Well, he left the house, and he allowed the divorce without fighting it. His wife had something to hold over him."

"True. And if he has Alzheimer's, as we've been told, I doubt he can tell us much."

She continued in her annoyed voice, "All right, where do

we go now? Do we turn the whole thing over to Martinelli? It's not my case. I can't go storming in on Matt Monmouth, or Nash, either. At this point we've got exactly nothing."

I murmured some honeyed words, hoping to calm her. She wasn't in a mood to be calmed.

"Don't sweetness me, Jason Lynx. I am not in the mood for tender sentiment. I'm expecting you to come up with something terribly original and clever. Don't let me down."

She stalked away in high dudgeon leaving me feeling unfairly assaulted and picked on. I had promised to love and honor and take care of and all the other time-honored oaths, but I had never sworn to be either original or clever. I felt my eyebrows going up, felt that pained expression sneaking over my face, and sternly repressed it. James Bond could no doubt be clever on order, but then, he was fictional!

As it happened, Mark had stayed late to work on an old marquetry table in the basement, so I took two beers out of the refrigerator and carried them down, perching myself on a desk while he struggled with recalcitrant veneer. It was trying to separate itself from the wood beneath, and Mark was determined that it should stay put. He was doing things with a hot iron and a hypodermic needle full of some new miracle glue we'd been touted on.

While he worked away, I told him the latest on the Maria Montoya case, including the fact that Steve had been gay. Mark is my expert on all things dealing with gayness, male or female.

I asked, "Would Steve, during those years when he

worked for Monmouth and lived on the place, have attempted to seduce the boys?"

"If he was a pedophile," muttered Mark. "Pedophiles can be attracted by children of either sex, but most prefer one sex over the other. Since he was working for Monmouth, however, it wouldn't have been smart of him to actively go after his employer's children. Now if one of the boys was gay and sexually mature, that would change the odds. Then there'd be no seduction involved."

I thought my way through this, but it didn't hold up. "Mrs. Monmouth more or less threw Monmouth out and told him to take the boys with him. Presumably Monmouth knew why. If Steve was part of the cause, Monmouth would have been angry with him, but he didn't show any anger. He didn't fire Steve. In fact, he put him on the payroll of his company. Therefore, it's unlikely that Steve was the cause of the upset."

Mark lifted his iron and frowned at the tabletop. "If Mr. Monmouth knew about the death of Maria Montoya, if that's why he left, would he have kept Steve on the payroll if Steve did it?"

I shook my head slowly. That didn't seem likely. "If one of the boys did it, and Steve helped cover it up, then Monmouth would have kept him on the payroll."

"Okay," said Mark, putting down his implements. "If Mrs. Monmouth knew that the body of that child was under her house, would she have gone on living there?"

I thought of her as described by those who had known her, neurasthenic, given to hysterias and complaints. "No. I think not."

"Therefore, it wasn't the presence of the body that Mrs. Monmouth used to get rid of her husband. She had something else to hold over him."

"She knew her son was gay, one or both? She knew . . . Lord, I don't know."

"Well, someone knows. If not Joanna, maybe Mrs. Monmouth's sister? Didn't you tell me Amelia said she had a sister?"

"Sister!" I struck my forehead with an open hand, accusing myself of all kinds of stupidity. "We've got letters! From the sister to Virginia."

"Letters you haven't read?"

"They're in German. I don't read German."

"Well, I have a friend who speaks and reads and teaches German. A slightly flaky but trustworthy friend if you're willing to pay for a translator."

I went upstairs and got the letters and brought them down to Mark, feeling like an idiot the whole time. Who would Mrs. Monmouth confide in if not her own sister? Of course I hadn't known when I first saw the letters that Mrs. Kettinger was her sister. Still, that was no excuse. Surely she would have told her sister why she had thrown her husband and sons out, why she was getting a divorce. "The only parts he would need to translate would be things dealing with her reasons for throwing her husband out and for his going without fighting over it."

Mark nodded, tucking the packet of letters away in his jacket pocket. After which I left him to his hot iron and glue and went upstairs, to report to my bride that we had gone yet another few inches toward solving our puzzle, and to find out what the lady fancied for dinner. She fancied Chinese, which was fine with me.

We got home about eight, fed the animals the leftovers we'd brought home in doggy bags—in my house doggy bags really are for the dog, and the cats—then I went into the office and checked the answering machine. Two nothing calls, one wrong number, and then a very strange voice:

"You'll find the answer you're looking for at the Monmouth yard. You've been there, you know where it is. You'll have to hurry. It'll be gone by tomorrow."

Grace came through the door just as I was listening to this.

"Play that again," she commanded.

I played it again, then several times more. It sounded more like a man than a woman though neither of us could swear it was.

"What does he mean, the Monmouth yard?" Grace asked.

"The construction yard. Where they keep heavy machinery and supplies. I met Matt Jr. there, the first time I talked to him. They still do some construction, according to Nash, though not so much as in their father's time."

"Where is it?"

"Clear south to hell and gone, off Titan Road, halfway to Castle Rock, with the railroad on one side and the South Platte River on the other."

"What's out there?"

"Oh, it's a sort of industrial area. There's a big container park and a place that sells drilling equipment and a couple of gravel pits."

"You're not going," said Grace.

"Why not?"

"Because it's too damn convenient, and it's obviously dangerous. It sounds like a trap."

"I think it's a follow-up to the letter. The letter said, ask elsewhere. This is elsewhere. The answer we seek is at the Monmouth yard, and it'll be gone by tomorrow.

Someone's there to talk to me who won't be there tomorrow."

"Why all the way out there?"

"If you had driven up from New Mexico, if you wanted to avoid coming into Denver, if you were familiar with the place from childhood, wouldn't it be a logical place to pick?"

"So you think it's Lucia?"

"Not necessarily. I think she picked the place, but it could be someone who knows Lucia, who's willing to do her a favor. Clare, perhaps, or someone from the Well of Silence."

"I'm coming with you."

"Now, Grace."

"Don't 'now, Grace' me, Jason! I'm coming with you. And, I'm carrying a gun, and I suggest you do the same. Also, don't erase that message on the phone. Take out the tape and put it in the drawer, so it doesn't get erased by accident."

"There's no one here but us. . . ." I complained.

"And no telling when we'll get back!"

I switched the tape, put the used one into an envelope and wrote on it, "do not destroy or erase," put the time and date on it, and put it in the top drawer of Mark's desk. If we vanished, as Grace seemed to think likely, Mark would find it. I went down to the basement and got the thirty-eight revolver out of the safe, made sure it was loaded, and put it in my overcoat pocket along with some spare ammunition.

Then I stopped, patting the pocket that weighed so heavily, wondering who it was that Grace thought we might have to shoot.

six

THE ROAD THAT had seemed heavily traveled when I had driven it last was almost deserted at this time of evening. Still, it was close to nine-thirty when we got to the intersection with Titan Road. Once we turned right from the lighted crossroad, the dark closed down around us. There had been a moon when we left home, but it had vanished behind wind-driven clouds, and we drove among hulking shadows. Warehouses. The container yard, full of truck-size shipping cartons, building blocks for some giant child. The moon appeared briefly, revealing the skeletal steel neck of a gigantosaurus, the invisible head up there fifty feet above the silhouetted body of piled gravel.

"What?" Grace asked, peering upward.

"Dragline," I said. "It's a gravel pit."

We went past even higher piles, a miniature mountain range to our left, and at the end of the chain came to the stretch of taut fence and an amber light shining discreetly on the M.M.A. sign. It now said NO TRESPASSING, PROPERTY IS SECURED BY HAMLITT AND HIER, ALARM SERVICE. I would have felt more sanguine about the effectiveness of that service had not the gate been slightly ajar.

Because it was ajar, I drove on past, a long way past, then turned and came back very slowly, lights out. The moon erupted briefly from behind a cheek of cloud, just enough to let me see the road.

"What?" breathed Grace.

"The gate shouldn't be open," I murmured. "Not if it's Lucia."

"You said it was a place she knew. She might have had a key."

"From twenty-one years ago? They haven't changed the locks in twenty-one years? Come on. That newly hired security company would have made them change locks, if not before."

"Oh. Right. What are you going to do?"

"I'm going to drive into the gravel pit property. When I came by here the other day, their gate looked permanently retired. And since the Monmouth gate is open, whatever alarms they've installed are probably off. We'll see if we can come in from an unexpected direction."

At the gravel pit, one side of the double gate hung on a single hinge, the other lay on the ground, just as I had seen it last. The dilapidated shack bore a large, light-colored FOR SALE sign, perfectly readable in the momentary moonlight. We drove past the angular monument of conveyor and loader, then around the foothills of the piled gravel range. The water-filled pit at the foot of the drag-line gleamed blackly around the moon that seemed to float on its surface, riffled into pearly fragments by a puff of wind. I glanced upward, glad to see the clouds moving eastward. The wind felt warm, a chinook wind, heated by friction in its race down the eastern slope of the Rockies, melting ice and snow, making midwinter feel like momentary spring. I drove around a gentle rise and then up it, stopping the car where I could see the road we had left. The fence line to the M.M.A. property would be to our right, past the pit and the higher gravel piles.

A level, snow-covered lane, wide enough to be a safe walkway, extended between the cab of the dragline and the pit. We moved in that direction, thankful for the thin blanket of snow that kept the gravel from crunching beneath our feet. Though ice edged the pit, the air was not cold enough to make the snow crunch or squeak as we walked, and our progress was almost silent.

Whatever improvements the security firm had made, they had not made them in the fence. The only separation between the gravel pit and the construction yard was three strands of barbed wire loosely tacked to assorted sticks and scraps of lumber between sporadic posts. For the most part, the wire sagged in rusty, dispirited swags. I held two strands apart for Grace, then she returned the favor. As I came through the wire, I stumbled over a straight chunk of sapling about four feet long, no doubt intended as additional fencing material. I turned and shoved it erect between the two lower wires, holding them apart. Our emergency exit.

We had come through the fence between two hulking machines, a huge front loader and an even bigger earth-mover, both on caterpillar treads. Standing there, careful to make no sounds of our own, we listened for any sound of people anywhere around us. We heard the wind and the approach of a train from the south as well as intermittent traffic noises from the main road. Nothing else.

We sneaked into the dark chasm between the machines, stopping when we reached the loader bucket and crouching to stay out of view. I was just readying myself to step out into the clear when we heard the unmistakable crackle of a radio as someone asked, "See anything?"

The answer came from so close beside us that we were almost surprised into betraying ourselves. The speaker was on the other side of the front loader, separated from us only by the hollow shell of the bucket.

"A car went by a while ago."

"I saw that," said the other voice. "Bret, you got anything?" The voice sounded familiar, but the person eluded me.

Ahead of us, to our left, among a cluster of smaller machines, a voice answered in a mumble that came more clearly through the radio beside us. "For God's sake, Corny, not from back here I don't. Ask James. He's by the road."

I put my hand on Grace's arm, nodding in the direction of that mumble. The moon reflected dully from the windshield of a car. As our eyes grew more accustomed to the dark, we saw another one behind it. Grace took my arm and dragged me away from the bucket, along the base of the crawler, back the way we had come.

"Bunch of damned amateurs," Grace whispered in my ear. "Chatting instead of keeping radio silence."

We reached the fence and lay full length beside it, heads down, waiting for the clouds to cover the moon again before we went through the fence. "James," I whispered back. "And Cornell, and Bret, plus an unknown. What does that tell you?"

"It tells me at least four of the sporty group are here, maybe more. You suppose the girls are here, too?"

I squeezed her arm. I doubted the girls were here, though they might have been. I didn't care. What had me in total confusion was that Lloyd Baldridge's couples club was here, on Monmouth property. Whose agenda was being conducted tonight? Was this a Matt plot or a Lloyd plot? Or had some unforeseen circumstance joined the two when I was unaware of it? It was like arriving to fight a duel and finding oneself faced by an army! Even though Lloyd knew Matt, he'd said nothing to indicate they were intimate friends.

The clouds gathered, the moon ducked behind a veil. In the transitory dark we slipped through the fence, and I removed the sapling, laying it in the dead grass along the fence.

"Damn," Grace whispered, her lips at my ear. "We don't dare try to arrest them, do we? We don't even know how many of them are here. There could be as many as ten or twelve."

"The cellular phone's in the car."

"Yeah. So I call the cops and what do I say is happening to warrant police attention? Trespassing?"

"Let's just get out of here, Sergeant. We're way outnumbered."

We went back the way we had come, past the hills of gravel and onto the narrow passageway beneath the great neck of the dragline, hurrying, more intent on what might be happening behind us than elsewhere. The attack came out of nowhere. A body launched itself at me from behind the hulking machine. All I saw was dim reflections from a form dark and smooth as a frog. As I went tumbling down the precipitous bank into the pit, I instinctively gasped a great gulp of air. Even before the two of us hit water, I realized he was wearing a wet suit and scuba gear.

Then I didn't realize anything. There was no time for thought at all. My body was totally engaged in frenzied, spasmodic action, blindly trying to twist myself out of the grasp that held me in the icy pit. Bubbles went gurgling past my ears, I couldn't move my arms. The attacker had his arms around me from behind. I kicked out with my feet, but motion was hampered by my heavy coat, trousers, shoes. . . .

Heavy. Everything heavy. The lump that hit my side, heavy. My gun. In the overcoat pocket. Not inches from my hand.

I struggled, getting the hand momentarily free, snaking it into the pocket, only to have the arm clamped tight against me again. I was almost out of air, the pressure in my head was building, in a moment I would have to breathe water.

Then he made a mistake. He tried to improve his grip to get me below him. For only an instant, my arm could move, and when I was gripped again, my arm was across my chest, the gun barrel pointing back under my left arm, the muzzle less than inches from his chest. There was no time for hesitation. I don't think he even heard it or felt it when it went off. The arms holding me jerked and released as I stroked awkwardly with my left arm, desperate for air but unwilling to let go the gun. Not every gun can fire under water without killing the person holding it. The fact that this one had endeared it to me.

My mouth broke the surface. I stroked weakly to the side of the pit, gasping and choking while trying to find something to hold on to. That's when I thought of Grace. It wasn't that I had forgotten her, only that there'd been no thoughts at all except survival ones. With the thought came the sound of her voice, almost whimpering, then Helen Baldridge's voice muttering, "You bitch, get down in there, get down in that pit, get down or I'll kill you right here, I swear I will."

I didn't think I had enough strength to move, but my body found it somewhere. I crawled out of the pit, water splashing, making no effort to be quiet.

"Over here, Lloyd," Helen whispered. "Help me with her."

I stood up and went toward her. She was also wearing scuba gear, her head smooth and round in the moonlight, as she thrust at Grace with the tip of a spear. She had her back to me, so confident that Lloyd had disposed of me that she didn't feel the need to look. As I approached, she drew back her arm, preparatory to spearing Grace in the face. I stumbled. She started to turn. I took one blundering step off balance, striking out at her. I hit her just enough to make her slip on the icy bank. She squealed, more in surprise than fear, and fell forward, almost on top of Grace, then slid off into the water. I saw Grace reach out to grab her.

My sweet Grace, who had somehow anchored herself to the bucket at the end of the dragline and refused to be moved. As I crawled out onto the bucket she opened her mouth to yell and I stretched to full length to put my hand over her lips.

"Shhhh. There are more of them!"

She gulped and was silent. I pulled her up onto the bucket, and across it to the bank. Below the shoulders, she was as soaked as I. I stood there, shaking, staring at the pit, waiting for Helen to swim to the top, ready to grab her. Nothing. Still I waited, panting.

"She's not coming up," Grace whispered. "Jason. She's not coming up. She hit her head on the bucket when she fell on me."

It was too cold and we were in too much danger for me to agonize over it. Still holding the thirty-eight tightly in one hand, I grabbed Grace with the other, holding her closely as we staggered along, looking in every direction, starting at every shadow. One shadow near the last gravel pile proved to be a couple of long, hooded parkas and two pairs of boots with a radio lying on top of the pile. It crackled and hissed. "Lloyd? Anything over there?"

I took out a saturated handkerchief, picked up the radio with it, thumbed the send key, and muttered in an anonymous whisper, "Keep it quiet. I hear a car."

Then I wrapped the handkerchief around the radio and took it, along with the coats and boots. Our car was as we left it. I put the stuff I was carrying into the backseat and got Grace behind the wheel. Her teeth were clacking together like those mechanical jaws one buys in joke shops.

"Where . . . ?" she asked as I started away.

"Just wait," I said. I sloshed around the nearest gravel pile and found the Baldridge car behind it, next to the fallen gate, keys in the ignition. Back to Grace. "Can you drive?"

"I think so. For a little way. Until I freeze."

"Just release the brake and coast out through the gate before you start the engine. Go to the first place you can turn off the road, leave the engine on, and wait for me. I'll be along in the Baldridge car."

"What? Who . . ."

"Grace, not now. Just go." I was freezing, but inside I was burning with rage. I wished Lloyd was still alive so I could kill him again. I wished Helen hadn't drowned so

I could see her arrested. My teeth were so tight together that my neck hurt.

She went as I had suggested, releasing the hand brake, letting the car roll down the slight rise we'd parked on. When she reached the road, she started the engine. I couldn't even hear it. She drove away and I slogged back to the Baldridge car and followed her. The engine started at once, almost soundlessly. I drove out and away, turning left at the crossroad. About a mile farther on, Grace had turned off in the long driveway of a builder's supply company. I drove past her, down the drive which led to a warehouse complex. She followed me. I found a place out back behind a storage shed that probably no one ever looked at, got out of the car, locked it, and slogged over to where Grace was waiting. I opened the back door and took the smaller parka out.

"The engine should be warm enough to turn on the heat," I said, reaching for the switch and then her hand. "Take off your wet things and get into this dry parka."

While she did so, I shed my own soaked outer clothing and put on the larger parka. It reached almost to my knees. The boots were way too big, so I didn't bother. Bare feet would do. Our dripping clothes went in the trunk.

"Where are we going?" she whispered.

"Home," I answered. "We never left home tonight, did we?"

"Oh, Jason, I'll have to report this."

"You do what you have to, sweetie, but think about it first." I barely got it out between uncontrollable shivers.

"You're wet," she said, as though she'd just noticed.

"I've been underwater," I replied, rather annoyed. "What did you think happened back there?"

"I thought Helen tried to kill me."

"Well, while Helen was busy with you, Lloyd—that is, I assume it was Lloyd—was trying to drown me. He very nearly succeeded."

"Where is he?"

"At the bottom of the pit, with a bullet in him. And Helen has evidently ended up joining him. Meantime, however, there are at least four other men back there, hiding in the construction yard, waiting to see if we arrive. If you feel compelled to explain all that to the police . . ."

I'd fetched a blanket from the trunk of my car, and I used this to cover our legs once we were in the car again.

Grace murmured, "The fourth guy is probably Dahlberg. What will they do, when Lloyd doesn't come back?"

Four men. Fourth guy. Something resonated but I couldn't pin it down. "I have no idea. We weren't there. As far as I'm concerned, you and I received an invitation to go out there tonight, but we didn't like the tenor of the thing, so we didn't go."

"I'm wearing Helen's jacket," she murmured.

"And I'm wearing Lloyd's. I also have the key to the Baldridge house, the one Lloyd gave me when we started the cleanup job. We'll replace Helen's jacket, and Lloyd's coat, and the boots at their house. And the radio. And first thing when we get home, we put the wet stuff in the drier and everything washable into the washer. First thing tomorrow, anything cleanable goes to the cleaners."

"And we don't tell anyone?"

"Who are you going to tell, Grace? Your colleagues? I

don't understand what happened back there! How do you intend to explain it?"

"What don't we understand?"

"Start with the phone call. I assumed it referred to the death of Maria Montoya."

She nodded. "I did, too."

"We assumed it because the place was a Monmouth place. But the caller didn't mention Maria Montoya. He or she just said we'd find the answer to our question. Then we arrive and we find Lloyd's sporty bunch after our skins. What 'question' did we have that they know about? If the call had come from Matt, the event would explain itself, but why Lloyd? Unless he's connected you to the fact that the DA is investigating all those recent accidents."

"The investigation is being done very quietly. It will go to a grand jury eventually, but it hasn't yet. Lieutenant Morrow's in charge of the case, and I'm not involved. I told Morrow better keep me out of it because of your professional association with Lloyd."

"Be that as it may, here is Lloyd, using Matt Monmouth's property. So maybe Lloyd and Matt are closer friends than I was led to believe. Maybe they're intimate friends! It was the letter from Lucia that got us here. . . ."

"No," she said, chidingly. "We received a letter from Lucia and we received a mysterious phone call that didn't mention Lucia at all. The two things might not be connected. We assumed so, but it was only an assumption. The caller may have known nothing about the letter."

I turned the heater vent onto my legs, gasping as the first hot air hit my ankles and feet, which felt like blocks of ice. "Lloyd's bunch either knows about it or they think we have some other question that relates to them."

"You remember that old quote, Jason, the one about the guilty fleeing when nobody's chasing them?"

"You mean the Bible one, the wicked flee where no man pursueth?"

She nodded. "Maybe that's Lloyd. He found out I was a cop. He'd been getting away with murder. He figured I was after him, and he fled where no man pursued. He used one of those universal come-ons. You know, 'I saw what you did,' or 'I can answer your question.' Everyone did something. Everyone has a question. So, he figured we'd follow the come-on, right into the pit."

"I can buy that, but only if he knew Matt Monmouth fairly well. The Monmouth gate was unlocked. The security was . . . well, notable for its absence. Matt would have had to arrange that. Matt himself might have been out there with Lloyd's bunch, we have no way of knowing."

She asked, "You think Slade and Rodale and Phillips and Dahlberg knew we were there?"

"No, I don't think they knew we were there. I hope to God they have no idea we were there. I think the Baldridges had assigned them to various places in the yard, just in case, while Lloyd and Helen themselves were probably across the road, watching for our car, which they had seen often enough to recognize. They came in behind us, and they waited for us to come back to the car. For all I know, Lloyd may even have had infrared surveillance gear. They figured either the others would get us or they'd get us when we came back."

"Lloyd just accidentally had scuba gear?"

"Oh, he intended to drown us all along," I growled. "If the others had caught us, they'd have dragged us back to that pit. No bullet holes for old Lloyd. Next time somebody worked that dragline, up we'd come, dead. It was to be another accident, Grace. They're getting good at staging accidents. The Monmouth yard has no connection to them, and besides, we wouldn't have been found inside the Monmouth yard. We'd have been found next door. We might never have been connected to Monmouth at all."

Grace said, "There's the phone message on the answering machine. If we were dead, somebody else might hear that."

"Maybe they intend to break into our place and remove it." Another dangerous escapade that they'd enjoy.

"Or they had someone unconnected to them make the call, so there couldn't be a voice print of anyone who was involved." She took a deep breath and sat up a little straighter, warmed by the car heater and ready to think once more. "Now what in hell is the connection between Lloyd's bunch and the Monmouths?"

"Damned good question, sweetheart. Damned good question."

We went on home without further conversation. It was almost midnight. I checked the answering machine for messages, finding one from an old friend in Seattle, whom I called back and chatted with for several minutes, casually mentioning that Grace and I had been over at our new house earlier in the evening. Then, dressed in dry clothes, complete with gloves, I put a sheet of plastic over the soaked front seat of the car and drove myself down to the Baldridge place, where I wiped the boots and put them and the parkas in the back-hall closet among other Baldridge jackets and boots and miscellany. The radio, which I had not touched with my bare fingers, was in the parka pocket.

As I was about to leave, I heard the phone ring. It rang six times, then clicked off. The answering machine was in the den, upstairs, so I went up, quiet as a cat, turned down the volume, and played back the messages.

There were several inconsequential ones, then one from Bibsie Slade. "Hi, this is Bibsie. You were rats not to let us girls help! If Corny comes home with you guys, tell him to call me and tell me what happened." She sounded giddy, like someone who'd been riding a roller coaster, high on the prospect of murder. The last message, the one that had just come in, was from a voice I recognized as James Rodale's. "Why the hell did you guys cut out before we did? Sorry we didn't do the job tonight. We'll get it done next time."

There was an extra tape in the drawer of the desk. Since I had the drawer open, I dropped Lloyd's car keys and house keys in it, then inserted the new tape in the machine and took the one with Bibsie's and Rodale's messages home with me. I have several small electric heaters with blowers, useful gadgets to keep one from freezing while appraising stuff in unheated houses. I opened the car doors and put heaters on both sides, where they could blow through to dry out the seat.

By now it was one in the morning. Grace and I made hot chocolate, we played the tapes again, both the messages left for us and the two left for the Baldridges, and when we'd said we didn't understand it about a dozen times, we got tired of that and went to bed. I think Grace fell asleep almost immediately. I didn't. At three, I was still staring dry eyed at the ceiling, wondering how in hell two separate puzzles had suddenly become the two halves of one.

At three-fifteen, I got out of bed, went into the office, cleaned the old Smith & Wesson thirty-eight revolver that had put an end to Lloyd Baldridge, reloaded it, took it to the basement, and put it away in the old iron safe where it had lived for years with the thirty-eight automatic and the two forty-fives, automatic and revolver. They were all target pistols leftover from my competitive shooting days with the navy, which, until the last few years, was all I'd ever used them for. In the last several years, however, each of the thirty-eights had killed a man. No. Unfair to blame the guns. I had now killed two men with them.

Of course, both of them were men who were, at the time, trying to kill me. Tonight it had been Lloyd Baldridge, two years ago it had been a man who sneaked up the stairs, intending to shoot me while I slept. That killing had been ruled self-defense. I hadn't thought of it until now, but I was glad the bullet from this gun would not match the bullet from that case, which might still be reposing in an evidence room somewhere, just waiting to be matched to the one that probably was still inside Lloyd's body.

Given the tenor of my life recently, maybe I'd be smart to get rid of the pistols. I certainly had no intention of taking them to the new house. Of course they could always stay here, where they were. As could the one upstairs in my desk, the twenty-two target pistol. I'd leave that one where it was, too. Grace hadn't seen the pistol I'd taken with me. As a matter of fact, she had never seen the guns I kept in the basement. If someone

asked for my handgun, I'd give them the twenty-two.
That one out of the five.

One out of five. One chance out of five. Of course.

I went upstairs to my desk and wrote those words on a
clean sheet of paper. Once chance out of five.

The following morning, Grace rolled out of bed, told
me with a troubled frown that she hadn't decided yet
what to do about our nighttime foray, she'd see me after
work. I got up, had coffee, and wandered down the hall
to the office. I sat down purposefully and figured Lloyd
Baldridge's bill, typed it up myself, put a copy in the file
and the original in the outgoing mail. The subcontractors
had billed him directly, but he owed me for the drapery
fabrics and the furniture I'd ordered. He'd already paid
for the cleanup and deodorizing job. If he didn't pay for
the fabrics, I could return them for a restocking charge,
and I could always cancel the furniture orders or sell the
furniture to someone else.

I told myself to forget that. I was pretending he was
alive, so of course he would pay his bill. I was doing
what I'd do if he were alive, hoping Grace could just let
the matter go. I felt no compunction about keeping quiet.
We'd been attacked; we'd defended ourselves. We'd
used no more force than had been used against us.

Mark brought the morning paper upstairs when he
came to work. I leafed through it idly. The fourth page
had a small article, ACCIDENTAL DEATH RULED HOMI-
CIDE. The story went on to say that acting upon a tip
received by local law enforcement, there had been an
investigation of the deaths of Carson and Eleanor Carlyle, previously thought to be accidental, but now definitely ruled homicide. The parachutes used by the couple

during sky diving, parachutes that had been in the sheriff's custody for well over a year, had been examined by experts and found to have been tampered with to prevent their opening. The sheriff's office had issued subpoenas for witnesses and friends of the dead couple, but thus far there were no suspects.

I called Grace. I read her the article.

"Damn," she said feelingly. "The sheriff's office was supposed to keep quiet about that. They were told it was part of a larger case!"

"It's definitely a case by now?"

"It's definitely a case, yes. Lieutenant Morrow has put the Benedict thing together with the Carlyle thing together with all the other so-called accidents and the arson. They've started talking to all the group, male and female. They've traced the money in the pot. They've got a handle on the whole thing."

"Did they talk to Lloyd?"

She hesitated a moment. "I don't know. I'm not in on it."

"Can you find out?"

"I suppose I could call Morrow. You think that Lloyd found out about this and that's what prompted him to . . . invite us to go scuba diving with them?"

I took a deep breath, staring at the words I'd written the previous night. They made everything so much clearer. "No, Grace. Sorry, it wouldn't matter if he had talked to Lloyd. The minute he talked to any one of them, the word was out. The first sporty group person Morrow interviewed would have called every other person in the group, including Lloyd, within the hour. There's no way this could have been kept quiet, except by jailing them all and putting each one in solitary. And my answer to your question is yes, that's why they kept trying to inveigle us down to Baja with them."

Baja. And Bibsie's excitement on the phone. Their thirst for thrills and danger. People risking their necks in Baja? Risking his neck?

"Do you think Morrow has all the names?" I asked.

"He has the ones we had. Why? You think there's someone else?"

"I know there is."

"You know?"

"I know. Those people you overheard at the New Year's Eve party said something about one chance out of five. And then we went on to name five couples. But one of the couples was the one drawing names, so it should be one chance out of the other four. They didn't say that, they said five. There has to be another couple. I'm going to talk to Bitts and Betts again."

My telephone call drilled into the Bitts-or-Betts gusher in thirty seconds flat. It took a moment for the flow to subside enough so that I could get a question in sidewise. "You said John Dahlberg's sister was part of the sporty group, she and her husband. What was John Dahlberg's sister's name and who did she marry?"

"Anita," she said, "and she married Nash Monmouth. She ran away to California when she was just a kid to be with him. She went with him on and off for years. They were always fighting and making up, fighting and making up. After her father died, Nash finally married her."

"And are Nash and Anita definitely part of that whole sporty group that includes the Dahlbergs and the Slades, et al.?"

"Well, yes, they are, though they haven't taken part as

much lately, because they've been short on money. Nash's brother supports him, everyone knows that, but Anita had money. Right now, however, the Dahlberg Oil stock is down, and that's where Anita's money comes from. In fact, Anita's money is why some people claim Nash married her. He dated her for years, but he never proposed marriage until the elder Dahlbergs died and she was suddenly rich. But money aside, I'd say Nash and Anita are definitely part of that crowd."

I thanked her. I called the local sweetshop and had a five-pound box of candy sent to her, thanking her. Then I called Grace again.

"Tell Morrow to add two more names to the sporty group list," I chortled. "Nash and Anita Monmouth."

"Anita?"

"Who happens to be John Dahlberg's sister."

"How in hell did you pick up on that?"

"Joanna referred to Nash's wife, Nita. Bitts and Betts mentioned John Dahlberg's sister, Anita. And we knew there had to be some link with Monmouth, didn't we? Nash is it. It was probably Nash who picked the M.M.A. yard as the battleground, even though it was Lloyd and Helen who led the assault. Nash, meantime, was probably far elsewhere, establishing a cast-iron alibi. He told me he'd get even with me for raising the Maria Montoya question."

"Why would Lloyd get involved?"

"Maybe just for the thrill of it, but more likely because he'd heard there were questions being asked about the Benedicts and the Carlyles and all the rest of it, and he thought you were doing that. Maybe thought he was acting in self-defense."

"Did he think if he stopped you and me, he stopped the whole police force?"

"Maybe. It's unlikely real thinking entered into it."

"Dumb," she muttered. "So now, what? You think Nash killed Maria Montoya?"

I started to say yes, then no, then . . . "I don't know, Grace. There's something blank and mysterious about that. The pieces don't seem to fit. I'm going to keep digging at it."

We said a few more sweet though essentially meaningless things. She went back to work and I went back to what I'd been doing, slightly amazed that neither of us had mentioned the fact that we'd almost been killed the night before. Were we that blasé?

The question answered itself when the phone rang. Bret Phillips was on, all hearty and smarmy, wanting to invite Grace and me to a party. He'd tried to call me the night before, and he'd left a message. . . .

He hadn't left a message. He hadn't tried to reach me last night. I gritted my teeth, then smiled, making my voice just as calm and comfortable as his.

"I'm sorry we missed you, Bret. Gracey and I were over at the new house all evening. And this damn answering machine is on the fritz. I haven't been able to get any messages off it for the last couple of days."

Well, said he, the party is next Friday. Gee, said I, we had a conflict next Friday, and besides, Grace's pregnancy was causing her a little trouble and we weren't really going out much.

Where is the new house? asked he. I told him, falsely, in great detail, describing a fictitious neighborhood, the remodeling, how thrilled Gracey was about it. I bored him. He said good-bye. I hung up and got out my handkerchief.

There was sweat all along my upper lip and around my ears. Grace was maybe blasé, but I wasn't. I had damned near been killed last night, but Grace and I didn't know a thing about Lloyd Baldridge.

Pertaining to which, I called the Baldridges' place and left a message on the machine, giving date and time. Question about the drapery fabric, have Helen call me. I then called his firm. Mr. Lloyd Baldridge, please. Oh? He wasn't in? Do you know where I can reach him? Well, this is Jason Lynx, please have him call me about the renovations at his place downtown. I've got a problem with the fabric Mrs. Baldridge wanted. Do you have that? Thank you.

Why was I doing this? Why not just go with Grace to the powers that be and tell them the story?

I'd been trying to justify myself ever since I'd dragged Grace out of that pit and had immediately, instinctively, ducked for cover. It had taken some time to come up with an answer, possibly because I didn't want to admit to cowardice. The fact was that I was afraid to involve the authorities. I was afraid for Grace, for our child, for myself. Once we told the police, the story wouldn't, perhaps couldn't be kept quiet. Even though I knew the authorities would hold us blameless, eventually if not immediately, I didn't want Lloyd Baldridge's friends and fellow travelers to know I'd killed him. The way I read the rules of Lloyd's world, killing Lloyd would require vengeance. We had stepped into Lloyd's world all unwittingly, but nonetheless, once in, one played by its rules. Or else.

Even if we had uncovered the entire roll call of the couples here in Denver, even if every one of them went to jail for decades, that didn't mean there weren't others in Acapulco and Argentina and France. Lloyd's kind of games was addictive. If he enjoyed his play here, he would enjoy playing elsewhere, with other dangerous men and risky women, licentious, lick-lip couples, high on tension and terror, eager to make a game of vengeance.

Perhaps, if it were only me, I'd feel differently. I told myself this in a weak attempt at justification, finally admitting that no, even if it were only me, I wouldn't want to play. It wouldn't be only me, in any case. In the Baldridge world, innocence was no bar to violence. The Benedict children weren't players, but they'd been blown to hell, right along with Mommy and Daddy. Setting masculine pride aside, I admitted that it was preferable that any friends of the Baldridges—including Bret Phillips— think Lloyd and Helen had run out on them, or had killed one another, or that they had been killed by parties unknown.

Grace and our baby were not involved. When our baby was born, there should be no stain or taint in his or her little world. Though, of course, there was still one smutch of darkness to be removed. Who was it who killed Maria Montoya?

Lucia Monmouth said she had written to those who were responsible. She knew who was responsible. She would have to come forward and tell me who they were. I sat at my desk, grim faced, grinding my teeth, planning how I was going to uncover the hiding place of Lucia Monmouth.

At which point, accompanied by a weedy and scraggly bearded youngster who smiled at me in the toothy manner of a stray dog seeking to ingratiate itself, Mark walked in and placed on my desk the packet of letters, the ones Bitts and Betts had found in the tin box, and introduced his companion.

"Jason, this is my friend Terry O'Dell, Terrence, the last of the Dense O'Dells."

I offered a hand, wondering what the hell.

"Terrence, though he claims to be as Irish as a shamrock, speaks fluent German. He has gone through the Kettinger letters."

"Have you!" I sat back down. "Did you find anything?"

O'Dell shrugged and spoke in a lilting tenor. "The lady liked to speak in euphemisms. I may have something for you."

"Well, by all means."

"My fee . . . ," he said with that same toothy grin, doggy begging a bone. "For translation?"

"Whatever Mark agreed to," I said.

"In advance."

It was a plea. I wondered if he were hungry. I wondered who had cheated him lately. "By all means. Mark, will you make out a check?"

We waited while Mark made out a check. I signed it, for form's sake, and passed it to O'Dell, who examined it closely before folding it once and putting it in his pocket.

"All right," he said with a sigh and a moue and a shrug, as though he had just finished the onerous and difficult task of being practical, a thing he had to do but much regretted.

He took a notebook from his pocket and opened it. "The earlier letters are not particularly interesting. In each letter, Olga speaks to her sister about her fears, that is, Virginia's fears. Olga reassures her and tells her things are not so bad, she has a nice house, nice children, and so on and so on. Then in 1974 Olga has a complaint of her own. She tells her sister of the trouble that has come upon Helmut, her husband, and in subsequent letters she talks about how unfair it is that Helmut, who was only doing what he was told to do, is in trouble whereas the people who told him to do those things are not in trouble. She says it has cost her, Olga, her entire inheritance to save Helmut."

"Not much to do with what we're after."

"Patience. This goes on for a few letters, then in March 1975 Olga writes that she cannot believe what Virginia tells her. It is impossible a brother should treat his young sister so. It is unconscionable. It is evil. Surely the girl is deluded. But, if she is not deluded, Virginia must stop her brother treating her like that, which he has been doing since she was ten. It must end."

"What was he doing?"

"What he is doing is never defined. Abuse? Torture? Whatever it is, is never specified. Words to do with ugliness are never used. We never learn what Helmut is supposed to have done, or what the Monmouth boy is supposed to have done. Specific words may have been in Virginia's letters to her sister, but they are not in Olga's letters to Virginia. Then, we have a letter in April of 1975 in which Olga says Virginia's husband is an ogre, that her son is worse, that the father has no regard for his daughter to treat her in that fashion, that the son is a devil to have done the awful thing he did and then to blame it on Lucia because Lucia refused to do what he wanted. Olga does not blame Lucia for running away."

"What can we extrapolate?" I looked at Mark. "Can we say Nash was molesting Lucia from the time she was ten? She got to be fifteen and refused to go on with it, so he raped and killed a little girl and blamed Lucia for it?"

O'Dell shrugged.

Mark said, "That's how it might be read. It's not, however, what it says."

"No, that's not what it says," O'Dell murmured. "It says, 'to have done that awful thing and blame it on Lucia.' It doesn't say rape or kill. I can't tell you that either Virginia or Olga knew the child was raped or dead."

I mused, "Virginia certainly didn't know the body was hidden in the house or she wouldn't have stayed there. She may have been told the little girl had been raped, and maybe she knew that the child was the niece of her maid, Rosabel. Certainly Rosabel would have mentioned her niece being missing! Though, come to think of it, maybe not to Virginia. If Lucia ran away, either she'd seen it happen or Nash had told her it had happened."

O'Dell nodded. "We don't know what either mother's or father's reactions were to being told about it. From the sense of the letters, I would guess that Virginia was rather weak. Her sister is constantly telling her to be strong, to act, to protect. My guess would be that if Lucia had told her mother something ugly, the mother would have fallen apart. When and if she or her mother told her father, her father would have accused her of being the one at fault, or maybe he would have accused her of lying. So, she ran away. It was the only choice she had. Either that or submit to Nash or see him continue doing whatever he'd done."

"Is any of that in the letters?"

O'Dell sighed. "Olga says to her sister, 'Virginia, when the child told you, you should have gone with her then to the police.' All that tells us is that the act was a criminal matter, it doesn't tell us what it was. Olga says

A. J. Orde

later, 'Of course you could have gone with her,' as though Virginia had protested that she could not have done so. Olga said, 'Virginia, when the child's father slapped her, you should have stood up to him.' Olga is right, of course, for all the good that does. Later she says, 'Virginia, why can't you stand up to him?'

"Then, in the next to last letter, Olga says, 'Virginia, Lucia is gone, she is gone, you must accept that and you must protect Joanna, or the same thing will happen to her.' Olga is still unspecific and uses no hard words."

"The divorce protected Joanna," I said. "How did Virginia get up nerve to do that?"

"She had help. In that same letter, Olga says she has called their older brother, the one who should help, and Edgar Ransome, Esq., will come from Massachusetts to Denver and take legal steps to protect Joanna. Ransome was Olga and Virginia's family name; Edgar was evidently an attorney."

Mark said, "Can we assume Matthew Monmouth Sr. was given an ultimatum? That Ransome told him, go and take Nash with you or we sue in open court and tell the whole sordid story."

"Something of the kind," said O'Dell.

"Then Olga and her family came to stay."

"In the last letter, written June of 1975, they say they're coming to live with Virginia, to protect her and Joanna."

"Then, when Virginia became ill, they stayed to take care of her, I suppose," I said.

"Likely. Or they may just have settled in."

"Did Joanna know about any of this?" Mark wondered.

I answered him. "I don't think any of them knew the body was there. Except whoever put it there."

I stared at the letters. Right there, all along, all the answers anyone could want, answers that would fit any preconception. Written evidence that could be interpreted as meaning anything one wished. The letters were not clear enough to be used as evidence in court. Bitts and Betts and I could establish their provenance, but it would do no good. Unless . . . Olga might still be alive. She would only be in her seventies.

"Mr. O'Dell," I said, "since you are fluent in German, would you undertake a further commission? Would you try to locate Olga Kettinger for us?"

He thought about it for a time, then nodded. "I am interested in this," he admitted. "It would be good to know how it happened, and who killed the child. Also, I can use the money."

"You're a student?"

"I am a poet," he said, rather sadly. "Poets starve, you know."

"Is he a good poet?" I asked Mark, half facetiously.

"In my opinion, he could be a great one," Mark replied, with a pat on O'Dell's shoulder. "If he can just get over being Irish."

O'Dell flushed. Evidently it was a matter he got teased about more than he liked. He started for the door, then stopped.

"I'm sorry, I almost forgot. In the letter of March 1975 was a picture of Lucia." He fished in his pocket, drew it out, considered it for a moment, then laid it on the desk. "Olga says she is returning it."

I looked down, for a moment confused. This was a head and shoulders shot, done by a good photographer or at an auspicious time, catching the tranquility of that face. It was utterly unlike the family snapshots I had

seen, and though younger, it was unmistakably the face
of Limpia Montaño Lujan.

I almost called out to O'Dell, to tell him not to bother
tracing Olga. Then I thought no, let him earn a buck.
Corroborating evidence is always useful. Meantime,
Grace and I were going to take a weekend trip south.

The Friday-morning weather forecast was for blizzard,
coming down from the north, arriving early on Saturday.
I asked Grace what she wanted to do, and she said she'd
take off an hour or two early, and we'd go that night.
That way, we'd beat the storm. I pointed out it might prevent our getting back, and she said that was all right. She
hadn't used all her accrued leave on our honeymoon, she
could take a day or so more if necessary.

She packed a bag before she left, and I picked her up at
the precinct at three. We'd get into Taos about nine or
ten. Around dinnertime we'd be in the unpopulated plain
of the San Luis Valley, so I'd stopped at a deli and put
together road food. Together with a thermos of coffee
and a bottle of milk, we'd stave off starvation for another
day. During most of the drive down, Grace slept. She'd
been sleeping a lot lately. I tried to remember whether
Agatha, my first wife, had slept a lot when she was pregnant with our son. I simply couldn't remember.

So, since there was no store of pregnancy lore to rumi-
nate upon, I ruminated on man's need for excitement.
When I was a teenager, I had done stupid things, risking
my neck and other people's safety. Most of the boys my
age had done equally stupid things. The girls I had
known were not into danger in that same way, but some
of them had been thrill seekers, too. The girls who started
smoking at fourteen, or staying out all night. The ones

who tried drugs. That had been the late sixties and seventies, drugs had been available.

In both high school and college, there were dangerous sports. I'd known more than a few men my age who had half killed themselves kayaking in white water, rock climbing, skiing the back country, or simply playing football or basketball so vehemently they broke bones and wrecked joints. I recalled an all-night beer party during which someone had hectored me across his body cast, "You gotta live on the edge, Jase! You gotta get out there on the edge!"

Navy underwater training had been edgy enough. We learned how to do very dangerous things, but we learned to do them with the least possible risk to ourselves. Even then, I saw men cutting corners, doing it the quick way rather than the safe way. Even then, I wondered at them. One of my friends, Alan McClean, had lived and died as a test pilot, but he had refused to go along with a "friend" on a sexual escapade in D.C. on the grounds it would endanger his family. The "friend" later told me about it, and when I heard Alan had died in a crash, I wondered if his wife would rather have had him alive with the clap, or dead but otherwise healthy. I suppose I was questioning the morality that avoided sex out of respect for his family but courted death without the same concern. And of course, he was right. The fact that he courted death as a test pilot was admirable to both men and women, no matter how foolhardy or unthinking.

Every street corner of every city had its population of young men high on machismo. Every gang had its armory of weapons to deal death in confrontations or drive-bys, no matter who caught the stray bullets. Young men have always died that way. That's what wars and frontiers have been for, to weed out those who courted death, leaving the steadier types to settle into civilization.

Courting death was rarer with older men, but here we had Lloyd and his whole coterie, all up to their ears in danger. In another age, Lloyd Baldridge would have been a train robber, a mountain man, an explorer. In another age, he would have led his clan against the other clans, or with the other clans against a common foe. In the past, even today in some places, even here in some high-risk jobs, danger could be sought, but that wasn't enough for Lloyd. He had to make his own danger, for the world no longer provided it on terms acceptable to him. No duels. No mountains to cross. No wildernesses to traverse. And Lloyd had to make his own danger among others of his kind, people who lived on their nerves, just as others lived on their minds and others on their gut and still others on their muscle.

"What are you thinking about," murmured Grace, opening one eye.

"Danger," I said. "How people go looking for it."

"You don't."

She was mostly right. Every time I encountered and survived a dangerous situation, I was plainly thankful. I had never since adolescence wanted to do something because it was dangerous, though sometimes I had done things that were dangerous.

"Where are we?"

"About forty-five minutes more, we'll be there."

"Where are we staying?"

"At the Kachina. We'll drive out tomorrow to see the Lujans."

"You think she'll tell us anything?"

"I think she will, now that we know who she is. She

has a life here. She's not footloose. She knows the police want to know as well. I think she'll tell us."

The storm came down upon us while we slept. We'd brought boots, luckily, for the pathway to the Lujan studio had not been shoveled, or even walked. A slight blue shadow lay along the snow, showing where the edge of the path was, possibly, and by sticking to this line, we made it around the hill safely. The statues were mantled in white and wore high white crowns, like people dressed up for an exotic ritual.

The studio was clamshell tight, the overhead doors squeezed down like eyelids, but a pale skein of smoke unreeled itself toward the sky, and the walk between the house and the studio had been shoveled. Someone was home.

We went down. We found a small door at the end of the shoveled path; we knocked; no one heard us; we opened the door. Same scene as before, sparks and smokes and trolls working around a statue. Different statue, this one a young man, bare except for a loincloth, sitting cross legged on a blanket spread with silver work and turquoise stones.

I waited until the scream of the burnisher stopped, then called attention to our arrival. As before, it was she who came to us, pushing back her visor. "Mr. Lynx."

I retreated to the door. "Lucia Monmouth," I said, "I'd like to introduce my wife, Grace Willis."

She stopped, dismayed, but only for a moment.

"How do you do," she said to Grace. Then to me, "You've found me."

"Your picture was in a letter that your aunt Olga sent

to your mother back in 1975. None of the other pictures looked as you do now, but that one did."

"Well," she said in a remote voice, as though she had not decided how to feel. "Give me a minute to take off these things. We'll go down to the house."

She divested herself, threw on a cape that was hanging by the door, and led us out of the studio, down the swept walk, across a little bridge to the portal of the house, and through the door. We entered a kitchen with tile counters and open shelves. She gestured us toward the chairs while she put on a kettle, then sat down with us.

"You didn't get anything out of Matt or Nash about the little girl?"

"They claim to know nothing."

She sighed deeply. "Well, they lie. Nash started sex with me when I wasn't even ten yet. When I didn't like it, he'd hit me, but it was between him and me, you know. I pretended it was a bad dream, and I didn't think it involved anyone else. He convinced me he had the right. When I got a little older, I realized that he didn't have the right. What he was doing was a sin, or at least a crime! I told him he had to stop. He said I had to go on, he was very sensitive and he needed someone. Nash always said he was very sensitive, too sensitive to act like a normal person. Other people had to toe the line, but Nash was special. I guess I had believed it. Dad and Matt always treated him as though he were special. Still, I said no and Nash said he'd make me. I said if he tried, I'd tell." She stared out the window, her face still remote and her voice calm.

"Well, next thing was he came to me and said he had something to show me. What he had was Rosabel's little niece in the storage room off the garage, her panties off and blood on her legs, and her crying and saying what I'd said, she was going to tell, going to tell. He told me he'd gotten off the bus at her stop, then he'd told her he had a pony she could ride and Rosabel would bring her home. He'd brought her all the way to our house. He sniggered. It was a nasty snigger. Joanna and I hadn't been on the bus because we had music lessons that day. Nash said he was going to keep her there in the storeroom, to use, unless I went on doing what he'd been making me do. He told me I'd have to feed her and take care of her.

"I went kind of crazy, I guess. I ran out of there, straight to Mother. She fell about, as she always did, but it didn't accomplish anything. She told me to go to my room, she'd do something. I guess that night she told Father, because next morning he confronted me, he slapped me, he accused me of lying. I told him Rosabel's little niece was in the storeroom, but when I took him there, she was gone. I told him what Nash had been doing to me. We went to Nash, and he denied everything. Father told me I was a filthy, rotten girl who was destroying the family. Then later Nash whispered in my ear that he'd find another little girl if I didn't give in."

"So you ran away," said Grace.

"What else could I do? I thought Nash had let the little girl go. I never imagined she was dead. I'd clipped out an article about the Well of Silence when I was in eighth grade. I had a little money I'd saved from birthday presents and from my allowance. I packed some clothes and dropped the suitcase over the wall. I left school in the middle of the day, took a taxi to pick up the suitcase, then downtown where I bought a bus ticket to Taos, then from there caught a ride out to the Well. I stayed there for almost ten years. After Mother died, once in a while I'd

catch a ride into town and call Joanna collect just to find
out what was happening."

"And then?" I asked, fascinated.

"Clare Simmons turned up. That was in '84. Back in
high school I'd talked to her about the Well, she said
she'd always figured that's where I'd gone, and she'd
come down to New Mexico in about 1981, intending to
find me, but instead she'd gotten herself hooked up to
Alfredo. She'd been with him for two or three years, but
she wasn't happy. I told her I'd been where I was for
longer than that, and I wasn't happy either. I'd been
experimenting with painting and sculpting, and by that
time I knew it's what I wanted to do. There's no time for
that at the Well. Making a long matter short, we decided
to trade lives."

"Just like that."

"Right. One day she left Alfredo's house and came to
the Well. I stayed with her for a little while, until I was
sure she was settled, then I left and showed up at
Alfredo's house. I told him my name was Limpia Montaño and I'd come to cook and clean for him. He doesn't
know I used to be Lucia. I never told him. Two years
later we were married. We have three children."

"Why were you so reluctant to help us about Maria
Montoya?" Grace asked.

"Because that happened to someone else." She stared
out the window at the sky, then at the steaming kettle.
Almost absentmindedly, she got up and made a pot of
tea. Bringing it to the table, she said:

"I'm Limpia Montaño Lujan. I'm the mother of Gre-
gorio and Benefiso and Gloria. I'm an artist. I help my
husband with his art, and I also do my own." She reached
across the table and took a teacup from the shelf, handing

it to me. It had that absolute integrity some utilitarian vessels have that are handmade for hands to use. The deep blue and violet glaze was lovely and not overdone. The shape fit my fingers.

"That's one of mine," she said. She filled the cup, plus one for Grace and one for herself, then spoke in that far-away voice.

"That Lucia, she was so wounded, so hurt. She was like a little rabbit in a hole, hiding from the world by pretending it wasn't real. She lived in her own world, inside her head, because the outside world hurt too much. She lived in silence for almost ten years, and she turned into someone else."

"Joanna said you called home after a few weeks," Grace said.

Limpia nodded. "I did. I wanted to know Joanna was all right. I'd written to Aunt Olga, and I'd begged her to have Uncle Edgar see that Joanna was protected. I told Aunt Olga not to tell Mama I'd written to her, because Mama would tell Father and all sorts of uproar would take place. The worst sin you could commit so far as Father was concerned was to talk about the family outside our walls. I told Aunt Olga just to get hold of Uncle Edgar and tell him what Nash had done to me, and about the little girl and that he must protect Joanna. I included my picture in the letter, because it made me look grown-up, and I wanted her to see I wasn't a child, making things up."

"You thought Nash would start with Joanna."

"Of course. Without me there, what else would he do?"

We sat for a moment, sipping tea. Finally, I asked, "Limpia, who killed the little girl?"

"I don't know. Until you came here and told Alfredo about Maria, I didn't know she was dead."

"But you wrote me an anonymous letter." I took the letter out of my pocket and showed it to her.

"I didn't write this."

"It's postmarked New Mexico."

She smiled and handed it back to me. "I didn't write it. I wrote to you recently, yes, but I didn't write this."

"It almost had to be Nash or Matt who killed her, didn't it?"

She shook her head. "I don't know. I wrote to Matt and Nash. I told them that one or both of them know what happened to that child. I told them that justice would catch up, that they ought to confess. But I really don't know who killed her. It could have been Steve, maybe, if he got paid for it. Steve didn't do anyone any favors out of generosity, but he'd do almost anything if he were paid for it."

I got up and wandered around the room, finding evidence of the Lujan artistry everywhere. Pottery. Paintings. Little clay figures and small bronzes. The house was alive with imagination and invention. Even the children's artwork on the refrigerator showed originality and expression. While I roamed, Grace led Limpia Lujan through the story once more, pinning down the sequence of events.

"If it was Steve, we could close the matter," Grace said. "Steve is dead. There was a similar murder four years ago, however, and we've been thinking the same person may have committed both, seventeen years apart. Or, maybe there were others that were never found, in between."

Limpia's face collapsed upon itself, mouth open in pain, eyes haunted. "Oh, surely not. Surely not!"

Grace leaned across the table and put her hands over Limpia's. "Not your fault," she said. "No matter how many or when, it was not your fault."

I asked, "May we tell Joanna we've talked to you, if we don't tell her where?"

"After you find out who," she said. "Not before. I'm a coward. I don't want Nash coming after my family, my children, threatening Alfredo. I'm not sure whether Joanne could keep it to herself."

Her ideas were so much like my own. We were both cowards when it came to people like . . . whoever it was. We finished tea and conversation almost simultaneously. Limpia walked us back past the studio, up the hill, and around it.

"You can write to me," she said. "We don't have a phone, but you can write to me." She brought a dog-eared card from the pocket of her cape and handed it to me. The name Lujan and the rural route address were printed on it, and that was all. If one knew who he was, that was enough. If one didn't know, there was nothing there to explain.

As we were about to leave, I was struck with a sudden thought. "Where's Clare? Do you know?"

She flushed. "Sometimes I go to see her. When she's on gate duty. She says she saw you."

"The Gatekeeper?" I laughed. It was the last thing I expected her to say.

"She likes it. She always felt guilty about everything when she was a kid. No matter what she said to her folks or at school, it was always wrong. Now she doesn't feel guilty. Nobody talks, so she never says anything wrong!"

"She knew? She knew where you were?"

"She would never have told. She knew all about Lucia, what she went through. She never told."

"And Alfredo doesn't know you're Lucia?"

"I'm not Lucia." She smiled at us, a radiant smile, the first time we'd seen anything but that remote, detached expression. "She was frightened out of herself, living in fantasy. Whoever I am, I'm not Lucia."

We went back into Taos. We had lunch. We checked the highway information to be sure we wouldn't encounter something nasty on the way home. The storm had blown over, eastward, and was now annoying the folks in Kansas and Nebraska.

We went home.

Lieutenant Martinelli was in charge of the Maria Montoya case. Grace invited him to drop over that evening, if he could get away from the family. He said he couldn't stay long, but he'd be there, around five-thirty. We gave him everything we had, including Limpia's story.

"You think she honestly doesn't know who killed the kid?"

"She didn't know the little girl was dead until I told her husband and he told her."

"So it was either Matt Monmouth, Nash Monmouth, or Steve what's-his-name."

"If the latter, on behalf of the former," Grace said. "He would have had no motive except money."

"Right. And how in hell do we get at either of them now? They each say no, we know nothing about it, and what the hell? There's no evidence."

"No DNA, I suppose," I gloomed.

Martinelli shook his head. "The lab says no. Not after

all this time. Besides, that might say who raped her but it wouldn't say who killed her. And we already know Nash raped her."

"Somebody . . . somebody ought to pay for this," I said. I should have been thinking about the Montoya child, but in fact I was thinking about Grace and me in that gravel pit. There was no question in my mind that Nash had set that one up. I wanted blood, for me. Vengeance. I sternly told myself that was Lloyd's game, not mine, but I still wanted it.

Martinelli yawned. "Let me think about it. I'll give you a call in a day or two."

He stuffed his notes into his pocket and wandered out, stopping in the front hall to admire the Gothic Revival chairs which I had finally found for the guy who was remodeling the church. They were excessively vertical with trefoils and ogives and little finials at the top of the side rails. We had a craftswoman making appropriately designed needlepoint seats, but the client already loved them.

"A church, huh? Seems like a funny thing to do."

"It's going to be a studio," I told him. "Actually, the space adapts pretty well."

"Huh." He yawned. "That's this whole case, Jason. So far as I can see, everybody adapted really well. This Clare girl, and Lucia, and the mom and the aunt. There was a murder at the heart of the whole family, and everybody just adapted and went on. A little murder didn't bother them."

"They didn't know there'd been a murder," I insisted.

"Funny," he commented. "Matt and Nash don't strike me as exactly the kind who can keep their mouths shut. What were they? Eighteen, nineteen?"

"A little younger, actually. Nash was a senior in high school."

"So Lucia tells her mom, then the mom tells the father, and the father hits Lucia across the face and tells her she's lying. Then she takes him to the garage, and there's nothing there. There's a space there, you know."

"Space?"

"Yeah. The mom tells the dad that night, and then there's a space. Next day, Dad hits the kid and says she's lying. What's he doing that night? Talking to the boys?"

He went on out and away, leaving me staring after him.

Grace called from the top of the stairs. "What's the matter, Jason?"

"Nothing." I thought a moment more. "Grace, get your coat. I want to go talk to Joanna."

The lady was home, sitting in her bay window with the big macaw on the back of the chair. I introduced her to Grace, then sat myself down across from her.

"We've got all the pieces but one, Joanna."

"You found Lucia." She said it flatly, as though it were the only thing left to say.

"Yes. She said Nash began molesting her when she was nine or ten years old. She said she told him he had to stop, and he responded by kidnapping Rosabel's niece, raping her, and telling Lucia he'd do it again, or to some other little girl, if she tried to stop. Lucia told your mom. Your mom told your father. He accused Lucia of lying. Somewhere in there, Maria Montoya's body disappeared under the floor. Who did it, Joanna?"

She stared out at the darkening sky, wearing the same expression Limpia had worn, that detached, lofty expression of someone who has hauled herself up by her bootstraps, out of the mire, into the clear light of day. She read my mind.

"Lucia means light. Ever since Mother died, Lucia has called me every few months from a pay phone, and the last time she called she said she calls herself Limpia now. Limpia means clarity and cleanliness. We talked about that, about clarity and light and seeing what reality is.

"When you're messed up in a family like ours, there is no clarity. There is only habit and obedience and trying to believe whatever muddy thing it is your parents believe without ever knowing what that really is. It's hearing them use words that don't mean what they seem to mean, saying things that have layers of meaning you can't uncode. It's being blamed when things go wrong, because you're a girl and therefore not valued like the boys are, and yet not knowing why you're being blamed. It's trying to accept a scapegoat role even while you're aghast at its unfairness. It's pretending to acquiesce and be good while your whole being is in revolt against an injustice you can't even define.

"I remember sort of stumbling through life, uncertain what I was doing or where I was going. I used to envy Lucia because she could find her way and I couldn't. For her, things were either quiet or noisy, and the noisy ones, she just . . . wrote off. They didn't exist. I was like a frog in a swamp. I'd never known anything but that swamp. I dreamed about somewhere else, something else, but when I woke up, there was that swamp. The swamp was real. The rest of it was only dreams. You don't know how to follow dreams. Dreams are scary. So you stay where you are, in the mud, and you hate it, but you stay."

She turned away from us, tears running.

She had turned away too long.

"Who was it, Joanna? Who killed her?"

"It was Dad. All that evening there'd been people talking behind closed doors, people whispering, going here and there. Rosabel had gone home early. She usually worked until six, but she left at five, and she'd been crying and whispering to Helga. Then there was Matt and Nash, whispering, going back and forth to the garage. Then there was Lucia running, screaming, tears streaming down her face. None of it connected. None of it made sense.

"I did what I always did. I hid, I listened, I followed, I tried to figure out what was going on. Then it was after supper, late, and Dad and Nash were in the den talking about the garage. So I went out to the garage. I didn't see anything, but I heard them coming, so I hid in the backseat of the car. Dad came into the garage with Nash, and he sent Nash away, then he unlocked the storeroom, and he went in. I heard a child crying, saying someone had hurt her, and she wanted to go home. Then she stopped. Then Dad came out and I looked out the back window of the car. He was carrying something wrapped up in his coat.

"For a long time after he was gone I stayed there, scared if I got out he'd see me. Finally, I climbed out of the car and sneaked into my bedroom. I didn't see him until the next morning. He was dragging Lucia around, and she was crying. I didn't know what happened to the child I'd heard, and by that night, Lucia was gone."

"Your father simply denied that anything had happened to Lucia?"

"He said she'd gone away. I was fourteen, but I didn't know why she'd gone. I didn't know until long after she left, and Aunty Olga showed me the letter Lucia had written to her. Incest wasn't the worst sin, not to Dad. The worst sin was disloyalty. Even if your brother screwed you when you were only a baby, you had to be loyal to him."

Grace said, "Joanna. There was another case, four years ago. Was that . . . ?"

"You think Dad did that? It never crossed my mind at the time, but I remembered it when I heard about Maria's body being found. The other child was found on an M.M.A. property, and four years ago Dad was behaving very irrationally. He used to reenact things, episodes. He'd get up in the morning convinced it was twenty years ago, the day of my piano recital or the day he and Mother were married. We paid a man to watch him, but Dad escaped every now and then. He could have done it. I don't know whether he did or not. He could have been reenacting that other time. When I read about that in the newspaper, I told Matt Dad had to be put in a home. He's been there ever since. He doesn't have many lucid moments anymore."

I looked at Grace and shrugged. No case, my shrug said. The murderer was dying, a death longer and lonelier than the one he had inflicted. "You wrote this letter," I said, showing it to her. "Death in life pays for death of life. You meant your father."

"Yes. I drove down to Chama one weekend and mailed it. I don't know where Lucia is, but I know she's in New Mexico. I thought you'd believe it was from her. Dad was the murderer. He did it so she wouldn't tell, so the family wouldn't be shamed. That's all that mattered to Daddy. That the family shouldn't be shamed. But what can you do to him now? He's not able to stand trial."

"What about Nash?" Grace asked.

"He did rape her, but I have no idea how you'd prove it. Lucia didn't see him do it. Neither did I."

"We'll see," said Grace. "He may have other troubles."

That night the weather turned bitterly cold, way below zero, and everything froze solid. I read in the business section of the paper, a day or two later, that the gravel operation out on Titan Road had been sold to a firm who wanted to build a warehouse there. In the accompanying photo, a large earthmover with the Monmouth logo on it was busy pushing a mountain range of dry gravel back into the pit it had come from. The caption explained that the pit had been ice covered, but the weight of the gravel would break up the ice for the blah-blah company, the buyer wanted to get a head start on site preparation.

The investigation against the couples club proceeded despite the absence of two of its members who were assumed to have fled the country. This very fact caused someone to break—Grace was told it was Bea Dahlberg— and that person incriminated another, and that one another until, when they had it all wrapped up, there were ten of them being charged with murder and conspiracy to commit and aiding and abetting and arson and God knows what. There were warrants out for Lloyd and Helen, too, though they hadn't shown up. Nash and Nita, however, were right in the middle of it. Nash, it turned out, was accused by his friends of sabotaging the parachutes that had killed the Carlyles. His brief career as a smoke jumper had taught him all he needed to know about parachutes.

Martinelli located Edgar Ransome, now in his late seventies, still living in Boston. He confirmed the story as we had it from the girls. He didn't know about the murder, but he had known about the rape, and he had had to threaten Matt Sr. in order to be sure the divorce was uncontested. He had threatened him with the thing Matt Sr. feared worst. Public ignominy. Martinelli could have charged Matt and Joanna, but he decided not to. As Joanna had said, they were only frogs in a swamp. They had had guilty knowledge, but then, all the knowledge they had had was equally guilty. All the information they had been given since childhood was guilty and false and wrong. There had been no innocents, as I remarked to Grace, in the Monmouth house.

"Which we will change," said Grace, busy trying on maternity clothes. "We will take the curse off that house."

I believe her. The east front bedroom is to be the nursery. It will be charming and the sun falls into it with intimate clarity and joy. If we do not live happily in this place, it will not be for want of care.

The Shirley McClintock series
by Anthony and Edgar Awards nominee

B. J. Oliphant

Published by Fawcett Books.
Available in your local bookstore.

MURDER ON THE INTERNET

Ballantine mysteries are on the Web!

Read about your favorite Ballantine authors and upcoming books in our monthly electronic newsletter MURDER ON THE INTERNET, at **www.randomhouse.com/BB/MOTI**.

Including:
- What's new in the stores
- Previews of upcoming books for the next three months
- In-depth interviews with mystery authors and publishers
- Calendars of signings and readings for Ballantine mystery authors
- Bibliographies of mystery authors
- Excerpts from new mysteries

To subscribe to MURDER ON THE INTERNET, send an E-mail to **srandol@randomhouse.com** asking to be added to the subscription list. You will receive the next issue as soon as it's available.

Find out more about whodunit! For sample chapters from current and upcoming Ballantine mysteries, visit us at **www.randomhouse.com/BB/mystery**.